N
MOUNT BRENNE
FIORAN
THE KEEP
FIORAN CASTLE
FORGOTTEN FOREST
WEST MARKET SQUARE
DOVENEER
RACINE
JACKLANDS

THE KINGDOM OF ELARIA
NORTHERN PORT
MORANA
KENDALL
EAST MARKET SQUARE
SOLUME
AGRONA SEA
SYNAN
MINES
ISSLOTS
T. MUNRO 2021

Other books by Emilee King

Arie's Story:

Surviving on a Whisper
Surviving through the Night
Surviving to the End
Surviving the After

Elarian Chronicles:

Pieces in the Cinders
Cracks in the Tower

PIECES
IN THE
CINDERS

EMILEE KING

ISBN-10: 1966173052
ISBN-13: 978-1966173052

Cover designed by MiblArt Map
designed by Tiffany Munro

Her father took a sharp breath as the short man laughed. "Not a friend, no. Merely a...collector." All at once, the devious smile vanished and a stony glare of warning took its place. "Your eighteen years are up, Henrik. I've provided you enough to keep your family sustained despite the harsh conditions. It's time you pay."

Margaret's mother screeched from her bedroom, making everyone but the short man jump. When her father didn't answer, Margaret smiled courteously at the stranger, ready to pay the debt and move on from the tense encounter.

"What does my father owe you, sir? I'm sure we can make it right."

The short man's small eyes flicked to Margaret, just as her father finally turned to face her. She stilled at his gaze.

"Me?" Margaret breathed. "You gave him your first—"

"He sold his own daughter?" Stella crowed in disbelief, nearly dropping the plate. "What an awful, despicable man."

Izzy finally looked up from the book, bronze hair spilling out of the haphazard knot on her head. "Maybe he had no choice."

"Clearly, he had a choice. He *chose* to make the deal."

"Maybe." Izzy went back to the book, eyes poring over the words while she tapped her pen against her bound notebook. "But remember what the troll said? 'I've provided you enough to keep your family sustained despite the harsh conditions.' The father needed help."

"Yeah. So?"

"So how bad would those conditions have to be for someone to give up their firstborn child?"

Stella scrubbed a resistant stain on the plate to buy her time to think of a response. As Izzy's best friend and roommate, Stella knew she was the only person Izzy really felt comfortable talking to, which meant she was often the designated partner when Izzy wanted to discuss her favorite topic: love. And since Stella had spent the day working for hours in Lady Pursbrough's house only to come home to a giant stack of dishes, she was in no mood to give anyone, even fictional fathers, the benefit of the doubt.

"I don't know. I guess bad?" She wanted to argue that a good father would never abandon his child—Stella's father would never have dreamed of it—but she kept that opinion to herself. No need to rub salt in Izzy's wounds.

"So what do you think that means?" Izzy asked, imploring, like this fictional story was the key to unlocking everything in life. "Of course, he made the deal before he even had children, so maybe he didn't understand the real cost. Or maybe he didn't think he and his wife would live long enough to have kids. Or maybe it was just a hasty decision he regretted instantly. Did Henrik not care enough about Margaret, or did he love the rest of his family more?" The sound of scratching on parchment filled the momentary silence as she jotted down notes. "Can love make you sacrifice that heavily and completely? Sacrifice something you love for something you might love more?"

Again, Stella thought of her father, sharpening the constant ache in the bottom of her gut. Instead of dwelling on it, she shrugged. "Love makes you desperate, I would think. If you love someone, you would do anything for them."

"Maybe. But does that mean he didn't love Margaret as much as he loved everyone else?" The idea caused her to grip the golden rose locket around her neck, twisting it around her finger. It was her nervous habit, but she was doing it *constantly*, so Stella assumed that by now nervous was just a part of Izzy's being.

"Maybe he didn't," Stella said, allowing venom in her voice, though she made sure to speak quietly enough that her stepmother couldn't overhear from the other room. Their house was nearly too small to be called a house. "Not everyone gets the love they deserve."

"No," Izzy replied softly, wide eyes lost in an ocean of thoughts. "They don't." Pages flipped again. "Maybe the love he had for each person added together—if it's Margaret versus the rest of the family, then there would be more love on the side of the family, because there are more people. More people, more love. So maybe it wasn't that particular child, so much as the fact that the others outweighed the one. He would've made the deal with any of the kids, not just Margaret." She sounded confident in this train of thought, and more scratches ensued.

Yes, more people, more love, Stella thought bitterly, reaching over to grab yet another dirty dish. She didn't believe that. Her life had been nothing but unparalleled happiness until her father decided to add in more people. Since his death five years ago, Stella's stepmother and stepsisters had brought nothing but misery. No love. If Stella's stepmother, Natalia, loved her, she wouldn't stick her in the shabby attic of their tiny house and pretend she didn't exist unless there were chores to be done.

That wasn't love. She knew what love was: her father was love. She didn't remember much of her mother, but she knew her parents loved each other, and she knew more than anything that they loved her.

If only love had more power. If only all their love could've kept them alive.

Suddenly, Stella understood Izzy's obsession with studying and defining love. It was what everyone wanted in the end, right? Love and acceptance?

The door flew open, interrupting Stella's thoughts and Izzy's pencil scratching. A tense chill clung to the air as Natalia rushed in. Though she hadn't been considered a noble for years now, she still held herself like near royalty: shoulders back, spine straight, and sharp eyes looking down on everyone else. Per usual, she was wearing a dress rather than pants—another small way she held onto her previous life. As a noblewoman, she'd always been in a skirt with bright makeup and an elaborate hairstyle. Of course, these days her dresses were shabby in comparison to her old ones, expensive makeup went from a daily staple to a luxury for special occasions, and she always had a handkerchief tied over her hair, somehow managing to make the scrap of fabric look regal. As if appearance really mattered in Racine, the poorest village in the kingdom next to the Jacklands.

Why did he have to marry such a vain little viper that only showed its true colors once he was gone?

Stella's shoulders instantly straightened, the hair on the back of her neck stood up, and she felt as Izzy tried to fold her own presence up into a tiny ball and stick it in the corner. Stella often dreamed of the day when she would finally stand up to Natalia; she told herself the right opportunity hadn't presented itself, but really deep down she knew she was too terrified.

Natalia didn't acknowledge either of them. Instead, she came into the kitchen and searched their few cupboards until she found an empty glass to her liking. Stella avoided looking directly at her as Natalia put a bundle of fresh flowers in the glass and set it on the table.

Flowers. That usually meant Natalia was expecting company, and she was trying to make their pathetic excuse of a house seem nicer than it was.

Stella went rigid as Natalia walked up to the sink and picked up a plate from the stack of dishes she had just washed.

Natalia clicked her tongue in disapproval and threw the dish back in the sudsy water. "Not clean enough," she said harshly, like it was a crime. She gestured around the small kitchen. "This whole place isn't clean enough. Get working on it."

Stella gritted her teeth, fighting the urge to both scream and cower. Miraculously, she held her tongue. There were only a handful of occasions Natalia had physically harmed Stella, though they were burned into her memory, always there to remind her it could happen again if she didn't keep herself in check.

"And be quick about it," Natalia went on. It was probably the most she had spoken to Stella all week, if she didn't count the screaming yesterday. "I have a meeting at seven. This place needs to be spotless and everyone needs to be out. Understand?"

Izzy nodded rapidly, face slightly pale. Stella mumbled, "Yes," but Natalia had already left.

Instantly, the tension in the room melted away. Stella gave a silent sigh, and Izzy regained movement. She stood without a word and started sweeping the floor, helping to prepare for Natalia's "meeting."

Since Natalia was a widow, the king sent several of his economic advisors once a month to discuss finances—the meetings were useless, in Stella's opinion, since they were still as poor as ever. But part of Stella did wish Natalia would include her in those meetings, extending even the slightest hand of trust or unity. Stella provided most of the family's income anyway. She was employed as a day maid for a noble household, and Natalia had seized Stella's wages from day one, claiming Stella needed to earn her keep.

Earn my keep in my own house? Her father would've never let Natalia say that. He would've never married the snake if he could have seen what she'd reduced his daughter to.

That's why I'm getting out of here.

Knowing it would help the chores go by faster, Stella let her favorite daydream take over again: the daydream in which she finally revealed the secret stash of money she'd been saving for years. The anger in Natalia's face. The triumph in Stella's eyes. The speech she would make before she took Izzy and left and never once looked back.

Stella practiced a version of the speech in her head as she and Izzy worked dutifully in the kitchen, slowly chipping away at the inescapable grime that came with living in such poverty. Izzy was less inclined to talk when she knew Natalia was nearby, so the two worked in companionable silence until the kitchen was clean. At least, as clean as it could get.

Just as Stella leaned against the counter to admire their work, Natalia burst in like a raging storm. "What are you doing?" she demanded. "Get out now." She glanced back nervously over her shoulder. "Now!"

Izzy darted out like a cat, gone without anyone realizing she had left. Yanking her apron off, Stella quickly leaned down to lace up her boots. She hadn't even gotten through the first one when Natalia was back, pushing her daughters, Isla and Noor, at Stella.

"Out, all of you," Natalia said in a frenzy as she herded them all out the back door. "Don't come back until sunset."

Noor, the little brat, turned her nose up at Stella and stomped out on her own, making sure to bump into Stella's shoulder. The eleven-year-old was short and stout—like a troll—but since Stella was kneeling, the blow knocked her off balance. Stella bit her lip to keep from yelling at her in front of Natalia.

Isla, on the other hand, awkwardly stepped around Stella and followed her younger sister, her steps unsure. The girl had sprouted nearly six inches in the last couple months, and now she was constantly tripping and knocking things over, unaccustomed to her height. Between her long legs and neck, she was on track to pass Stella despite being two years younger. Another thing Stella couldn't stand.

A knock sounded in the front room and Natalia disappeared to answer it. Stella ushered the two girls out the back door, and they rushed after Izzy. Muffled voices sounded in greeting, getting closer with every word. Stella was about to duck out when something caught her eye: a rogue platter on the counter and the broom leaned up against the cupboard. Natalia would hate that.

With a huff, Stella darted forward and stuffed the broom back in its place, heart pounding at the voices getting louder.

"...it was invaluable, what was taken," one man was saying.

Another man added something she couldn't make out, then said, "...the investigation regarding the crimes is still ongoing..."

Stella paused, platter in hand. Crimes? Had someone stolen something? Had *Natalia* stolen something?

She glanced around the ugly kitchen just as she shoved the platter in a drawer. This place didn't fit Natalia—Stella had known that for a long time. Were the guards here for something other than helpful conversation? What theft could warrant that kind of attention from the crown?

"Of course, with Damon gone," the man went on, his voice clearer, too close, and dripping with disgust, "it's logical to assume his resources fell to you."

The mention of her father's name, especially by a stranger, made Stella's blood go cold. For a split second she was torn—was there somewhere she could hide and listen?—but her quick search came up fruitless. No matter how badly she wanted to hear the conversation, survival instinct won out. Just as the kitchen door swung open, Stella ducked out the back door, running after Izzy.

* * * * * * *

"Good morning, Isabelle," Lady Pursbrough greeted with a dimpled smile. "How are you on this beautiful morning?"

Izzy set her books down on the writing desk at the front of the classroom, a bead of sweat trickling down her back from carrying her things. "I'm fine, Lady Pursbrough. Thank you for asking." She gave the same answer every day—well, every day since her father had been taken away—and Lady Pursbrough had graciously learned to accept it. "How are you?"

"I'm doing well, thank you. Ready for another day of learning and growth." She began dusting the chalkboard clean, but was too short to reach more than halfway up. Izzy was about to offer to help, but Lady Pursbrough just flicked her wrist. Izzy watched, mesmerized, as the cloth suspended higher on its own and wiped away the dust, then settled back in Lady Pursbrough's hand.

Lady Pursbrough turned and saw her looking. Izzy dropped her gaze and fiddled with the locket around her neck.

"I'm sorry. I didn't mean to stare."

"Oh, no worries at all, dear, of course." Lady Pursbrough beamed again and her face crinkled. "You probably don't see much magic where you live, do you?"

"Not really," she said, then added in her mind, *not anything legal, anyway.* It had long since been law in the kingdom of

19

Elaria that only certain nobles were allowed to practice magic. For anyone else, especially in her community, it was strictly forbidden to use magic unless they trained and became licensed. A few people in Racine had a license—Natalia was one of them—but most were either too poor for training or didn't have the skill to begin with, and magic there tended to draw unpleasant attention anyway. Watching Lady Pursbrough use her power with ease was startling.

Shaking off the encounter, Izzy leafed through her notebook for the day's lesson plan. "How's Christian doing?" she asked, trying to be polite.

Lady Pursbrough's chestnut eyes brightened at the mention of her son as she went about the room straightening desks. "He's doing really well. Doctors are in high demand these days, you know, especially one as well trained as he is. And so young! He and his wife keep busy, and they're still happily, madly in love." She winked. "Though I tell him he needs to carve out some time for grandchildren. I'm in dire need of a new baby to coddle."

Izzy smiled. "That's good to hear. I'm happy for them."

"I am too."

Children started trickling into the classroom, buzzing with excited chatter. Lady Pursbrough greeted each of them by name as they entered, while Izzy began writing the day's vocabulary words on the chalkboard, unable to keep a grin off of her face. She'd been a peasant girl her whole life, but that hadn't stopped her thirst for knowledge and knack for learning, and the only thing that made her happier than written words was the chance to teach them to others. She'd been ecstatic when Lady Pursbrough had noticed her talent and offered her a teaching position at the refined primary school she opened in her late husband's honor. It gave her more purpose than anything else she'd found in her seventeen years of life, and the academy was the only place she felt centered. Plus, it gave her access to the library upstairs, a major bonus since Racine didn't have any kind of library.

The students continued filing in and found their seats just as Izzy started on the last line of words. She was midway through 'predilection'—a new word she'd found in her book the night before—when she heard it.

"Crazy Izzy," a boy murmured.

Izzy stumbled, and the chalk made a screeching sound when her hand jolted. Several kids snickered.

"Crazy Izzy makes me dizzy," another boy said, and Izzy knew without looking the way he dragged his finger in circles on his temple and rolled his eyes.

Izzy closed her eyes and tried to remember how to breathe. How did the kids learn it? They were *noble* children, for star's sake, and had never seen the harsh realities of the outer villages. The cruel nickname had first originated when her family lived in Solume—a village on the other side of the kingdom. Sure, gossip had trickled through the grapevine and found her hiding in Racine, but these kids, this academy...this was supposed to be her safe place.

"What was that, Blanche?" Lady Pursbrough demanded, steaming like a fresh pot of tea. Izzy wasn't sure if her gratitude outweighed her embarrassment. Either way, she couldn't make herself turn around.

Coward.

"Nothing, Mrs. Pursbrough," Blanche answered with feigned innocence. Izzy cracked her eyes open and continued writing vocabulary words, focusing intently on her penmanship while grasping her rose locket in her other hand.

"All right, then," Lady Pursbrough said sternly. "Now all of you pay attention to Isabelle today. Understand?"

"Yes, Mrs. Pursbrough," the children repeated in unison.

Steeling herself, Izzy turned to face the class. Her hands were warm with sweat and grimy with chalk dust, and she felt the room closing in on her slowly, the walls pushing in even though she'd always been able to stand here and teach just fine...

Izzy took a deep breath and forced herself to begin the lesson. Her voice was thin and fragile at first, but eventually she worked her way into a numb rhythm. Lady Pursbrough stayed in the classroom for a few minutes, eyeing the students like a circling vulture, waiting for someone to say something fatal, but the kids behaved themselves even after she'd left. Izzy didn't let go of her locket for the duration of the lessons, even when the classes rotated and nothing else happened. The chain left a line imprint on her palm.

When the hours finally passed and the final bell rang, she excused her last class for the day and began gathering up her things. Several of the boys lingered behind, to ask a question, she thought. She straightened up to face them and the boys burst into laughter.

"Crazy Izzy's head is fizzy!" one of them shouted before they bolted out the door, nearly crashing into a newcomer in a well-tailored suit and handsome, slicked-back hair.

"Hey!" Christian yelled down the hallway at the boys, his hands balling into fists. "You show some respect!"

Izzy ducked her head, both from the sting of the remark and the fact that Christian had heard it.

"It's okay," Izzy told the floor. "I'm used to it."

"It's most certainly *not* okay." Christian took a breath and strode into the room. "And here I thought we were raising decent citizens, not miscreants."

"What did you need, Christian?" Izzy asked, wanting to change the subject. Grabbing hold of her locket again, she glanced up to meet his eyes. Despite knowing Christian for years, his face still surprised her at times: it was virtually perfect, except his nose, which had been born at an odd angle, so it looked like it was constantly hanging off his face. Between that and the dent in the middle of it, she didn't know how he was able to breathe. She'd never been brave enough to ask.

"Well I came to talk to you about your father," he continued, still fired up, as he gestured to the door, "but those delinquent offenders probably deserve my attention more. I should talk to their parents."

Izzy deflated. Of course Christian came to talk about her father—he was a doctor after all. But Izzy was sick of those superficial conversations. Everyone wanted to 'talk' about her father, but never in any way that actually mattered or helped. At least Christian was genuinely concerned, though, and Izzy had to be grateful for that.

He opened his mouth to say something else just as Izzy did, and they both stopped for the other. Izzy hiccupped nervously and grasped her locket tighter out of habit, which stole Christian's attention.

"You only have half a locket," he said, then shook his head and smiled. "Obviously. You must have realized that by now."

Izzy gave a small grin and nodded, tucking a loose strand of hair behind her ear.

"Where's the other half? Did you lose it?"

She looked down to inspect the gold rose pendant with broken hinges where the other half should've been clasped. "I don't know. It's my…" Taking a sharp breath, her eyes darted back to Christian's.

"Your mother's?" he asked softly.

Izzy bit her lip. People loved to talk about her father, but nobody ever spoke of her mother. People could make fun of her father, of Izzy even, and pity them in a situation that was largely out of their control. But her mother...her mother had chosen to leave them, to walk out years ago without any warning or explanation. It marked her as a traitor to the community, as if she had somehow betrayed an apathetic village more than she had her own precious daughter and fragile husband.

"Yeah," she finally breathed. "Hers."

Christian looked like he was going to say something, then he shook his head and seemed to change his mind, getting back on track. He pointed to the hallway again. "How did those boys even come up with those phrases anyway?"

"They didn't. They must've...I don't know. They must've heard them from somewhere else, I guess." At that, Izzy turned and started stacking her books—it was more than time to go home.

"Who would make up something like that?"

Izzy picked up her books. "My best friend. Well, obviously he's not *anymore*, we're not together any…" She trailed off when she saw the all too familiar look in Christian's eyes. Pity.

Izzy used to think anything—even pity—was better than the hurtful stares and whispers and remarks people would aim at her and her family, but she'd come to realize pity was just another dirty lens people chose to look at her with, rather than cleaning the glass and seeing her for who and what she actually was.

To be seen as she was, and to be loved for it. Isn't that what everyone wanted, in some way, in the end? It would seem so impossible to Izzy if she hadn't seen it happen before to others.

"How did you know you loved your wife?" she blurted suddenly. She felt her cheeks turn pink at the outburst, but she had to admit she wanted an answer. Christian and his wife had been a prime case study in Izzy's research—without him knowing, of course.

Christian blinked in surprise before stuffing his hands in his pockets. "Hm, um, well, I don't know. It's a feeling, I guess…one day, I just knew."

Izzy pursed her lips. She hated that answer. It was vague and left too many things unaccounted for. "How do you know she loves you?"

"Well…she told me so."

"Huh." Izzy nodded to herself. "That's what they said, too."

Christian's eyebrows furrowed; Izzy stepped around him before he could continue the conversation.

"Goodnight, Christian," she mumbled as she stepped out of the classroom and began the long walk home.

It took her over two hours most days to walk from Pursbrough Academy to Stella's house. She didn't mind it much except in the rain or snow, as it was nearly impossible to keep every book from water damage, and wet socks were some of the worst torture she could think of.

But she walked. She wouldn't ask Stella to dip into her secret stash of money just for a carriage back and forth, and she didn't dare bother Natalia. She barely spoke in Natalia's presence. Natalia had let Izzy live in the attic with Stella after her father was taken—Izzy had no other family, nowhere else to go, and she would never ask Natalia or Stella for anything else. As long as nobody bothered her, walking was just fine.

Izzy walked the dirt streets with her head down, hoping nobody recognized or stopped her as she finally entered Racine. The village remained largely destitute, and people weren't friendly or neighborly like the Pursbroughs. Life had too much hardship to be friendly. Out here, it was everyone for themselves, as Izzy had so brutally learned, and though the thought made her toes curl with fear, she longed for the day when Stella announced they had enough money to leave. Start over. Write any story they wanted to.

The idea gave her legs strength to make the last stretch to the Amaranth house. She snuck in the back door quietly to avoid being noticed by Natalia or her daughters and climbed the stairs to the attic where she shared a room with Stella. Sighing in relief, she put her hand on the doorknob and pushed her way inside.

Izzy jumped when she nearly ran into Stella, who must've been standing by the door, waiting for her. She left no time for Izzy to question the state of her hair or the frantic look in her wide, blue eyes. Instead, Stella took Izzy by the shoulders and pulled her inside the attic, shutting the door behind them.

"Izzy, I've got to talk to you."

* * * * * * *

"Are you sure that's what you heard?" Izzy asked for the millionth time.

25

Stella let out a frustrated breath through her teeth as she plucked a flower from its place in the earth and started ripping apart the petals. They were sitting out in the meadow watching the sunset, taking their traditional secluded spot so no one would overhear them. Stella wouldn't trust anyone but Izzy with her new information, but she felt like their conversations had just gone in circles. Isla and Noor had been with them all last night—Stella hadn't wanted to talk about their mother's crimes in front of them in case they snitched—and by the time she had the chance to get Izzy alone again, she was half asleep in bed and mumbling things in response. It had driven Stella insane to wait this long to really talk about it.

"*Yes*, Izzy, I am *sure*. Get your head out of the clouds and just *listen* to me for once, will you?"

Izzy seemed to curl in on herself slightly in response. That's when Stella realized her mistake: wrong choice of words.

Crazy Izzy's head is fizzy, the snotty village children would yell at her, back when her father was still home and suffering from delusions. Her best friend Gannon spread the rumor Izzy was just like her father, just to be cruel, and kids loved to jeer at her. Somehow the gossip had stuck to her even after she'd moved to Racine with Stella, and they heard 'Crazy Izzy' jokes way too often. It made Stella's blood boil.

Before she could apologize, Izzy, knees to her chest and arms around her legs, said, "I believe you, Stella," like nothing had happened. "I do. I'm just afraid your emotions are getting in the way. A lot could go wrong if you're...if you're wrong about this." She sighed. "But tell me again. I'm listening."

Stella took a breath, slowing herself down, until the edge was out of her tone, then told Izzy *again* what she'd heard.

Izzy pursed her lips, hesitating to show her skepticism. "Okay...so there's an investigation for a possible theft of something valuable. Is that all you know?"

Casting her eyes to the darkening sky, Stella reached inside herself for patience, crushing the flower in her hand. "Yes, it is, but think about it, Iz. The crown is *investigating* Natalia. And if all these years the meetings have been about the same thing, they've been investigating her for a really long time. Since my father died. Five whole years."

"Maybe." Izzy nodded, still unconvinced. "It's not very promising on her part."

"Not very promising?" Stella repeated. She was fighting the urge to pull out her hair. "Izzy, the *crown* is *investigating* my stepmother. They don't do that unless it's something huge."

"I know, Stel, but it doesn't have to mean something bad. Maybe they're investigating her finances. That's what they've always said it's about, right?"

"Yeah, but if they were *helping* her with finances then they wouldn't have said it like that. And they wouldn't have brought up my father that way—like they were disgusted she was given what he had. Like she *took* it all from him."

"We don't know what Natalia has been dealing with," Izzy reasoned, fiddling with her locket. "It could be—"

Stella whipped her head around to look at her. "Are you *defending* her?"

Izzy's face turned white despite the golden glow from the sun illuminating her cheeks. "No, I don't...I mean, I don't know...she's..."

"She's a wicked witch, is what she is," Stella finished for her with finality. Her resolve had only grown over the past twenty-four hours, going from an inkling of an idea to firm, concrete knowledge. "I think she got desperate. I think she robbed my father, the stress and betrayal caused his heart to fail, and now the crown is investigating. Did anyone else notice how we were high middle class until my father died? He's gone and the money goes right with him." She dragged her fingers through the dirt and squeezed it in her palm. "Natalia brought us to this ruin. I know it. This is all her fault."

Izzy's voice came so quietly, Stella thought it could've been the whispers in the wind of ghosts long forgotten. "She took me in. Nobody else would."

They both stopped talking then, the discomfort from the topic settling between them in the uneasy silence. The sun was sinking below the tips of the trees in the forest miles and miles away; the beautiful, idyllic scene had no place in such a grimy, rotten village, and was often the only beautiful thing people could find in their side of the community, besides Miss Leed's garden down the road. And, of course, the meadow.

Stella and Izzy had fallen in love with the Elarian sunsets when things had started to take a turn for the worse. When Stella's mother died and her father was arranging the funeral, Izzy sat with her in their pumpkin patch while she cried. The same happened when Noor accidentally broke her favorite china doll, or when Natalia told Stella she couldn't have seconds on chocolate pudding even though Stella's real mother had *always* allowed her to, or when she'd received word that her father had suffered heart failure while on a business trip.

Izzy was good at comfort. She was small and quiet and soft, and it was incredibly easy to forget who you were and just fall into her. Stella always felt awkward around sadness—she had enough of her own she couldn't manage well, so how was she supposed to nicely deal with someone else's without saying the wrong thing?

Stella tried, though, for Izzy. The day Izzy's mother left them, she'd been inconsolable. The day Gannon had turned on her, told her she was insane just like her father, spit in her face, and spread the "Crazy Izzy" jokes like feed for the chickens these people were...that day had been awful. That day Stella and Izzy had gone to her flower bed in Solume and, surrounded by a sea of blooming blue and yellow petals, the bright flower that was Izzy shriveled up and crumbled. She barely even cried the day they finally took her father away to the mental ward. Stella thought she must've already cried all the tears she had.

"Look, Iz," Stella broke the silence, the extra fire out of her system now that she'd had a moment to cool down. "I'm not sure what Natalia is mixed up in, but I know it's something. I can feel it. And I have to figure it out. If it has anything to do with my father's death—or the fact that his money dried up as soon as he was gone and we plunged headfirst into peasant

28

life—then I have to make it right. I owe it to him to find the truth, no matter what."

"I know." Izzy pulled the locket from one side of the chain to the other, back and forth, lost in thought. "But if...Natalia...if she finds out what we're doing...she'll be livid."

Stella breathed a silent sigh of relief that Izzy was still on her side. "That's why we'll be sneaky about it. She hardly pays attention to us anyway."

"If they just closed the investigation, she's not going to want us poking around. Digging stuff up."

"Exactly. She thinks she's in the clear. It's the perfect time to gain the upper hand."

Finally, Izzy tore her eyes away from the scenery and gazed at Stella. "And what if we do? What if you're right? And we...she thinks she's cleared and we...ruin it. She would come after us." She shuddered softly. "She would be so *angry*. What do we do then?"

Stella jerked out her chin with resolve, refusing to be shaken by the idea of Natalia's venomous wrath. "Then we will pack up and run, and she'll never hurt us again."

CHAPTER 2

TEARING OFF PETALS

Izzy sat alone at the kitchen table wringing her hands over and over, the chain of her locket pursed between her lips as she repeated the words in her head again.

Good afternoon, Natalia. How are you today? I was...I was just curious if you stole money from Stella's father and possibly contributed to his death. No? Okay great, I'll let Stella know.

No, of course it couldn't be *that* easy. Besides, Stella hadn't tasked her with asking about the money—just getting more information. Since Natalia often pretended Stella didn't exist, she thought it might be better if Izzy tried broaching a conversation with Ms. Amaranth.

Amaranth. That was another bad sign about Natalia, one that Izzy had just realized. Right after Stella's father died, Natalia shed her married name, Madeus, took on her maiden name again, and changed her daughters' names back as well.

Izzy sighed, the knot in her gut tightening. She really didn't want to believe Natalia would steal from the family she married into—from the man she claimed to love. Before that man was taken from them, Natalia had been kind and happy. She used to teach Stella how to cook, play hide and seek with her daughters, and make warm sweet rolls whenever she knew Izzy was coming over. But life had hardened Natalia Amaranth just like it seemed to harden everyone else eventually. Could that hardship drive her to not only break the law, but also break the trust of those closest to her?

Izzy wasn't sure. She didn't know how love worked in this situation—she'd yet to come upon it in her studies. If Natalia believed her daughters were in danger of having less than they needed to survive, would her love for them override her love for Stella and her father? That was plausible, if Natalia Amaranth hadn't come from a family of wealth with a nice inheritance from her previous husband, who was of higher class than Damon. Why would she have needed money in the first place?

The front door slammed, making Izzy jump and gasp softly. Her locket fell from her lips as she doubled over her books on the unsteady kitchen table, pretending she'd been absorbed in them for hours.

Natalia rushed into the room and set the vegetables she was carrying on the counter, dark brown curls flowing out from under the beige handkerchief tied around her head. Without acknowledging Izzy's presence, she grabbed a giant, rusty pot from off the shelf, filled it with water, and put it on the stove. A putrid smell of burning wood and broiled crumbs filled the air as their stove spluttered to life. Natalia began chopping vegetables—she was the only chef in the house since Stella tended to blacken everything and Izzy was too quiet and usually overlooked. The furious tapping and occasional crackle of the stove were the only sounds in the solid silence of a house stitched together.

You can do this, Izzy. You can do it. Stella's counting on you.

"Good aft—moon," Izzy mumbled under her breath, then hiccupped. Her hand automatically reached up to clutch her locket. The scrawled words in her notebook blurred as the tapping continued, and Izzy knew Natalia would run out of vegetables eventually. What would happen then? She'd miss her chance.

Come on, Izzy, come on.

"Natalia?" she blurted, surprising both of them. Natalia jumped, her shoulders tensing and the knife scraping across the cutting board. Izzy's heart leapt in her scratchy throat.

"Izzy?" Natalia seemed to choke on the name and Izzy internally recoiled at the sound. Natalia turned halfway to face her, one hand still gripping half a squash, the other clutching the knife like she'd have to fight her way out of their conversation. Izzy couldn't even remember their last conversation, and Natalia's uncertain words stumbled over each other, as if she'd forgotten how to talk with Izzy altogether. "What are you...um, did you need something?"

"Oh, uh…" Izzy pulled her locket back and forth on its chain. "I was just wondering how you were."

"How I am?" Natalia repeated, like she'd never once considered the question. But with two young daughters—ages fifteen and eleven—and a seventeen-year-old stepdaughter who came with an abandoned teenage best friend all under a husbandless house, it was easy to believe the pale haggardness to her face.

Izzy tried to recover herself. She had to save this. She picked up her pen and tapped it against her book, nonchalantly, she hoped. "Yes. I haven't asked in a while so...so I thought I would."

Natalia was frozen, hazel eyes hazy while they stared at nothing. She didn't say anything for so long, Izzy wondered if she'd made up the whole encounter in her head.

"I'm okay," Natalia finally answered through unmoving lips. "One day at a time. Just like everyone else." Then she jerked herself back around and kept cutting vegetables, but now the tapping sounds were awkward and clumsy rather than the methodical background music it had been moments before. To Izzy's utter shock, she went on, as choppy as her knife work. "How's...um, how's your father doing?" The question was forced and clunky, but it was out in the space.

Now it was Izzy's turn to freeze; she was grateful Natalia wasn't looking at her anymore. "I'm going to visit him today," she finally offered because it was all she could give.

Natalia nodded, like she'd done her part. "Good." The word easily closed the book of their interaction, and Izzy could feel Natalia putting it on a high, dusty shelf so she wouldn't have to open it again anytime soon.

The knot in Izzy's gut tightened. She didn't want to keep talking to Natalia—she didn't like talking to *anyone*, really, except Stella—but she didn't know when she'd get this opportunity again, especially when Natalia was this calm and...weirdly nice. On the other hand, she didn't know how successful she could be. It wasn't like she could just bring up Damon Madeus—Natalia barely even acknowledged Stella's father had ever lived, let alone loved her. Izzy would never bring him up in a million years, and doing so would be suspicious.

The pot on the stove started rattling as the water boiled and Natalia reached for her last squash. Izzy tapped her pen harder against her notebook, glancing down at her notes again, which gave her an idea.

Taking a deep breath, she steeled herself for the words to slice her tongue on the way out of her mouth. "Natalia?" She didn't wait for her to respond. "When did you first meet my mother?"

Natalia didn't jump as much this time at Izzy's voice. Her work rhythm stumbled for a second, but she regained herself much easier. By the time she'd turned around to look at Izzy, her face was a mask of carefully crafted curiosity, caution, and pity. Her thin eyebrows pulled down in concentration.

"I met her early on," she finally answered, each word its own decision. "Early on in our courtship—" She hesitated for a fraction of a second, her eyes darting to the front door and back, but Izzy still caught it. "Stella's father introduced us. Me to your parents, then to you. He...honestly, he spent so much time with her, at first I thought they were courting in secret.

But then I met your father, before…" Her hazel eyes snapped back to Izzy's, afraid she'd overstepped.

Izzy buried her pain at the bottom of her heart. "Before he got bad?"

"Yes." Natalia nodded, relieved. "Yes, before that. Your mother was a very bright woman—not just smart, but sophisticated. Dedicated. She saw the good in the world. Aside from my slight jealous streak before they reassured me they were just friends, I really liked your mother from the moment I met her."

Yes, Izzy remembered that. She remembered how easy it was to love her mother—Izzy herself had made the same mistake.

"You two were friends then?" Izzy couldn't help asking, completely floored at Natalia's open response. Why had she never thought to ask about this before?

Natalia's shoulders relaxed, like she had finally decided the conversation was permissible, and she turned to pour her diced vegetables in the pot of boiling water.

"Yes we were, especially over the years. I'd say she was one of my best friends, eventually." She reached for a wooden spoon and began stirring the pot. "With you and Stella always being together, it was natural that Sofia and I grew together too."

Izzy's insides flinched at the use of her mother's name; she made a conscious effort to never think it, ever. "So did you…did she tell you…before…why she…" her voice nearly cracked, and she strained to keep it together, "…why she left?"

This time when Natalia froze and turned to look at her, there was no fear or contempt in her expression. It seemed the despair and grime that was a permanent feature to her face fell off, replaced with understanding and compassion. Suddenly, she looked like a ghost of the noblewoman Izzy remembered from years ago. She stared at Izzy for the longest time, as though by sheer force she could fix the hurt that Izzy knew was splayed out all over her face. She couldn't hide it.

"No," Natalia finally answered, though the strain in her voice said she wished she had another answer. "No, I didn't know she was leaving. I knew she was worried about your father, but I never would've guessed…" Natalia sighed, and Izzy was shocked when her voice nearly cracked now. "She loved you, Izzy. Both of you. Very much. I didn't know she had it in her to leave you."

Many people had posed their theories as to why Izzy's mother had left—the most popular theory was that she didn't want to deal with her husband's worsening insanity. Perhaps that theory made sense. Izzy might even believe it, at this point, except it didn't account for one major detail: her daughter. If Izzy's mother didn't want to deal with the public and personal cost of a crazy husband, why would she leave her beloved daughter behind to face the fate on her own?

She wouldn't, Izzy had decided long ago. Izzy's mother couldn't have loved her, since she left her. And that made most of Izzy's childhood memories a hideous lie.

Natalia cleared her throat and it snapped Izzy back to the real world. "If you ever…Izzy, if you'd ever like to talk about her, you can. I know that…that other people can be cruel, but I won't be. I loved Sofia."

Izzy was stunned to silence, her mouth hanging open. They stared at each other for a few seconds. Izzy realized she should say something else, something about Stella's father—that was the whole point after all—but a knock sounded on the front door, making them both jump. The sound immediately cut the tentative tie they had formed with each other in the past few minutes. Nodding to herself, Natalia placed her wooden spoon on the counter, smoothed out her wrinkled, lavender skirt, and went to answer the door.

With a heavy sigh, Izzy buried her face in her hands. She knew Stella was waiting upstairs in their room for Izzy to come back with whatever information she could get from Natalia, and Izzy squirmed at the thought of going through that ordeal again just to get Natalia to talk to her. She'd squandered their opportunity by getting distracted with thoughts of her mother.

She needed to focus. When was she ever going to get Natalia to be that nice again? Stella wouldn't believe it when Izzy told her; Izzy hardly believed it herself.

Men's voices sounded from the front door, issuing a greeting. Izzy lifted her head from her hands just in time to see Natalia dashing into the kitchen with wide, frantic eyes.

"Get out," she hissed at Izzy with enough force she might as well have screamed. She slammed one of Izzy's books shut and started pushing Izzy to the back door. Izzy snatched them all off the table before Natalia could touch them again. "The girls are down the road at the Bale's house." Natalia's words were harsh and sharp. "Pick them up in three hours and walk them here."

"What's going—"

"Is Stella here?" Natalia demanded in a frenzy, her beautiful face contorted with furious desperation. "Is she?"

"Um, she...no," Izzy managed. "No, I think she's at work right now."

Natalia nodded to herself, calming a degree. "Good. Get out and don't come back for a few hours. Bring the girls on your way." And with that, she gave Izzy the final push outside and slammed the door in her face.

Unsettled, Izzy checked to make sure her books were okay, then shook herself out before taking timid steps down the dirt road. After a moment she glanced back at the window in the attic.

Please be quiet, Stella, Izzy silently pleaded. *Be smart, be quiet, and find out what Natalia's up to.*

* * * * * * *

The bed gave a croaking groan when Stella sprawled out on it, exhausted, ignoring the familiar musty smell so thick it made it difficult to breathe. She'd been up late last night working overtime—Lady Pursbrough had thrown a party and it had taken ages to clean up, even with the help of the two other

39

maids. Lady Pursbrough had paid extra, though, an exciting fact that Stella didn't share with Natalia. A few more months, a few more parties, a few more late nights, and she'd have enough to leave Racine. She could feel it.

Casting her eyes up at the dank ceiling, Stella imagined the place she and Izzy would have. It wouldn't be anything fancy, to be sure, but it wouldn't be like this shack Natalia had found for them. No, it would be open. Airy. Bright. There wouldn't be any bugs or mice or cobwebs; no backed up sinks or missing lights or wood so worn you thought the floor would come out underneath you. The walls wouldn't be thin and narrow, angled so they seemed to press in on you from all sides. They would be wide and welcoming, giving Stella and Izzy space to breathe. And they wouldn't be cracked and empty either, like they were now. They would be covered in maps of every kingdom, cave, and ocean, every nook and cranny in the world. The corners would be full of rare antiques, like the kind Stella's father used to find and sell. And, of course, she'd give Izzy a wall for her bookshelf. A whole room for a library, if they had the space.

As a trade for the library, Izzy would put aside her distaste for animals and let Stella get a cat, just like Natalia's old cat, Lucy, that died years ago. The cat would sit on Stella's lap while she plotted her next adventure, and Izzy would sit in the big chair next to the fireplace, reading. The place would be filled with smiles and laughter and memories worth hanging on to.

Stella's vision melted away and reality took its place. Scowling, she threw her arms over her face to hide Natalia's shack from her eyes. This wasn't a home, she'd decided long ago, after the millionth night she'd sprawled out on this bed facing the dim ceiling, the sheer weight of loneliness pressing her so hard that tears came out. Homes were happy and cheerful and full of love, not dark and quiet and full of heartache no one dared speak of.

She had to get out. She had the right to a home. Her father would want that for her.

My father. Izzy should've been in conversation with Natalia now, trying to get more information on the money Stella was sure had been stolen. Though the plan had seemed somewhat solid earlier, Stella felt doubtful at the thought of Izzy striking up a conversation with *anybody*, let alone Stella's guarded and unnerving stepmother.

A knock sounded downstairs, drawing Stella out of her musings. With a huff, she pulled herself off the bed and looked out their small window, squinting her eyes to see through the dirty glass. Her heart skipped a beat when she saw the carriage parked in front of the house: it had a royal crest on the door.

The royal advisors had visited Natalia regularly since Stella's father died, but never had they come twice in one week.

Stella lurched to the door, prepared to barrel downstairs, but she stopped herself. Natalia would throw her out again if she knew Stella was in the house—if she knew Stella were still here, she would've shouted up at her already, since she rarely, if ever, came up here. Why hadn't she driven her out?

Izzy. Izzy must've lied. Terrified, brave little Izzy must've told Natalia that Stella was gone.

Beaming at her best friend's ingenuity, Stella tiptoed across her small room to the door, opening it painfully slowly so it wouldn't creak. Then, holding her breath, she took the winding staircase down one step at a time, forcing herself to pause at each break so she didn't make a sound. The slow pace was absolutely maddening—she could be missing everything!—but Stella forced herself to be patient. Getting caught was not an option.

Stella's breaths were shallow and quiet, her fingers tingling with anticipation, as she approached the door at the end of the staircase that would lead to the kitchen. Gingerly, she pressed her ear to the crack and listened.

The voices were muffled, but Stella could pick out two distinct male ones—probably the same ones that had been coming to check on Natalia for years. Stella strained her ears with all her might, begging the stars to let a word or two slip through.

"...we apologize...any inconveniences or hardship..." one man was saying. "But...the investigation regarding you and...has officially been closed."

Closed? The tingling in Stella's fingers turned to a painful buzzing in her veins. They couldn't be closing it. Natalia was guilty!

Stella heard Natalia choke. Her response was mumbled, but her tone was one of awe. Shock. Relief. In the dark, Stella shifted on her feet, pushing herself harder against the door. There had to be a mistake.

One of the men cleared his throat. "The crown will no longer be...or investigating you or your family." His voice took on a harder edge. "We know...can't right all the damage...the shameful murderer...retribution for Damon...his death..."

Stella gasped and stumbled backward, barely catching herself on the bottom step before she fell to the ground. She had to stuff her hand in her mouth to keep silent, though the urge to scream engulfed her throat, the same word drilling over and over again in her mind.

Murder.

Murder.

Murder murder murder murder murder murder.

She shook her head, as though the royal visitors could see her. No, her father wasn't murdered. He'd died of heart failure, having been too caught up in his travels to see a doctor until it was too late. He'd left, just like every other trip, and she'd watched out the window every night for him, just like every other trip. Except that time, instead of a loving father and doting husband bringing home a cart of strange treasures and fascinating stories, Stella received devastating news from a royal guard with uneven eyebrows and a brown moustache.

Why had a royal guard come to bring the news? That thought had never occurred to Stella—she'd been too overcome with disbelieving anguish to question it.

An investigation. A *murder* investigation.

As quickly as the sucker punch shock came, it was replaced with boiling indignation. Her father was *murdered* and the crown itself was holding an investigation to find the culprit. Why had nobody told her? Why had Natalia, as cruel as she'd turned out to be, kept something like that from her?

Then the next punch came, harder than the last: they were investigating Natalia. For murder.

Natalia murdered my father.

She held her hand to her mouth, blinking back hot tears. The sentence sounded like blasphemy in her head, but some instinct in her gut told her she was right. But how could Natalia do that? Stealing from her husband and treating Stella like dirt was one thing. *Murdering* someone was an entirely different story.

Then again, it had been Natalia who had refused to have a funeral for Damon. Stella had begged and begged until her stepmother allowed a thirty minute service with only the two of them, her stepsisters, and Izzy.

When Stella had asked for help in trying to contact her godmother, who was like an aunt to Stella and a sister to Damon, and let her know of his passing, Natalia was the one who ignored her request and refused to give her any contact information.

And the day after he died and twelve-year-old Stella ran to her stepmother sobbing for him, Natalia was the one who had slapped her across the face and told her to never say his name again.

Natalia murdered my father.

Stella pressed her ear to the door again, only to catch the tail of Natalia's endless thanks and the men's dismissing departure.

She needed to get out of this place. She needed air. She needed to think.

Exhaustion long forgotten, Stella stole back up the stairs to grab her boots, sneak out the window, and head to her father's makeshift gravesite.

If anywhere could give her the peace and space to think through all this, it was her father's grave.

Her *murdered* father's grave.

Natalia murdered my father and she just got away with it.

Balling her fists in hate and resolve, Stella ducked her head away from the carriage and ran toward the rising sun.

* * * * * * *

The mental ward was always cold. Izzy hated that.

Her gut squelched with each step forward, but Izzy forced her feet to be firm. Strong. The moments spent in this place were always the most isolating of Izzy's life, and she knew in those moments she had no one to pick her up but herself.

The cement stairs seemed to wind forever, dragging her down to bury her in eternal gray stone. She clutched a book in one hand and her locket in the other, holding both next to her heart as though they were her lifelines, tying her to a brighter, warmer world. That was in part why she read so much: the reminder that there were happier worlds out there somewhere. Worlds that understood her and accepted her.

She used to tell her best friend Gannon about those worlds. There was once a time when he would've listened to her ramblings with a twinkle in his eye, waiting politely until she was done dissecting a story before he kissed her. Now, he used Izzy's wandering and imaginative mind as a weapon to attack her, and Izzy was careful to keep her thoughts to herself.

There's a happier world out there somewhere, she reminded herself with a glance at the book cradled against her chest. The thought propelled another step down. *There's a happier world where love is boundless and people are enough.*

Like every time she visited the mental ward, Izzy saw almost no one besides the lady at the front desk who let her in and the occasional guard she passed in the hallway. The oppressive silence was like a dense weight, bearing down on the building and suffocating everyone inside. Her hands were trembling by the time she reached her father's room, whether from the cold or her nerves, she wasn't sure. Her knuckles ached when she tapped them softly against the door.

There was no response. There never was, but Izzy still felt she should show respect. She placed her hand on the glass panel, just as the guard had taught her the first time she'd come. The cell that kept her father prisoner was spelled to only deactivate for a select few people's touch: basically just the workers and Izzy, as nobody else ever came to visit Merel Aelius. She shuddered at the thought of how much time he spent all alone. Then, taking a deep breath, she pushed the door open and stepped gingerly inside.

As usual, the cramped space was filled with a thin mattress on the floor, a single chair, and a bucket in the corner. A small bulb on the ceiling provided the only light, made dimmer by the metal cage around it that kept residents from breaking it. And clustered on the mattress in the corner was a lump—a lump that had been lying unconscious the past four times Izzy had visited, but was now sitting up and very much awake.

"Papa?" Izzy asked softly, the word nearly getting stuck in her throat. Tentatively, she took a step closer. Two more would have her at the foot of the bed. "Papa, it's me. Izzy."

Her father sat with his back against the wall, blue eyes cloudy, with sporadic tufts of white hair that stuck out at odd angles. He gave no acknowledgement of her presence.

With another step, fist tightening around her locket, Izzy tried again. "Papa, are you there?" She held her breath and kneeled down on the mattress. Her knees pressed into the fabric and settled against the hard stone underneath. "It's me. It's Izzy."

There was a time when even the mention of Izzy's name would make Papa spark with excitement and pride. "Ah, it's my beautiful Izzybelle," he would say, an easy grin already stretched across his wrinkled face. "Here to ring my favorite song."

But the cruelty of people and circumstances had beaten that spark out of him. Now he looked at her with a vacant expression, caught up in things that only he could see. Izzy jumped slightly when a few of the clouds in his eyes cleared and his gaze shifted to her.

"Izzy," he said, his once teddy bear voice now ragged and hoarse. "You came to visit."

Izzy couldn't help a small smile. "Yes. Yes I did." She cleared her throat and settled herself better on the small mattress. Slowly, so as not to spook him, she took his hand in hers. His papery skin was like ice. "How have you been, Papa?"

Papa gave a lopsided shrug. "Been better, been worse. You?"

She matched his shrug. "Been better, been worse."

"Hmph." He gave her hand a little squeeze. "You've always been a tough one."

Izzy kept herself from refuting him; never in her life had she been anything close to tough. "Stella says hello," she offered. Stella hadn't, of course, but Izzy liked to think she would've if she'd known Izzy was coming today.

"Tell her I say hello too."

"I will." She traced her finger on the leather cover of the book in her lap. "Papa, do you...do you remember much about Stella's father?"

His bushy eyebrows furrowed as he thought. "Damon, was it?"

Izzy beamed and nodded; it had been ages since he'd been this...well, normal. "Yes, Damon. He married Natalia."

He nodded slowly. "Damon—Sofia's friend."

A lump rose in Izzy's throat and she swallowed it down. "Yes. Do you remember much about him?"

"They were inseparable, I'd say," Papa started, leaning back further against the wall. "More so as the years went on." He pursed his lips thoughtfully. "Why ya asking, Iz?"

"Oh." She fiddled with her locket. "Stella...Stella thinks something may have happened...with Natalia. She thinks Natalia may have...may have stolen from him and that may have caused his death."

His eyes widened and he whistled. "Now that's a serious accusation from Stella."

"I know. I…" Izzy sighed. "I don't want to believe it, Papa, but Stella…I do trust Stella, more than Nat—"

"Trust?" he exploded, making Izzy jump and nearly shriek, her locket falling back against her chest. "Trust is poison. Futile. They're everywhere, Izzy, everywhere! You can't trust the lot of them!"

"Okay, Papa, okay." She put her trembling hands up in a show of peace. "It's just me."

"No!" he roared, his eyes cloudy again as they searched the room in a wild frenzy. "Beasts! Everywhere! From all sides! They are always there!"

"No, Papa, it's okay. Please…" Izzy nearly choked. "Please don't leave me."

As quickly as they had come, the clouds departed from his eyes, a clear sky after the heaviest storm. He took her shoulders in his wide hands. "There are beasts, Izzy," he said, his voice solemn. "Beasts everywhere. Beasts in them all."

Izzy nodded frantically, if only to appease him. "I know. I know. It's okay."

Having said his piece, Papa collapsed back against the wall, breathless. His eyelids slid closed hesitantly, fighting exhaustion and the darkness it brought.

Izzy waited a few moments to give him space and collect herself. "Papa?" she asked timidly. "During my last visit I read you a story. I never got to finish it." She stroked the book reassuringly, to comfort herself. "Can I read you the rest?"

Papa's head moved up; Izzy took that as a nod. Settling against the freezing wall next to him, she opened her book and began to read, the words coming up from the pages and engulfing both of them in a blanket of warmth, promising a better world somewhere, someday.

* * * * * * *

Stella's boots were caked with mud by the time she returned to the house. It was late, and there was nobody awake in the village now to catch her as she stole down the dirt path in the inky night. She had only the moonlight to guide her steps and find the rope she'd used to climb out of her window earlier; thankfully, it was still tucked safely against the wall when she returned.

Carefully, she placed the rectangle box she was carrying underneath her arm, then took the rope in her hands, braced her boot against the side of the house, and began to climb. It wasn't too hard—their house had low ceilings, making it short for two stories, and the paneling wasn't completely aligned, allowing for a few footholds along the way. She was grateful she'd ditched her maid skirt for the sturdy black pants she always snuck underneath her dresses.

Within a few minutes she had forced her way up the house and through the attic window. The top half of her body was barely through the pane when two hands snatched her shoulders and helped pull her inside.

"What are you *doing?*" Izzy demanded quietly, breathless, though she wasn't the one who had just scaled the wall. "Do you have any idea what time it is?"

Stella collapsed to her knees, panting, sweat beading on her forehead. "I don't know," she huffed. "Midnight?"

Izzy put her hands on her hips. "Well after! You've been gone all day and I've been worried sick!" Her eyes tracked the dirt and mud that decorated Stella's skin and hair. "Where have you been?"

Once she'd caught her breath, Stella regained the urgency that had propelled her to run through the night.

"I heard it," she said, rage boiling underneath her skin. "I heard the guards come back and I heard them talking and…" She forced a breath through her teeth.

"What did they say?"

"More than Natalia ever did," Stella snapped. "And now everything...it all adds up. It all makes sense—everything that *didn't* make sense makes sense, and now…"

Izzy appraised her hateful spluttering with wide eyes. "Stella, what happened?"

"He left. He left on his trip just like he always did, and then he never came back. Heart failure, she told me. I've thought that, believed that all these years, and it took eavesdropping on royal advisors to hear the truth. I can't...I can't believe it."

Izzy kneeled down next to her, imploring. "Believe *what?*"

The words tasted like bile so Stella spat them out. "She lied. It wasn't heart failure. My father was murdered."

Izzy's face crumbled. "No."

"Yes." The harsh reality only fueled Stella, her words almost tripping over themselves as she raged on. "They were talking to Natalia about a *murder* investigation, and she didn't tell me, and I know she won't because *she did it.* She killed him and she's covered it up for five years and now they've closed the case. So I've got to solve this on my own. First I went to my father's grave and dug up the—"

Izzy's mouth dropped open. "You did *what?*"

"Closed-casket funeral," Stella said, impatience oozing out of every syllable. "He had a closed-casket funeral. Natalia said it was because his failing health left the body so mutilated, but now I'm not so sure. I went to his grave and dug up his casket and you know what? It was empty."

Izzy gasped but Stella pressed on.

"Then I sat in the graveyard for a while, thinking. I have no idea who would want to murder my father, except for Natalia, if she wanted his money *that* badly. Although a lot of good it's done her now," Stella added bitterly, glancing around the shack.

Izzy looked like she might object, but Stella didn't give her the chance. "Because he had no enemies except her, he might not have known he was going to be murdered. If he suspected anything, though, I knew he would leave something behind. Something for me."

The weight in Stella's chest grew heavier at the thought. She shifted her position on the ground so she was sitting cross legged. "I took a carriage out to the seaside—to the spot he always used to take me."

Izzy gasped again. "Stella! The sea isn't safe! You know that."

"My father was always safe on the sea," Stella argued, despite Elaria's terribly high record of sunken ships.

"Maybe, but that was just good luck."

"No, it was skill and love." Stella jerked her chin out defensively. "That's why he was so successful at what he did—he loved the sea, so it loved him back. He would take me there all the time. You remember, don't you?"

Hesitating, Izzy finally gave an unconvinced nod.

"Anyway, I went to our spot and spent hours snooping around. It took some time but I finally found a suspicious rock off the shore that had been hollowed out." She held up her hands, which were covered in rubble and scratches. "It was hard work, getting into it, but…" She reached behind her and pulled the box into her lap, slowing down for the first time at the thought of showing Izzy what it held. "Inside was this."

When Stella didn't move, Izzy took the box and set it in her own lap before taking off the lid. Her eyes widened at the contents, and the lid dropped from her grasp.

Stella knew what she'd see first: the metal crest, about the size of her palm.

"What…?" Izzy inspected the insignia, barely touching it with her fingertips as though the slightest pressure would shatter it. "It's almost…it almost looks like the king's crest. The royal family symbol. Except…" Her eyebrows furrowed while she studied it. "Except—"

Stella huffed. "Except the royal family symbol is red, not ice blue, and the shape is symmetrical and circular with smooth designs, while this one looks like someone took a hammer to it."

"Right. What does it mean?"

"If I knew that, I would tell you."

Ignoring the bite in Stella's tone, Izzy set aside the crest and peered back into the box to find the second puzzling object: a long and slender rod of what looked like glass or ice, broken into two perfect pieces, rendering it useless.

A magic wand.

"But…" Izzy stuttered, pinching a piece between two fingers as though it were a venomous snake. "But I thought magic wands were outlawed years ago. After The Great War."

Stella nodded grimly. "They were. My current theory is that whoever it belonged to may have been the one to murder him. They must've been mixed up in whatever this is—" she gestured to the crest, "—and he found out, was going to do something about it, but they killed him to keep him silent or retaliate."

"That rules out Natalia," Izzy offered, already bracing herself for the backlash from the remark.

"No, it doesn't. Natalia has a motive, and she's from a noble class—one much higher than my father when she married him. Technically she still has her magic license; she's allowed simple magic in Racine, if people wouldn't mob her for it."

Izzy shook her head. "Magic wands aren't for simple magic, Stel."

"Exactly. What was she into?"

"I don't know if…" Izzy trailed off, the last item in the box catching her eye, and the color drained from her face. In slow motion, she reached inside and pulled out the faded photograph. The corners were bent and yellowed, and there was a large crease down the middle, but the image was shockingly clear, taken, Stella guessed, about six years earlier. In it were four figures lined up next to each other, smiling as if they were all old friends. The king was on the far left, as regal and powerful as ever, only a half smile on his perpetually stern face. The vivacious dark-skinned woman on the far right had dredged up Stella's memories from before her father's death.

"Zaria?" Izzy breathed, her thumb brushing the beautiful woman's face.

Stella nodded again, her whisper matching Izzy's level of incredulity. "My godmother. She used to visit all the time until he died, remember? Everyone thinks she went missing." That was the only excuse Stella wanted to believe regarding Zaria's disappearance from her life.

Izzy nodded absently, her attention already snatched away, dragging her back in time. For wedged in the middle of the pack, beaming with excitement, were Damon and Sofia.

"You know what this means, don't you?" Stella asked, fidgeting with impatience. She had made a plan hours ago, on her way back to the house, and she was ready to get going on it.

Still dazed, Izzy shook her head.

"Well this photo is in this box for a reason. These people mean something. Obviously, my father is in it because he wanted me to find the truth about his death, and Zaria isn't around." Stella skipped over the part where Sofia was unreachable too—Izzy didn't need the reminder. "So that only leaves one avenue. The closest one, anyway."

"One aven…" Izzy trailed off, glancing at the picture again, and her expression filled with dread and understanding.

Stella nodded through Izzy's silent protests. "We need an audience with the king."

CHAPTER 3

DANCING ON BROKEN GLASS

"Natalia is going to be so angry."

That was at least the fifth time Izzy had mentioned that to Stella. And for the fifth time, Stella brushed her off with a wave of her hand and said, "Natalia is never going to know."

Izzy grasped her locket as they walked down the dirt road, glancing around every few seconds to make sure nobody had seen them. She hated walking through the west market square; she felt like she was on display, waiting for someone to throw the first figurative egg. But just like Stella had said before they snuck out their window, everyone was too busy to pay attention to anyone, especially two social outcasts. Nobody would notice them today.

Today was the day of the king's ball.

All around them, villagers were bustling about, washing grimy skin, mending fancy clothes, and dusting dancing shoes that hadn't been used in ages. The streets of dismal, collapsing shacks full of grungy and hardened people seemed a little straighter and brighter, genuine smiles on people's faces as they rushed about preparing for the magical evening ahead.

There was once a time when Izzy had dreamed of going to the king's annual ball too. She and Stella had gone one year with Natalia and Damon, and she had vivid memories of tables that stretched out forever, full of extravagant food Izzy had never even read about; of giant swan statues that were spelled to sing the sweetest songs; and the biggest, most amazing, and most ridiculous gowns Izzy had ever seen. And before that, when the girls were too young to attend, she and Stella used to sneak into Natalia's closets with Isla and Noor and dress themselves up. Amid compliments and fits of giggles, they'd all pretend they were going to the ball to meet a prince.

Natalia would scold them for stealing her things, but it was always half-hearted, and she'd always take photos of them. Damon would whistle and clap and dance with each of his daughters, while Papa would play his harmonica and Mother would sing. The parents would promise them that one day they'd get their chance too.

And here they were, years and lifetimes later, dressing up again to attend, this time in reality. Only now, Damon was dead, Sofia was gone, Papa was detained, and Natalia was unrecognizable. In fact, Natalia had strictly forbidden everyone from ever going to a palace function again—no exceptions, even for the annual ball celebrating King Rowan's defeat of the rebels nearly a century ago.

She'd made that rule shortly after Damon died. Stella had been too depressed to fight her on it, and Izzy had learned that staying home was better if she didn't want to be ridiculed in public. They'd never had a real reason to break that rule.

Until now.

Izzy would never dream of defying Natalia if it weren't for the photo that Stella had found. The photo of King Asher of all people, Stella's missing godmother Zaria, the murdered Damon, and Sofia. *Her mother.* Sofia and Damon had been best friends as long as Izzy could remember, but what were the two of them doing with the king, just months before both of them were gone for good?

Izzy's fingers tingled at the thought. It meant something. And both she and Stella were determined to find out what.

Stella pulled on Izzy's shoulders to stop her. Blinking through her daze, she realized they were out of West Market and had reached their destination: Lady Pursbrough's house.

Dread coiled in Izzy's stomach as they walked up the grand marble steps to the stark maroon double door. "This isn't going to work, Stella," she whispered, fumbling for her locket.

"Of course it will." Stella gave a mischievous grin and rang the brass bell. "It was your idea."

The peal of the bell rang through the house—magically enhanced, of course—and Izzy didn't have time to hide before the door opened and Lady Pursbrough greeted them. She was already dressed up in a round, red corset gown, looking like a rosy apple rolled in glitter.

"Isabelle. Stella. Welcome girls!" She extended her arms out, gesturing inside. "Come on in."

Izzy wrung her hands, eyes darting every which way. Surely, Natalia had told Lady Pursbrough they weren't allowed to attend. Not that the two ladies ever talked to each other, but there was *some* probability that they crossed paths...

"Thank you for letting us borrow some dresses, Lady Pursbrough," Stella said as she pulled Izzy inside with her. "We just didn't have anything good enough for the occasion."

"Oh well of course, dear," Lady Pursbrough gushed, maroon skirts swishing around her stout frame. "I'm so glad you thought to ask me for help! I've collected so many gowns over the years, and it's good to put a few of them to use. We all have to look our best to celebrate our great King Rowan's victory, don't we?" She smiled. "Of course, Stella, you know the way up to the spare powder room—you must've cleaned it just yesterday."

"Sparkling clean," Stella replied with a grin. "Only the best for you."

"Oh you are just too sweet. Come on up."

Lady Pursbrough led the way up the iron spiral staircase; Stella had to grab Izzy's hand and drag her up the stairs. Izzy's eyes were everywhere, as if they could somehow detect the moment their plan would be discovered.

Izzy wasn't sure Lady Pursbrough would be upset if she discovered they were breaking Natalia's rules. She'd probably just stay out of it or advise them to go home. But if Natalia found them out somehow...she could be terrifying when she was angry. Izzy hadn't seen it much, but she'd seen enough to know she didn't want to be on the wrong end of Natalia's wrath. Especially now that Natalia might be a murderer.

Might, she reminded herself. *Innocent until proven guilty.*

Izzy had long been trying to figure out Natalia Amaranth. She doted on her daughters—not as much as she used to, of course—and Izzy remembered a time when she'd gaze at Damon with so much love in her eyes, a time when she told Stella to call her 'mother' if she felt comfortable with it. Natalia loved her daughters; she'd loved Damon. Izzy had thought she'd loved Stella too, but now it was difficult to find any indication of that. Not that Izzy was a leading expert on motherly love, but still…

"Isabelle?" Lady Pursbrough asked, concern coloring the edge of her tone. "Are you okay, dear?"

Blinking, Izzy yanked herself out of her thoughts. With a start, she realized they were already in the parlor upstairs, a wide room with four floor-length mirrors, two silver vanities, and a vast wardrobe overflowing with fabrics.

"Um, what…" She hiccupped with nerves, and Stella elbowed her in the side. "Yes, Lady Pursbrough. What were you saying?"

Lady Pursbrough gave a smile, though it was weaker than her usual. "You are both welcome to anything in here. Most of the fabrics have been spelled to fit the frame they're put on." She gestured to her wide hips. "You girls are quite a bit smaller than me. Too many chocolate cream puffs, I tell you, but there's just no other way to live." She gave another glance around the room. "Alrighty, then, I've got to catch Christian's carriage, but there'll be one here waiting whenever you'd like to go. Have fun girls!"

"Thanks Lady Pursbrough!" Stella exclaimed as the noblewoman sashayed out the door. Izzy mumbled, "Thanks," but she was already gone.

* * * * * * *

The carriage ride took longer than Stella had anticipated, thanks to the stalling traffic that came with an entire kingdom trying to get to the same place at the same time. Ever the terrible traveler, Stella kept tapping her hands against her legs, barely feeling the motion underneath the plush fabrics of her ice blue gown. The magic-driven carriage Lady Pursbrough had let them borrow, while spacious and luxurious, could not move fast enough.

Izzy had read for the first half of the ride—Stella had no idea exactly where in her yellow dress she had stowed the novel—but by the end she had the book cradled to her chest, locket in hand, as she gazed out the window with glassy eyes. Stella tried to do the same. She watched out the window with fascination as the kingdom passed her by, but the constant stop and start of the carriage grew tiresome and boring. No matter how hard she tried, she couldn't quiet the distracting thoughts in her head.

Soon, though, those thoughts would find a resolution. She'd get her answers, no matter how badly Natalia wanted to keep them from her.

Eventually, the carriage came to a stop and the door opened, jolting Stella from her stewing. She shoved her borrowed shoes on and all but jumped out of the carriage. The shoes were slightly too big, but they were the only shoes in Lady Pursbrough's closet that would somewhat fit her tiny feet. She must've forgotten to spell the shoes like the dresses.

It doesn't matter, she told herself. *Let's just get on with it.*

The castle stood before her, shooting up into the sky and alight with the festivities it held inside. Lush, green grounds seemed to roll on forever, dotted with shocking reds, oranges, and yellows from the exotic plants, framing the castle in an expanse of growth. Iron torches lined the stone pathway to guide their way, and guards were stationed periodically with the charge to keep any potential threat contained. Since they had to wait until the coast was clear to sneak out without Natalia knowing, Stella and Izzy were some of the last to arrive, the people outside dwindling and the party in full swing inside. Stella heard Izzy take a sharp breath when she got out of the carriage.

"It's huge," Stella said, tipping her head back to see where the highest spire touched the sky.

Izzy hugged herself, the novel now hidden again wherever she'd put it. "It looks angry," she whispered.

"Now you're being ridiculous." Stella took Izzy's gloved hand and pulled her forward. "Let's go."

Stella had to drag Izzy up the pathway that led to the palace entrance. The air outside was cooling down as evening began morphing into night, but there was still a trickle of sweat running down Stella's back by the time they made it to the doors and up the stairs to the ballroom. An elegant guard dressed in red nodded to them as they entered.

"Good evening, ladies," he said, and the girls curtsied. "Names?"

Izzy went pale and Stella shook her head. "No announcement needed for us, sir, but thank you."

If the man was surprised, he didn't show it. He just ushered them inside the ballroom.

The aromas hit Stella first: roasted lamb, steaming vegetables, fresh pastries, enough food strewn along the banquet tables to feed the kingdom many times over. Red banners bearing the king's crest hung over the crowd of people, nobles and villagers alike, that had come together one night for an evening of celebration. The dancing was well underway, and the orchestra in the corner played a faster tune that people were clapping and whirling along to.

"Look at that, Izzy!" Stella gasped, pointing. At the far end of the ballroom stood a giant statue of a bird. It flapped its wings to the beat of the music, and once the song ended it made a wide arc up to the ceiling, then dove back and exploded into flame. A second later, it flew back up and flapped its wings again to the next song.

"Wow," Izzy murmured at the symbol of the late King Rowan, who was as close to deity as a mortal had ever become. "A phoenix rising from the ashes."

They watched the bird for another moment, mesmerized, before Stella broke her eyes away and found the throne, set back and on a raised dais to look over the crowd of guests. Queen Sarafina dazzled in an elegant wine gown that clung to her frame, a half smile on her face as she watched the dancing from her seat on the right. The chair on the left was empty—Prince Roman must've been enjoying the party somewhere else. And sitting on the middle throne was King Asher himself, looking as regal as ever in a fiery red suit. His salt and pepper hair had been swept up like a flame, and the jewels on his crown sparkled in the light.

Stella nodded to herself. That was the man she needed to talk to.

Izzy seemed to follow her gaze. "How are you going to do this? Just walk up to him and ask?"

"We need to be direct but not suspicious," Stella decided, unwilling to admit she didn't have a set plan. "We'll meander close enough to get a conversation started, then just mention my father used to come around the castle before he died. 'Perhaps you knew him, Your Majesty?'" Stella curtsied, mimicking a noble's gracious tone. Then she smirked. "Easy. We get back home before Natalia notices we're gone, and she has no idea we're one step closer to finding her out."

Izzy sighed, unconvinced. "Whatever you say, Stel."

"I say this will work."

Stella and Izzy descended the stairs, and the masses seemed to absorb them into the throng. Stella linked elbows with Izzy so they wouldn't be separated as they navigated through the guests, being sure to stay on the edges where people were mingling and eating. The sounds of music, clapping, and dancing steps overwhelmed the massive space, but Stella caught snippets of lively conversation and laughter. She wondered if it was heartening for the king to see his people come together and have fun. Not that anyone could tell—King Asher rarely managed more than half a smile.

They lost sight of the king for a minute and struggled to make their way across the ballroom. Stella wanted to plow through the crowd and make them part for her, but Izzy steered her by the elbow, a master of finding the small spaces between groups and weaving through them unnoticed. The song had just ended, the phoenix exploding again, when they finally made it to the other side.

The dais was empty. Both King Asher and Queen Sarafina were gone, leaving a trio of vacant thrones in their wake.

Izzy muttered something under her breath, but Stella was determined. The king was not getting away from her, not tonight. She barely hesitated before surging forward with Izzy in tow. Following a servant with an empty platter, she made her way closer to the thrones. When the servant went through the door to the kitchen, Stella ducked to the other side, darting through the door behind the dais.

The room was small and shockingly quiet compared to the noise just on the other side of the wall. There were two vanities on the far side of the space, full of makeup and gels and discarded jewels. A square table took up the center with a few chairs and a pitcher of water. The opposite wall had another door, presumably leading deeper inside the castle. It seemed even the royal family needed a place to take a break from the party.

Unfortunately, it was empty, but Stella could work with that. King Asher had to come by sometime, right? Stella pulled the photograph out from where she had stowed it in her dress. She was ready.

Izzy clutched Stella's arm tighter as she looked around, realizing where she was. "Stella," she squeaked in a whisper. "We aren't supposed to be in here."

"No, you aren't."

Stella whirled around to find two figures in the doorway they'd just come through: Prince Roman and his advisor. Izzy took an automatic step back, then gave an awkward curtsy. Her elbow was still linked with Stella's, yanking Stella's left side down and back up with her.

The prince appraised them without expression, a wiry, silver crown settled in his dark hair, devoid of the jewels his father's held. Behind him, his young advisor glared at them with his hand on his sword, the glower made more menacing by the severe scars that disfigured his face.

Stella's resolve froze—the idea of talking to a royal seemed much easier moments ago, before she'd been trapped underneath the sheer power and prestige the prince's presence brought.

"Your Majesty." Stella finally managed a half curtsy. "We were just trying to find—"

"The ladies' room?" Prince Roman interjected, empty humor in his tone as he surveyed her, unimpressed. "Believe it or not, I've heard that one before. Surely you have something better for me than that."

Stella gritted her teeth at his arrogance. "Actually, I don't have anything for *you*. I need to speak with the king."

A flicker of surprise went across Prince Roman's bored face. Izzy glanced at Stella nervously, fingering her yellow gloves, but Stella held her ground. She would not be intimidated by a spoiled prince.

"Inquiries for the king should be taken up elsewhere," his advisor growled, his voice fierce, choppy gravel compared to the prince's low, rolling thunder. He began pulling out his sword. "I will—"

Prince Roman raised his palm, and the advisor paused. "What's that?" he asked, caramel eyes on the photo clutched in her hand.

Stella took a step back, and Izzy stumbled with her. "It's none of your business."

"My kingdom, my business."

"It's not your kingdom yet."

The prince's face darkened and the advisor hissed under his breath. Izzy squeezed Stella's elbow. "Stella," she breathed, a mix of a warning and a whimper.

Prince Roman set his jaw and walked forward, a powerful ease about him, as though he were commanding the floor to meet his foot with every step. The advisor shadowed him, hand still on the hilt of his weapon. Despite her resolve, Stella couldn't bring herself to move when Prince Roman reached around her and pried the photo from her fist.

The room almost paused, time slowing down, as the royals looked over Stella's precious photo. Prince Roman arched an eyebrow, elbowing his advisor so he would take a look at the photo too. His friend gave no discernible reaction upon studying it himself, though there was a new flame that danced in the prince's eyes. Izzy moved from fingering her wrinkled gloves to holding her locket. Stella grew more jittery by the second, wanting to see what they saw. Clearly, they saw *something*.

"That's my father," she finally said, feeling the need to defend him somehow. The cloud of haughtiness in the room grated on her nerves.

Prince Roman's lips quirked to the side, almost a smile. "No, that's *my* father."

Stella huffed and forced her tone to stay polite. "Point taken, Your Majesty."

Tearing his eyes from the photo, the prince regarded Stella again, this time with calculation. "And why did you need to speak to my father about this?"

Stella lifted her head higher. "I'll let your father know that when I speak to him."

"Maybe I can pass along a message."

"Somehow I doubt it would reach him, Your Highness," Stella responded, her voice dripping with fake pleasantries. Pleasantries as fake as this prince. "But thank you for the offer."

Prince Roman moved to say something else, but the door across the room swung open, revealing several servants. The distraction let Stella snatch her photo back, dash around the boys with Izzy, and duck out the other door, allowing themselves to be swallowed whole by the crowd.

* * * * * * *

"Well that could've gone better," Stella muttered to herself, leaning back against the wall as she took a bite of a pastry. "Haughty little prince in his fancy castle, high above us all. Ridiculous."

Izzy twirled her locket and drank some punch, quietly surveying the dancing and letting Stella stew. Izzy knew better than to tell her she shouldn't have talked to the prince that way—not if she didn't want to be in trouble.

Instead, she offered, "He seemed interested in what you had to say."

Stella scoffed, crumbs falling from her mouth. "He was only interested in knowing everything. Probably meant to turn it around as a rumor."

Izzy refrained from rolling her eyes. If Stella would let go of her stubborn pride every once in a while, she'd get closer to where she needed to go.

"Maybe," Izzy replied before another drink of punch. The sweet, strawberry-citrus taste left her tongue bubbling; she wasn't sure if she liked the sensation or not, but she kept drinking it. "So what should we do now?"

"I still need to talk to the king." Her determination didn't sound nearly as sure as it had when they'd arrived. She must've noticed it herself because she blew out a breath in frustration. "I just want to know what happened to my father. And these shoes are killing me!"

Without hesitation, Stella lifted her skirt and threw off the borrowed shoes, kicking them against the wall next to her, then huffed and grabbed another pastry from the banquet table in front of them.

Again, Izzy waited and drank her punch. Stella would cool off eventually, especially if free sweets were involved. She just hoped it would be sooner rather than later; Izzy didn't have Stella's brazen comfort in the palace, and she'd had to pause her book at a really great part. More than anything, Izzy just wanted to hide in their room and read.

But Izzy had promised she'd help Stella, and she was going to keep that promise. If Stella wanted to stay and eat against the wall and come up with half plans that wouldn't really work, then Izzy would resign herself to the same.

The moon shone through the big window by the doors, though the party showed no sign of slowing down despite the increasingly late hour. The laughter had only gotten louder and the dancing slightly sloppier as people drank to their heart's content and let themselves have a night off from their work and worries.

It amazed Izzy that so many poor peasants were able to come to such a lavish party without shouting the embittered profanities she'd often heard in their village, but, then again, maybe those angry people had put their frustrations aside to celebrate the kingdom's victory.

Izzy had started on her third cup of punch—it was a good concoction, she decided—when something caught her eye, making her choke and cough. Amid the throng of dancing guests, a boy was twirling a beautiful girl around, her burnt orange gown swishing around her with grace and flirtation at the same time. The boy's black hair had been slicked back into a ponytail, and his muscled arms caught and twisted and dipped the girl with ease, both of their faces alight with smiles.

The sight was like a blow to the gut. Izzy wrapped her arms around herself, as though she could keep herself together, but she'd started to wonder why she should bother.

"What is it?" Stella asked, remnants of her annoyance still smoldering in her tone. "What's wrong?"

"No-nothing," Izzy stuttered. She tried to drop her eyes, to stop the pain of looking, but she couldn't get herself to obey. It had been years since she'd seen him. "Nothing. It's nothing."

Not to be deterred, Stella followed Izzy's gaze, and Izzy felt when the air around Stella crackled, her anger catching fire again.

"Gannon," she spat. "Talk about people that deserve to die."

Finally, Izzy tore her gaze away to look at Stella, who had her hands balled into fists like she was going to jump into a fray. If anyone in the kingdom had a reason to fear for their life, it would be Gannon, the boy that had stolen Izzy's heart for years only to brutally crush it. Stella had it out for him, to put it mildly, and he likely wouldn't have survived that year if they hadn't moved away to Racine.

"No, Stella, don't...just...I'm not...I don't know. Just don't. Please. It'll make it worse."

Stella jerked her chin up at Gannon, as though he weren't worth her time. "You're right, we have much more *important* things to worry about. Focus on the king. How can we find answers?"

Izzy bit her lip and nodded, but she knew it'd be useless. Of course, she shouldn't have been surprised that Gannon would be here, but even the thought of his name sent a blade in her side. Knowing she was in the same room as him again made it more difficult to breathe. What if he saw her? What if he said those horrible things to her, called her those awful names, *here*, in front of the entire kingdom?

The thought sent her backing up further, curling herself in the corner of the wall and a giant decorative pillar. The new position hopefully kept her hidden from Gannon, and allowed her to catch a glimpse of him every time a woman a few feet in front of her swayed to the beat. It also allowed her a new angle to see a slight part in the crowd, which paved the way to someone else.

Izzy realized Stella had been in the middle of saying something, but she cut in.

"Stella," Izzy gasped. "I see Natalia."

Stella straightened up and moved closer to Izzy. "What? Where?" she whispered, even though nobody would be listening anyways.

"Straight ahead, slightly to the left. Next to the man with the eyeglass."

Stella pursed her lips at the sight of Natalia shining in a marigold gown—shining not just in her wardrobe, but in her smile. The grime and hardness had been washed away, and her skin was radiating, both with the makeup she was wearing like she used to, and in the genuine brightness on her face. Apparently she thought to share such a fine evening with her daughters, because Isla and Noor were there too, dancing around Natalia while she laughed with the woman next to her. Natalia looked like the wife of a noble again. A happy one.

"I hate her," Stella said under her breath. "And she can have her night of supposed freedom, because I'm going to bring all of her buried skeletons back to light. She's not going to get away with it."

Izzy opened her mouth to say something—like how they had to watch for when Natalia left so they could beat her home—but a voice behind Stella interrupted her.

"Ladies."

Stella jumped and a silent squeak escaped Izzy when she saw Prince Roman standing on the other side of Stella, slightly too close to be casual. The intimidating advisor once again towered behind him, his mane of hair barely contained in a ponytail, and lips pursed as though he were trying not to growl.

Prince Roman nodded at them before extending his hand to Stella. "Care for a dance?"

Stella raised an eyebrow. "A dance? You can't be serious."

"I don't joke about dancing."

Stella exchanged a glance with Izzy, but Izzy's limbs felt frozen and she couldn't think of a way out of this, of what the prince must want with them now that they'd shown their hand…

"I, uh…" Stella cleared her throat. "I was just leaving. We both were."

People were looking now, their gazes prey to the gravity of the royal. She turned to go, but the prince stepped in front of her, blocking her path and trapping Izzy against the pillar. Again, he extended his hand.

"You're going to turn down your prince in his own house?" he asked, his lips quirking to the side in an arrogant half smile.

"I'm sure there are plenty of other girls here that would ecstatically accept. Now, excuse us."

Again, the prince blocked her path. "I insist."

Izzy practically felt the steam coming out of Stella's ears, but thankfully, Stella didn't make a scene. She took the prince's hand like it was a live snake, then gave Izzy a last nervous glance before stepping hesitantly after Prince Roman.

Unsure what to do, Izzy took a step away from the pillar, but instantly backed right up to it again when Prince Roman's advisor stepped toward her and turned his back to the wall. He was too stiff to be casual, and Izzy recognized what he was doing: standing guard over her.

What did these boys want with them?

Clearly, Izzy wasn't going anywhere, and she wasn't brave enough to challenge him like Stella would. Instead she leaned back in the corner of the pillar and pulled out her novel from a slit in the waist of her dress. She needed a story to distract her before her nerves ate her up.

She'd only barely settled into the chapter when the advisor interrupted her. "What are you doing?" he demanded through his teeth, part disbelieving and part annoyed.

Izzy glanced up and blinked in surprise. "I'm reading."

"You brought a book to a ball?"

She shrugged. "What else is there to do?"

The advisor stared at her heatedly, and Izzy couldn't decide if he was trying to understand her or trying not to strangle her.

The effect was heightened by the scars down his face and neck, and despite the chill in her spine when he glared at her, she wondered what had happened to him. Though he was the prince's named advisor, he couldn't have been much older than Izzy herself.

After another moment of glowering at her, he turned his head back to the crowd, which reminded Izzy of her job as watchman. Closing her book, she stretched up on her toes, trying to see over the scores of people.

"Are you looking for someone?" the advisor asked, exasperated, like he was babysitting an unruly child.

"No," Izzy answered absently, eyes poring over hundreds of faces. "I'm trying to stay hidden."

* * * * * * *

Stella gave a last glance to Izzy as the prince pulled her onto the dance floor.

"Your friend will be safe with Griffin," Prince Roman said, pursing his lips in amusement. He picked a spot toward the middle of the crowd and stopped, seemingly oblivious to the people—mostly girls—watching them intently.

"I felt safe until now," Stella muttered. "Was that a threat, Your Majesty?"

The prince smirked at her before wrapping an arm around her waist and pulling her into a mild-paced dance. "Why would I threaten a guest at my party?"

Stella's retort got lost in her throat as her focus fell to her feet. She hadn't danced in years, and her bare feet stumbled against the smooth floor—a stark contrast from Prince Roman, who obviously had practice, grace, and shoes.

"You don't get out much, do you?"

Realizing she was watching the floor, Stella snapped her gaze back up to see the prince's mocking smile. "I don't get out *at all*," she snapped. "Some of us don't have a castle to go home to and have to work for a living. Work hard."

70

"Ah." The prince nodded to himself. "So you *are* political. I wondered, with the color of your dress."

"What?" Automatically, Stella glanced down at the icy blue dress she was in. She'd grabbed the first reasonable one in Lady Pursbrough's closet; it hadn't been a conscious choice. "I don't know what you're talking about. I don't care about politics."

Prince Roman appraised her with a raised eyebrow as he turned them around to the music. "You are either incredibly brash or incredibly naive. I'm not sure which makes you stupider."

Stella gritted her teeth. It was an effort not to yell at him. "And you are either incredibly arrogant or incredibly insecure, both of which are rather pathetic."

The mocking amusement fell from Prince Roman's face, cold resolve taking its place, and for a second Stella was reminded she should be afraid of him—or at least a little wary. He was the prince, after all.

His arm around her waist tightened, pulling her closer to him despite her hesitation. He lowered his voice and spoke in her ear. "My father wants to be with his people this evening, as a show of unity, but security is still thick. You won't get close enough to him to ask whatever you're here for. I'm your best chance at any royal help."

Stella watched over Prince Roman's shoulder as people twirled by. "Why would you help me?"

"Well, now, I'm always out to help my loyal subjects."

She made a face, which, unfortunately, he couldn't see. "Not good enough."

He sighed in exasperation. "Because I'm bored. I'm bored, resourceful, and endlessly curious as to what you're up to."

Infuriated, Stella tried to yank away but the prince held her fast, so she resorted to digging her fingernails into his hand in an effort to inflict pain. "I don't care who you are, *Your Highness*. My father's murder is *not* some glorified puzzle to fill up your free time because you're *bored*."

Prince Roman stiffened, missing a step in the dance, and it took a few beats for him to recover. "I'm sorry," he said with sincerity, loosening his hold on her. "I didn't realize. You wanted to speak to my father about investigating?"

Without the fire from the prince, Stella's angry energy depleted too. She felt her shoulders sag as she sighed. "I found that photo. I thought maybe the king would know something—anything. I think...I think my stepmother killed him."

The song ended, but Prince Roman didn't stop dancing despite the line of hopeful girls watching him. He kept going until the next one started, then adjusted to the new rhythm, taking in what she said. "Has there been an investigation with her?"

"The crown just closed it."

"And you don't believe them." He said it as a fact, without surprise.

"No. I know she had something to do with it."

Stella felt him nod to himself. "All right. Are you still living with her?"

She forced herself not to gag at the thought. "Yes."

"Are you in any danger?"

A lump formed in Stella's throat at the deep fear she'd been trying to bury for days, casting an anxious glance in Izzy's general direction. "I don't know."

The prince broke their stance to spin her around, then brought her back, giving her a chance to see his concentrated gaze, as though he were strategizing his own military force as they spoke. "Do you know who the others are in the photo? Maybe they know something."

Stella nodded. "One is Sofia, Izzy's mother. She walked out on them a few months before my father died—she's a dead end. The other is my godmother, Zaria. I haven't seen her since he died."

"Missing?"

"Some think." Stella shrugged. "I was too young to go find her on my own, and my stepmother didn't care to help. Zaria was a thrill-seeker, though, always out doing crazy things. I guess after so long I figured she got caught up in adventure and forgot about me. But now...now I'm wondering if she was involved somehow. If my stepmother kept her away from me."

"Hm." The prince nodded again. "So you're going to find Zaria, then?"

The thought hadn't occurred to Stella, but it seemed obvious now. Of course Zaria would be the perfect person to find—she knew Stella's father long before Stella was born, and even if she didn't know exactly what had happened, she'd be eager to help Stella figure it out.

"Yes," Stella said, as if that were her plan the whole time. "That's exactly what I'm going to do. I just thought I'd check with the king first."

"Sounds logical to me," Prince Roman said, still in military mode. "I take it you have leads then as to where she is?"

Stella couldn't stop the nod that came; there was no chance she would admit to the prince she didn't. "Of course I do."

"And what—"

The prince kept talking, but Stella stopped hearing him. With another twirl, she had a new line of sight over his shoulder, and a puff of frantic yellow fell right into that line. Izzy's face was screwed up in a panic as she waved Stella down, mouthing one word over and over again while pointing to the door.

Natalia.

Stella sucked in a sharp breath and let go of the prince; he was so startled, he let her go automatically.

"I have to go."

His eyebrows pulled down in confusion. "Go? Why—"

Stella lurched forward, her eyes following Izzy's ducking escape from the watchful advisor. She heard a girl ask for Prince Roman's next dance, but Stella spared no other thought for him as she forced herself through the crowd.

Izzy met her at the doorway, breathless too, but neither of them stopped. They balled their skirts in their fists and raced to their borrowed carriage waiting for them at the end of the arrival line. Stella's head smacked against the roof as they threw themselves inside.

"Go!" Stella slapped her hand on the magic panel, as Lady Pursbrough had instructed, before they were fully situated, and the carriage jerked forward, throwing the girls backward. Stella felt she would suffocate underneath the mounds of blue and yellow fabric.

Finally, Izzy got herself upright in a seat, and she helped Stella get up too. Her yellow gloves had slipped off onto the floor; she gripped her locket in both hands, her face as pale as the moon shining through the window.

"I don't know when she left," Izzy blurted, her voice trembling, confessing like it was somehow her fault. "I was watching her, making sure we were safe, and then I got distracted and lost her and then I couldn't find her again, and I knew, somehow I knew, that she—"

"It's okay," Stella said, trying to make her words strong, though they wobbled a little. "We'll make it. We'll climb through the window and she'll never know. She never goes upstairs anyway. We'll be okay."

The fear in Izzy's voice just confirmed what Stella had been trying to ignore. So far, she'd mostly been able to think of Natalia's guilt as a narrative separate from her own, a hypothetical question that Izzy would pose in the kitchen on a calm evening. But the truth, the reality, of that prospect had been a sharp nagging in the back of Stella's mind since she'd overheard that awful conversation.

If Natalia really could kill Damon, she could kill them too.

We'll make it. They had to make it. They had to.

Time seemed to speed up while the landscape around them slowed down. The carriage had no competition like on the way to the ball, and it had no trouble making its way down the road. It was fast, it just wasn't fast enough.

Finally, the carriage came to a halt, and Stella threw herself outside without the slightest hesitation. With a sinking boulder in her gut, she realized they were at the Pursbrough house. Of course, the carriage had been spelled to go *home*.

Neither Stella nor Izzy spoke. They just started running. Stella's dress stuck to sweaty skin, her hair falling free from its braids, while her bare feet slapped against the ground. She noticed occasional gravel dig into her toes, but she hardly felt the pain.

They ran for ages, the long walk they took daily to work whipping by yet stretching out at the same time. Stella's legs cramped and she heard Izzy breathing hard, but they pushed on, refusing to stop.

A jolt went through Stella's veins when she recognized the grim of Racine and their house finally came into view: candlelight flickered through the window. Natalia was home.

She never goes in the attic. She never checks on us. She'll never know. We'll be okay.

Stella scaled the wall with ease, then helped Izzy up as well. They both collapsed onto the floor, limp and panting.

"See?" Stella said. "We made it. She has no idea we left." Removing the photo from where she'd tucked it in her bodice, she reached underneath her bed and grabbed her father's box. The broken wand and crest were still inside. She tucked the photo in its place, then pulled out the crest. "I hope Zaria knows what this means."

Izzy sat up, regaining herself. "Maybe—"

Suddenly the door opened. Stella jumped, accidentally smacking the box halfway back under her bed.

"Girls," came Natalia's voice from the other side, nearly sing-song. "Guess wha—"

The door swung open completely, revealing Natalia in her plain work dress again, though her hair and makeup were still done, carrying a tray of sweet rolls. Natalia stopped when she saw Stella and Izzy in ball gowns, and the happiness froze on her face.

Time slowed. Natalia dropped the tray. It clattered when it hit the floor, smearing frosting on the wood, and the sound ripped through the thick atmosphere.

Stella's heart thudded in her chest, genuine fear coursing through her. She couldn't move. She couldn't think. She could only stare back at the woman who had murdered her father.

She waited for the explosion, the demand of where they'd been—the dresses made it so obvious, and Stella knew she couldn't lie her way out of it—but Natalia wasn't watching them anymore. She didn't seem to even care about their blatant disobedience of her 'don't set foot in the palace' rule. Her eyes were locked on the blue crest still in Stella's clenched fist.

"Where did you get that?" Natalia finally whispered, her mouth barely moving.

Stella just stared. She wasn't sure Izzy was breathing, but she didn't dare take her gaze off Natalia to check.

Natalia's voice grew sharper, though not louder. "*Where* did you get that, Stella?"

Hearing her name said in Natalia's voice snapped Stella out of her daze. "I found it."

"Found it," Natalia repeated, lifeless. "Found it."

The lack of fight produced confidence in Stella. She raised her chin slightly, defiant. "I know my father was murdered. You can't keep that from me anymore."

"Murdered." That word awoke something in Natalia, the dark side of her that made Stella believe she was capable of killing. She raked her fingernails through her hair, then glanced around wildly, words frantic. "Stella, Stella listen to me. Listen to me very carefully. Drop this. Drop all of it. Get rid of that, get rid of all of it, and forget."

"Forget?" Stella demanded. "How can I forget about my father? You've been lying to me!"

Natalia's face contorted into a kind of monster Stella had only seen hints of in the past; both she and Izzy scrambled back against the wall. "I've done everything for you!" she screamed back. "I've done everything for you—for *us*—to keep us safe! To keep my girls…" She trailed off, then held her head in her hands and doubled over.

"I heard the royal guards talking to you," Stella told her, remembering vividly the sting of her cheek the time Natalia had viciously slapped her, when she was just a grieving kid. What had this woman done to her father? "I know they closed the investigation on you, but I'm not going to let them. I'm going to report you."

Natalia's head snapped up, so fast she could've broken her neck. Her eyes scorched Stella to ash. "No. No, you won't."

Stella gestured to the crest. "Yes I will, and I'll find out what this means. I'll find the truth, and I'll make sure the world knows it."

Deep lines dug crevices into Natalia's beautiful face, making her look years older. "One chance, Stella. I'll give you one chance. Drop this. Now."

Despite her fear, Stella managed to meet her stare evenly. "No."

"Fine." Natalia pressed her lips into a hard line. "Then you leave me no choice."

She lifted her hands in some intricate pattern, her forehead creasing in concentration, as she backed up slowly out of the room. A bead of sweat was falling down her face when the door slammed shut on its own.

Izzy jumped and whimpered at the sound. Stella leapt up and dashed to the door, closing her fists around the knob. It wouldn't even budge. Breaths uneven, she raced to the window, only to find it had been sealed shut too.

Horror sunk deep into her bones as realization dawned, and she felt the color drain from her face.

"She used magic. She locked us in." Stella turned to see Izzy huddled on the ground, and her eyes filled with tears at the thought of what awaited them. Of the lengths Natalia had gone to cover things up. Of how much she had lied.

Numbly, Stella trudged over and sank to the ground next to Izzy. "She did it," Stella whispered. "She murdered him. What if...what if..." She couldn't make herself finish the sentence.

Izzy gave a half nod, knowing what she meant. Clutching her locket in one hand, she put her other arm around Stella, squeezing her tightly and leaving the question to hang in the air over their heads.

What if she kills us too?

CHAPTER 4

IF THE SHOE FITS

"Are monsters born? Or are they created somehow?"

Izzy posed the question thoughtfully, though Stella could sense that her fear bubbled close to the surface and threatened to break through her contemplative expression. She was lying next to Stella on their bed, facing the opposite way, so her feet were on the pillow next to Stella's head.

Stella sighed, staring at the ceiling like she'd done all night. Any frustration she may have felt at Izzy's ill-timed pondering had been numbed in icy anticipation of what Natalia could be planning for them. "I don't know. Does it matter?"

"Of course it matters."

"But aren't monsters monsters for a reason?"

"Exactly, that's what I'm—"

"Then it doesn't matter, really. A monster is still a monster, no matter how it came to be." She gave another nervous glance to the sealed bedroom door—her fiftieth glance in the last hour alone. "And monsters need to be destroyed."

Izzy's response came a few seconds late. "Maybe," she mumbled.

Stella tapped her hands against her leg. Both she and Izzy had changed from their borrowed ball gowns into sensible dark pants and shirts—clothes they could run in, if the opportunity presented itself. After a whole night of trying to break whatever curse Natalia had put on their attic room, Stella was starting to think that they really would never get out. After all, she was a rake—someone born without the capabilities of using magic—and while Izzy had a little capability, she'd never been taught, and had no idea where to start in harnessing the magic around her.

They were stuck. Hopelessly, desperately stuck.

Eventually their unsuccessful attempts and mounting desperation gave way to exhaustion, and now both of them were collapsed on the bed, every thought muffled by the fear of waiting for what was coming. Night turned to dawn, and Natalia still hadn't come back. Stella didn't know what would happen when she did. Thinking about it made her dizzy and nauseated.

"If you could go anywhere," Izzy began again, "anywhere in the world, right now, and stay, where would it be? And let's say the closed borders don't count—you can pick somewhere outside of Elaria too."

Stella considered the question, eager for any break in her forlorn thoughts. Her eyes glanced over the rotting beams in the ceiling, and in her mind they twisted into the strong beams of a magnificent ship.

"The ocean," she finally answered, pressing on to interrupt the objection she knew was coming from Izzy. "I would find a safe place to sail on the ocean, and I would explore everywhere."

"'Everywhere' is kind of cheating," Izzy scolded halfheartedly.

"Yeah, it is."

"Well I think—"

A pounding sounded on the front door downstairs. Both Stella and Izzy bolted upright, glancing from their room door to each other.

"Who would come over this early?" Izzy asked, twisting her locket around her finger. "You don't think she...you don't think Natalia would…"

"I don't know what she would do," Stella said grimly. "Not anymore." Pushing herself off the bed, she looked out their window to see a black, unmarked carriage parked out front. It wasn't shiny or luxurious by any means, but it was still a carriage, and that meant whoever was inside didn't live in their poor village.

Izzy came up behind her and looked out over her shoulder. A little gasp went through her lips. "Would she sell us? Or maybe it's just to scare us. Or maybe she didn't want to...she didn't...she…" Izzy trailed off quietly.

"She didn't want to do the dirty work herself?" Stella finished for her, unable to make her voice as strong as she wanted. The Jacklands were just southwest of Racine and made their grimy village seem like a luxurious city. It was a place for the desperate and murderous, a place crawling with all kinds of nasty criminals. Everyone in Racine had heard the rumors of what atrocities went on in the Jacklands, and everyone knew to stay far, far away.

How easy would it be for Natalia to hire some criminal to make them disappear? Is that what she'd done to her husband?

Izzy opened her mouth—likely about to voice the same nightmares Stella was thinking about—when they heard the front door open, and Stella motioned for Izzy to be quiet. Voices sounded below, but they were too faint to make out what was being said.

Moments passed, but it felt like eternities. Stella and Izzy stood frozen by the window, scarcely breathing, silently linking arms without looking at each other. They'd have to run. It would be quick, Stella knew, and it would probably be unsuccessful, but they had to try. Stella was not going to let Natalia take them down without a fight.

The knob on their door rattled. Stella's heart skipped, then pounded erratically, and Izzy gasped and pressed herself against the wall.

Nothing happened.

They waited. More nothing.

Stella had been sure she'd heard the knob rattle. She couldn't have made that—

Suddenly the door exploded. Izzy gave a shriek and Stella jumped back, both of them covering their heads with their arms, trying to shield themselves from the onslaught of wood shards. When Stella glanced back, the door had been blown clean off its hinges, and standing on the other side, scarred and unkempt, was Prince Roman's advisor.

Stella's formalities dropped to the floor with her jaw. "Griffin? What are you—"

"Get back," he growled, his harsh face tight with concentration as he raised his hands. The air between them seemed to ripple, bend, and sizzle. A smell like burning rubber filled the space, something snapped unexpectedly, and the rippling air disappeared. Griffin hesitated before taking a step forward, then passed through the doorway with ease.

"Grab your belongings," he said, regaining a formal posture, though it didn't quite match the inherent ruggedness he had about him.

Stella and Izzy exchanged disbelieving glances. Griffin cleared his throat.

"Are you coming or not?"

Numbly, Stella nodded. She mentally checked her pockets, where she'd stowed her father's photograph, broken wand, and crest, in case they had needed to run earlier. Izzy squeezed her locket before letting it fall back against her chest, as though reminding herself it was there. Both of them stepped forward at the same time.

"You don't want to bring anything?" Griffin asked.

Again, Stella and Izzy glanced at each other. "We don't have anything to bring," Stella answered. "We're all we have."

Griffin assessed them quickly, then gave a curt nod. He turned and made his way down the staircase; Stella and Izzy waited a beat before following.

Stella could feel the tense atmosphere before she finished descending the stairs. They entered the kitchen to find Isla and Noor gripping each other's hands in the corner behind Natalia, who had her lips pursed in an effort to be expressionless, but the paleness of her face showcased her anxiety. Standing across the room from them, looking so regal among the shabby furniture it almost hurt, was Prince Roman.

Griffin nodded to the prince when they entered. Prince Roman glanced at Stella and Izzy before turning back to Natalia.

"Now that wasn't so hard, was it?" His tone was that insufferable hybrid of serious and mocking. "Ms. Amaranth, while the official investigation regarding your family has been closed, I would make an effort to be docile before the crown. If there appears to be anything wrong or suspicious about your innocence, there will be no hesitation or warning before corrective action is taken."

He did nothing to hide the threat that hung in the air, and it looked like Natalia would be crushed under the weight of it. She managed to dip herself slightly on wobbly legs, a poor excuse for a curtsy. "Yes, Your Highness. I understand."

Prince Roman nodded to himself before turning to Stella and gesturing to the front door. "Shall we, then?" He didn't wait for them to answer; he strode out the door, showing himself out, with Griffin following close behind.

Izzy took a hesitant step forward, as if testing to see if something would hold her back. When that experiment worked, she gave Natalia a last glassy look before leaving too. Stella started after her, but Natalia lashed out, gripping Stella's arm. There were fierce tears in her boiling eyes, though when she spoke her voice was low, smooth, and strong with resolve, concealing the feral animal underneath.

"If you walk out that door," she said slowly, distinctly, with her nails digging into Stella's skin, "then you never *ever* come back."

A lump rose in Stella's throat, and she swallowed it down. With a jerky nod, she yanked her arm from Natalia's grasp and stalked after the prince, turning her back on the place she'd never once called home.

✳ ✳ ✳ ✳ ✳ ✳ ✳

"How did you find us?" Stella demanded the second they were all situated in the prince's carriage and driving away. Izzy sat next to her, across from Griffin and the prince, twisting the chain of her locket around her finger. While the boys had made no hostile moves toward them—they'd only been respectful—the sheer power of their presence alone was enough to have Izzy shrinking back into the plushy carriage seat.

Prince Roman smirked at Stella. "This morning a servant found a pair of discarded shoes in the ballroom. A noblewoman named Pursbrough was happy to have them back and kindly directed us toward your house." He cleared his throat a little too ostentatiously, faking a serious expression. "And now that I've boldly rescued you, fair maiden, do I get the honor of knowing your name?"

Stella rolled her eyes. "You really are pathetic."

"Not even a thank you?"

"No—"

"Thank you," Izzy cut in, her voice too small in her own ears, but both boys gave her their attention. She twisted her locket tighter. "I was...I was afraid...of what she might have done. Thank you for coming. Both of you."

Griffin nodded at her; Prince Roman regarded her for a moment before saying, "You're welcome." Then he looked back at Stella. "See, it wasn't too hard for your friend here."

Stella scowled and turned to look out the window. "You're insufferable."

86

Izzy glanced out the window herself, noticing they were leaving Racine. She shouldn't have been surprised—why would the prince want to stay there longer than he had to?—but the thought of leaving made her get nervous all over again.

"Where are we going?" she asked as dirt and gravel gave way to street and grass.

The question seemed to sober up the prince. He smoothed out his shirt, which was when Izzy realized he and Griffin were wearing matching maroon jackets with the royal insignia. It was hard to notice: they both wore it so powerfully, but with very different kinds of power. She didn't know royalty ever allowed their employees to match their clothes.

"I tried to look into Damon's death," the prince started, snatching Stella's attention back. "It's sealed up. Tight. It must've been quite the ordeal, if I couldn't even get into it. I agree with you that finding your godmother is the best and only lead we really have."

Izzy mentally nodded along with him. Stella had filled her in on their dancing conversation while they were locked in their room. She agreed that finding Zaria could be a key in figuring out what had happened. They just had no idea where to really start.

"I checked into her," Prince Roman continued. "You're right about one thing: it seems she did just disappear. She isn't on any travel visas or any kind of crown-sanctioned transportation records, which means—"

"She's either still in the kingdom or she somehow managed to slip through the borders illegally," Stella finished, matching his strategic tone. "She could never stay in one place for too long—I'm sure she's been all over, whether she managed to get out of Elaria or not." She frowned. If Zaria did leave the kingdom, it was going to be incredibly difficult to find her. "What are the best ways people travel illegally?"

"Without papers," Griffin answered. Though he spoke at normal volume, the inherent force to his voice made Izzy lean back slightly. "You can't cross kingdom borders without them, no matter what kind of transportation you use, and they are nearly impossible to get."

The prince nodded. "I imagine you know how cut off Elaria is: we are surrounded by ocean to the north and east, frozen mountains to the south, and forest to the west—security is lax in certain areas, seeing as all of them are a death trap. I guess the easiest ways to slip by the checkpoints are to attempt to climb the Isslotts, go through the Forgotten Forest, or get on a boat. But, like I said, all are incredibly dangerous and usually result in death."

Izzy gave Stella a pointed look, and Stella echoed what they were both thinking. "My father was a merchant. He travelled by sea constantly and never had any problems."

Griffin scoffed. "That's unheard of. Over eighty percent of ships sink. Anyone who somehow survives the wreck is killed by sirens."

Stella jerked out her chin. "My father's ship never did. If Zaria were to escape by boat, she could do it with him."

"Didn't you say she went missing after your father died though?" Prince Roman asked.

That deflated Stella a little; she sat back in her seat. "Yes. She did."

"That doesn't mean she didn't still have his resources," the prince amended. "But it's not as likely she would have survived."

Maybe she hadn't survived. The thought occurred to Izzy, but the memory of Zaria, such a lively person, made it hard to believe. Stella had probably already considered the possibility— considered it and then tossed it out. She could be ruthlessly determined, as though through willpower she could bend the universe to do what she wanted. Sometimes it annoyed Izzy to no end, but other days she wished she could match that kind of conviction.

"There are other options," Prince Roman continued when nobody commented on Zaria's survival. "You say she's brave: maybe she did go through the Forgotten Forest."

"The Forest is as much a death trap as the sea." Izzy jumped slightly when she realized she'd said the words out loud. Her three companions looked at her, and she felt herself curling inward. "It's infested with all kinds of creatures. Few are stupid enough to try, no matter how desperate."

"But if Zaria were trying to get away from Natalia," Stella reasoned, "she might have been very desperate. Natalia may have tried to track her over the ocean using some of my father's old contacts, but Natalia would never go into the forest. She'd leave Zaria for dead."

Prince Roman nodded, as though proud she'd made that conclusion. "That's what I thought too."

Griffin sighed, like he was bored and everyone was taking too long to decide where to go. "Didn't you say you had leads on your godmother?" he asked Stella.

Leads? Izzy's eyebrows pulled down and she looked to Stella, who set her jaw evenly, and Izzy knew what she'd done.

"I didn't *lie*," Stella said, defensive even though Izzy hadn't reprimanded yet. She folded her arms across her chest. "I just stretched it a little bit."

Griffin scowled at her. "You have nothing?"

"We have *something*. I'm just not sure what to do with it yet."

Izzy cocked her head to the side, an idea coming to her. "They're good with magic," she told Stella, willing her to understand so she wouldn't have to give up their secrets just yet. She glanced at the two boys. "Royals are some of the most powerful magicians, aren't they?"

The prince's face locked up, expressionless, and Izzy imagined Griffin's would've looked the same without his scars and perpetual glare.

"You broke through Natalia's shield," Stella offered as evidence. "That means you can do more than we can, at least."

The prince regarded them with cold calculation for a moment. "What did you have in mind?"

Her eyes narrowed. "Why should we trust you?"

Izzy nodded in silent agreement at the question. Why did the prince care so much?

Prince Roman sat back, thinking. "We haven't already convinced you we are honorable then, huh?"

"Why would you help us?" Stella asked, more forceful.

"Just being good neighbors."

Stella scoffed. "Not *our* neighbors. Clearly we come from different places."

"Look—" The prince cut himself off and glanced at Stella with a raised eyebrow.

Izzy didn't understand the significance, but Stella huffed, "It's Stella."

"Look, Stella," the prince went on, "I'm going to be king one day, and—"

"Exactly." Stella folded her arms across her chest again. "Why would you concern yourself with us?"

Prince Roman gave Izzy a 'can you believe her?' look before taking a breath, and Izzy almost smiled in spite of herself.

"If you'd let me finish: I'm going to be king one day. I plan on being a very good one. Until then, my days are rather mundane and repetitive, and not nearly as exciting as you might think. I meant what I said at the ball: I'm bored." He held up his hands in a show of peace. "I mean that in the best way possible. I'm curious about your situation, and staying shut up in the castle doesn't teach me anything, really, about how Elaria really works. I want to know the affairs of my future kingdom, and with the rising complexity of what you're facing, I'm very determined to solve this problem." His caramel eyes burned with sincerity. "And you'll find that when I'm determined enough, nothing will get in my way."

Izzy was torn: half of her believed Prince Roman, believed what he said, believed that he wanted to help them and that he would be a great king someday. It was so difficult to doubt his passion and dedication. On the other hand...people often didn't mean what they said, even if they once thought they did.

"That's great," Stella said flatly. "But what I have...well, you just have to swear you won't arrest me. It isn't mine."

The prince raised his hand, the corner of his lips pulling up. "Of course not. You have my solemn oath and burning curiosity."

Izzy glanced at Stella, uncertain. Stella blew out a breath, then, making up her mind, she reached into her pocket and took out the two glass pieces of magic wand.

Both Griffin and Prince Roman's eyebrows shot up, in near perfect synchronization with each other. Again, Izzy found herself wondering how deep their connection went.

"Where did you get that?" the prince asked in disbelief.

"It was with the photo," Stella answered, holding the wand with reverent care, though the object still made Izzy cringe a little. "My father hid them in a box. I think he meant for me to find it, to help solve his murder."

Prince Roman exchanged a glance with Griffin, something like animation lighting up his face. "We could spell it," Griffin said. "The magic wand itself will be useless, but we could spell it to lead us to its owner. Like a compass."

"You can?" Stella asked, as much awe in her voice as Izzy felt.

The prince frowned. "It's very difficult magic." Griffin gave him a long stare, and Prince Roman nodded, gaining confidence. "But it can be done. We can do it. If we find the owner of the wand, they may lead us to Zaria, or give us an idea of where she is."

Stella nodded, tucking the wand pieces safely back in her pocket. "When do we start?"

"Two days should give us enough time to prepare everything." He winced slightly. "Unfortunately, I can't actually bring you to the castle. It's a bad time for visitors—we'll put it that way. I've arranged for you to stay with close family friends."

Izzy grabbed her locket out of habit, her first question coming out of Stella's mouth.

"A noble family?" she asked, not hiding her disdain.

The prince nodded. "They're good people. They'll take care of you."

This time, the words jumped from Izzy's mouth. "But we're just peasant girls. They won't...we aren't like...we won't..."

A small, mocking smile played on Prince Roman's mouth. "For claiming to fight for equality, peasants are awfully prejudiced against the nobility."

"They treat us like dirt," Stella spat. "They think we *are* dirt."

"Not all nobility are so self-important, just as not all peasants are undeserving, mindless laborers." The prince gestured to the two of them. "You two are examples of that. My belief, though, is that it's a two-way street. The kingdom will always be divided by wealth and magic if the people think of themselves as separate."

Izzy raised her eyebrows, impressed. With outlooks like that, Prince Roman might be the king Elaria desperately needed. She wanted to ask what his plans were when he was king, but he didn't give her the chance.

"While I agree that some of the nobility can be—I'll use your word, Stella—*insufferable*, you'll find there are a lot of them that have hearts of gold." He grinned wryly. "They just happen to have a lot of gold too."

Lady Pursbrough, Izzy thought, trying to comfort herself. *She's nothing like snobby nobility. She's always been very sweet.*

Stella just shrugged, unimpressed. "If you say so."

Prince Roman nodded. "This family is the best of the best. They're good people. I trust them with anything." He stopped himself, his eyebrows pulling down and creasing his forehead as he looked between the three of them. "In this case, though, I think it's best if we don't tell them what we're really doing. They think we met two *fascinating* girls at the ball and have decided to take them on a tour of the kingdom. Let's keep it that way."

Stella rolled her eyes. "We shouldn't tell them we're going to spell an illegal wand to try and solve a closed, restricted murder case?"

For once, Prince Roman was unfazed by her sarcasm; his serious expression stayed steady. "No. I don't trust anyone with that."

* * * * * * *

Stella had planned on hating the Coronas, but as the hours passed by, she found that to be increasingly difficult.

First of all, Genevieve Corona was the warmest lady Stella had ever met. She couldn't think of another word to properly describe her, but it wasn't the cozy, fireplace, hug-you-like-a-grandmother warmth like Lady Pursbrough. Genevieve was the warm earth under your feet on a summer day—simple, natural, but regal. A flower so beautiful that the sun itself dropped a bit of its magic, making the plant truly shine.

When Prince Roman dropped Stella and Izzy off on a massive marble doorstep with promises to be there in the morning, Genevieve welcomed the girls into her home with open arms. Half of her honey hair had been pulled up into a bun, and the other half fell down her back in cascading waves. She said they could call her Genevieve, rather than Lady Corona, and immediately pulled them into her sky room: a spacious area with a glass roof and walls dotted with dozens of paintings. In the center of the space was a canvas set up on an easel with all sorts of paint tubes strewn out on a table.

"It's going to be a sunset," she told the girls of her work in progress. "I haven't gotten it quite right yet, but…" She trailed off when she saw Izzy's locket. "That's a beautiful gold color. That would be absolutely perfect on my canvas."

Izzy beamed at that. Stella tried not to care, tried not to let Genevieve's magnetic brightness overcome her too, but she found herself failing.

93

After several hours spent in Genevieve's workroom listening to the inspiration behind each painting, then watching the mesmerizing way she brushed the paint on the canvas, just blobs of color prodded gently into images, Genevieve took them on a tour of the rest of the house. While elegant and classy, it lacked the gaudy extravagance Stella had been expecting. The earthy tones were accented with deep golden yellows and rich purples, and the large spaces felt open and light without swamping itself.

Somehow, the upstairs felt colder. Genevieve padded quickly down the hallway, her eyes on one of the doors. It seemed she was just going to pass it, but at the last second she jerked to a stop—the girls nearly crashed into her—and knocked softly.

"Rosalind," she called, her melodic voice a little stiff, as if she were in a play and wasn't sure of her lines. "We have guests."

Nothing happened for a few moments, then the door swung open. The girl, Rosalind, wasn't much younger than Stella, but she was nearly a head shorter, and had the palest skin Stella had ever seen. The contrast was starker thanks to her raven hair that fell in tousled tangles down to her ankles. Like Stella and Izzy, she was dressed in simple pants and a shirt, and, unlike her mother, the air around her was frigid. Not angry. Not mean. Just cold.

"Hi," Rosalind offered. Her tone was polite but empty, like her cavernous eyes, and she too sounded like she was reading a script. "I'm Rosalind Corona. Welcome to our home."

"Stella," Stella replied with a tip of her head.

Izzy did some kind of half bow. "I'm Izzy."

A tiny flame of interest caught in Rosalind's expression. "That's a unique name. I like it."

Izzy smiled. "Thank you. I like it too."

"Your father will be home soon," Genevieve said, swelling with hope, and her sweet voice snuffed out the spark in Rosalind. "Can you come down for dinner?"

Rosalind balled up her fists and looked between the three of them, as though she'd been cornered. Stella and Izzy exchanged glances, suddenly very uncomfortable, but the girl put the struggling silence out of its misery.

"Of course, Mother." And with that, Rosalind slid back into her room and shut her door.

Genevieve deflated and sighed before walking on. "I apologize for her lack of hospitality. I'm not sure what to do with her these days."

"That's okay, Lady Corona," Izzy said, having found some confidence somewhere. "You've been very kind to us."

Genevieve finished the tour in the dining room, leaving the girls in lush dining chairs while she spread out a feast of roasted chicken and potatoes. It was an effort for Stella to keep from drooling on the rich wooden table.

Then they met Sterling Corona, the master of the house. He shook both of their hands and welcomed them as sincerely as his wife had.

"If you need anything at all," he told them, "please don't hesitate to ask. It's an honor to house Roman's guests."

"Thank you, sir," Stella and Izzy had replied at the same time, garnering laughs from the Coronas.

Rosalind came to the table last. Her parents exchanged wide glances when she walked in, but she just stared at the ground until she sat down, moved her shockingly long hair out of the way, and stared at her plate. She didn't seem angry, just...empty.

Stella couldn't help but feel a twinge of resentment for her. Here in the Corona house, she had everything she needed and she could get anything she wanted, and as a noble she had many more opportunities in her future. Genevieve was a loving and dedicated mother, and Sterling was a soft, strong leader of the house. Why did Rosalind seem so blindly apathetic to the amazing life she had?

"It's good to see you and your hair out and about, Rosalind," Sterling finally offered to his daughter with a teasing smile.

She didn't look up from her empty plate. "You too, Daddy."

Sterling and Genevieve shared another glance, then he sat at the head of the table, and invited his guests to sit too. Genevieve sat to his right, leaving a space in between her and Rosalind. With a start, Stella realized there was a place setting, but no chair.

"Zachary," Genevieve called into the hallway, making Rosalind flinch and scrunch herself smaller. "It's time to eat, sweetheart."

"Coming, Mother!" a young voice yelled back. Stella almost choked on her own breath when Zachary came rolling into the dining room.

The chair was self-propelled somehow—probably magic—but that wasn't what stole Stella's attention. The boy in it, probably eleven or so, had a smiley face full of freckles and dimples, a kind of zest in his eyes that Stella had never known. His right ear was missing, the skin scabbed over, and one shoulder sat higher than the other. His right arm was bent too far, and short, shriveled limbs took the place of his legs.

Genevieve beamed at her son and ruffled what hair he had, while Sterling greeted him and introduced the girls. Zachary gave an enthusiastic wave, then lit up when he saw Rosalind sitting in her seat.

He beamed at her. "Hi Rosy!"

Rosalind just winced at his voice and mumbled something back without looking up.

Suddenly, Stella understood this house a little better: things were broken. Magic could fix nearly anything, but not everything.

Izzy discreetly elbowed Stella, which made her realize she was staring. Quickly, she dropped her gaze.

"The food looks amazing," Izzy said, slicing through the thick atmosphere. "Thank you all again for having us."

Genevieve gave her a grateful smile, and they began the meal. Conversation was light and fun: Sterling gave an account of his day serving on the royal council, Genevieve spoke of her renovation plans for the spare room, Rosalind gave half responses about her day when prodded, and Zachary told a story of the toad he'd found on their grounds today and decided to keep as a pet. Even Izzy offered conversation of her own, asking questions to all members of the family, but Stella remained stuck in her head. Though the Coronas behaved as normally as anyone may have expected—besides Rosalind's distance, of course—Stella couldn't help but wonder how they could be so ordinary with such a glaring difficulty.

She was itching for more information. The next day, Prince Roman stopped by to report on their progress with spelling the wand. To Stella's dismay, he went straight up to visit Rosalind and was gone for a long time—too long, in Stella's opinion. They had a mission to complete, after all, and there was no time for social hour. Some of her annoyance ebbed, though, when the prince finally returned and suggested he and Stella take a walk for a private discussion, and she brought up her curiosity the second they were alone.

"What happened to Zachary?"

Any light that had been in the prince's expression instantly went out. "They don't...talk about it much, so..."

"I won't tell anyone."

He sighed, pushing a hand through his dark hair. "It was an accident. The Coronas are some of the most magically talented people in the kingdom, but the talent doesn't always pass on through bloodline like it should." He watched the ground, his tone somber and lacking its usual prestige. "It was several years ago. They were trying to teach Rosalind how to harness her magic. She just doesn't have a knack for it, like her parents, and things went...wrong. Zachary was too close. He's lucky to be alive, but...but sometimes there are scars that just can't heal. Rosalind has locked herself away, literally and figuratively, ever since."

Stella didn't know what to say to that, so she settled with, "Huh."

"The Coronas were always political, but Sterling threw himself into it afterward. They are huge supporters of restricted magic, as you can imagine, and heavily advocate the magic licensing program. They believe anyone without a licensed level of skill shouldn't be allowed to practice without supervision, like an academy or private tutor. For them, it's a matter of public and personal safety."

Stella bit her lip, chewing that over. "I always thought that the magic restriction was just another way to keep the peasants poor and the nobility on top."

Prince Roman shrugged. "Unfortunately, you're right. That's not the intention, but it often ends up that way. The whole system needs a lot of help."

She stopped walking to look at him, so he stopped too. "And you want to help that? When you're king?"

He considered her question thoughtfully, though Stella guessed he already had his answer. "Of course I do. There are a lot of problems with Elaria, as much as I love it. The magic restriction is the first place I want to start. Then, of course, there's the poverty issue, so many imbalances and instabilities, ever since the Great War—"

"The Great War?" Stella cut in. "That was almost a hundred years ago."

Prince Roman shook his head, deep lines piercing his face. "Not at the castle. The closer you get to the throne, the more you feel that disaster was just yesterday. Elaria needs a strong king, one to help it truly come together after so many years of fracture." He said the words methodically, like he was reading it off a statue or speech card.

Stella folded her arms across her chest, suddenly feeling vulnerable, though she didn't know why. They weren't talking about *her* life. But it had been ages since she'd had such a real conversation like this with anyone besides Izzy.

She looked across the Corona's grounds where Zachary was showing his toad to Izzy, both of their expressions alight with excitement, while Griffin looked on, the usual grimace on his face.

"I can tell you believe in it," Stella said without looking at him. It was probably the nicest tone she'd ever used with him. "Elaria. The kingdom. I can tell you care. Putting it all back together again...it sounds intimidating. A lot of threats."

Out of the corner of her eye, she saw him nod. "Elaria is my life. It can be a scary world, and we have to be able to defend ourselves."

Stella looked down at her hands, hands that were usually dirty and used for work but not much else. When it came down to threats—like Natalia—she was completely defenseless. "I don't know how," she admitted.

Prince Roman turned to her, looking her up and down for a few moments before nodding to himself. "We still have a day or two before the wand will be ready—I'll teach you. Come on."

He brought her to the Corona's recreation room, where shelves of equipment for a half dozen sports lined the walls, all of it caked in layers of dust.

Prince Roman strode up to the fencing equipment and took two swords down from their hangers, then handed one to Stella. It felt strange in her hand—she wasn't sure how to hold it, let alone hurt someone besides herself. Meanwhile, Prince Roman held his in balance with ease.

"We'll start with sword fighting, then I'll teach you how to throw a good punch."

Stella rolled her eyes. "I can show you that right now."

After illustrating how to hold the unfamiliar weapon and balance it correctly with the rest of her body, he made her practice simple movements. Once she'd mastered the basics and started complaining for a challenge, he waved his sword in the air in an intricate pattern nearly too fast for Stella to follow. "Good luck keeping up."

She gritted her teeth in determination, but despite her will, he had her disarmed in less than ten seconds. Her weapon clattered to the ground, useless. She fought the urges to either yell in frustration or run from further embarrassment.

The prince picked up her sword from off the ground, and she took it back from him.

"Again." He gave her one of his signature royal smirks. "If we're really going into the Forgotten Forest, you must be able to hold your own better than that."

* * * * * * * *

"It's just down this hallway," Griffin said, leading Izzy down the palace corridor.

It had been two days since the prince and Griffin had taken Izzy and Stella to the Corona's house, and those two days had been some of the strangest and greatest of Izzy's life. Whatever time she didn't spend exploring the household grounds with Zachary was spent painting with Genevieve. During their stay, the prince and Griffin had successfully managed to spell the wand; sure enough, it pointed northwest, toward the Forgotten Forest. With the wand and travel provisions ready, the boys had stopped by to report the news and tell the girls to prepare to leave the next morning. For the rest of the day, Stella and the prince decided to continue with their defense lessons. Griffin didn't seem to like not having a job to do or something to work on, so Prince Roman suggested Griffin return to the library in the castle to do any last minute research they thought would be necessary before their departure.

Izzy's spirit had perked up at the mention of the library—it sounded so much better than learning to use a sword, which she had no desire to do—and the prince gave her permission to go as well. Now she was coiled in excitement and trying not to appear too giddy or common as she walked down the palace halls with the prince's stoic and quiet advisor.

Though her thoughts went to imagining the library, Izzy couldn't help but notice how Griffin responded to the castle. His shoulders were still straight and proud, the permanent scowl etched on his face like his scars, and clearly he had no problems being in the castle, but...there was something about the way he glanced around, the way he tensed when people, even servants, passed by, the way only some of them even acknowledged him while others half glared or ignored him entirely. It made her want to ask how he got to be the advisor anyway, especially being so young, but before she got the chance he stopped at a double door and pushed his way inside.

Izzy gasped. She couldn't help it. Her hands flew to her mouth as she gazed in wonder all around her, eyes scanning the shelves and shelves and shelves and shelves of books. They seemed to stack all the way to the sky, and she had to crane her neck back to see the top. It was magnificent. So many shelves, so many desks filled with books, thick ones and thin ones, and the *smell*...the smell was the perfect combination of must and ink and parchment that came with old books that had been loved so long.

"It's amazing," Izzy breathed, turning around again and again. "I've never seen anything like it."

Griffin glanced around, as though trying to find whatever amazing thing she saw. When he couldn't, he stalked over to one of the desks, gesturing to an open book next to the stack of volumes he'd pulled out a few days earlier, before coming to free the girls from Natalia.

"These list the creatures we may run into in the Forgotten Forest, as well as beyond. They should give us some guidance and safety precautions."

Izzy nodded, making herself focus. She had a job—Prince Roman had given her a job—and she was going to do it successfully. She'd be an expert on the creatures before the night was over.

"Okay." She marched over to the desk and sat on a stool next to Griffin. "Where should I start?"

Griffin regarded her with curious disdain, stepping away so there was more space between them. "Start with the top one. You can skip the chapter about sirens—I don't think the forest will take us anywhere close to the sea."

Nodding, Izzy started flipping through the pages, shivering at the drawn images of the gorgeous, razor-toothed sirens. She could not understand why Stella loved the sea so much.

It's because of Damon. This is all because of Damon. That thought just fueled her with more determination. They had to bring justice for that man, and for Stella, and for Izzy too, in a way. She'd be lying if she said she wasn't also looking for information about what happened to her mother, though she hadn't decided yet whether she'd actually want to see Sofia ever again.

With that, Izzy pursed the chain of her necklace in her lips and began reading. When she came upon something interesting or of possible worth, she snagged some parchment and a pen to jot her notes down. While she was constantly flipping pages, scrawling notes, and mumbling to herself, Griffin sat on a stool one desk over and didn't make a sound.

Hours later, he came back to trade books, having just finished his first one, only to find that Izzy had worked through nearly a dozen and had over twenty pages of notes, front and back.

"They're just some bits of information I thought might be helpful," she said timidly as he stared at the papers. She pushed the bits of hair that had fallen from her bun out of her face. "We don't have to take them with us; it was mostly just to keep me busy."

Griffin cleared his throat. "They, uh, they might be useful. It's always good to have more information." He didn't scowl as much when he spoke, and Izzy took that as a compliment.

"I think I hit all the major possible creatures in the forest," she said, flipping through her pages. "Although there were some pages missing about the fairies. I think most of them are dead, but any remaining ones may have hidden out in the forest. Their lifespan is much longer than a human's. They're practically immortal."

Griffin glanced at the fairy book. "Most of the fairies are dead, yes. They were a deadly part of the rebellion. After King

Rowan's victory, he outlawed and hunted them down, for everyone's safety."

"Hm," Izzy mumbled to herself, already lost in her notes again. "Well, danger aside, it might have been interesting to meet one."

"I'd like to meet one too."

Izzy snapped her head up, wondering if she heard him right, if he actually said something personal for once, but his head was already ducked into another book. She looked at his reddish-blond hair for a moment, speculating why he grew it so long just to keep it in a ponytail all the time—especially when it didn't seem to stay in very well. And on him it looked too wild, almost, to really fit into the court, but maybe he didn't fit into the court at all, maybe—

"Keep reading," Griffin called to her without looking up, as if sensing her wandering thoughts. "We're leaving for the forest in the morning, and I don't want to be eaten by anything."

CHAPTER 5

SNIPE HUNTING

Stella was surprised at the little rock that settled in her chest when she said goodbye to the Coronas. She hadn't ended up hating the noble family like she'd intended; when she got into the prince's carriage and turned to wave back at Sterling, Genevieve, and Zachary on the front porch, Stella felt a twinge of sadness that she was leaving the beautiful family.

The sadness easily melted into determination and a bit of fear as Prince Roman held up the wand pieces. Now spelled, they had a radiance about them, and would supposedly influence the person holding it to go in the direction of the owner. Stella had been skeptical until she held a piece in her own hand, and some kind of outside force pulled her mind toward the forest. It was an odd sensation; she didn't like it. When Griffin volunteered to be the guide, Stella didn't argue. She let him keep a piece and stowed the other in her pant pocket.

"I have no idea how long we'll be gone," the prince confessed, wrapping up their strategy session, which, admittedly, had little strategy. "We have enough provisions packed for four days. Any longer than that, we may need to return and come up with a new plan."

Stella tapped her hands against her legs, frowning at the prince's unremarkable clothes. He could pass for a commoner now, if he worked on lowering his authoritative aura and arrogant attitude. "Won't someone recognize the prince is gone? You didn't tell anyone what we were doing, did you?" She wondered what the prison sentence was for endangering the prince of Elaria's life—the *only* child of the king and queen, no less.

"Of course not. My staff members think I'm taking a solo trip with Griffin. It happens." Prince Roman dropped his gaze. "Nobody will notice there. They don't care much about what I do. Not yet anyway." He took a breath, composing himself before Stella got the chance to press the issue. "We'll be covered. You have your weapons, right?"

Stella patted the sword on her hip. She wasn't a master by any means, but Prince Roman had joked he was confident she could defend herself against a tree sprite. Stella had rolled her eyes at that.

"Yes," she told him. "I've got my sword."

Griffin glanced at Izzy. "And you?"

Izzy hadn't been interested in learning how to fight, but she'd taken the small dagger Griffin had given her, just in case.

"Yes."

"All right then." Prince Roman rubbed his hands together. "I guess there's nothing left but to start." With that, he exited the carriage, Griffin and the girls following. They each grabbed their packs out of the trunk and slung it over their shoulders. Prince Roman sent the magic-driven carriage back to the castle, leaving them on the side of an obscure dirt road on the edge of Elaria. The top spire of the castle was barely visible in the distance if Stella squinted hard enough.

Steeling herself, she turned around and faced the Forgotten Forest: a wall of deep green so thick, she couldn't see more than three feet past the first tree. The air was different here, cleaner but almost heavier, like the magic from the creatures in the forest had given it its own life. The greenery seemed to breathe on its own, as much alive as Stella herself felt.

"Wow," Izzy murmured next to Stella, gazing up at the trees that stretched on forever.

"You feel that too?" Stella asked, unable to speak at normal volume, like the forest would hear her.

Izzy nodded. "It's alive. It's beautiful, but...scarred. The leaves sag with the weight of what they carry—what they want to forget." She nodded again. "I had hoped it would be kind to us, but I don't think it knows what kindness is."

Both boys stared at Izzy, and Stella was glad Izzy didn't catch—or ignored—their skeptical glances. With a grunt, Griffin started for the forest, and Izzy followed. Prince Roman gazed after her with his eyebrows pulled down, then gave a questioning glance to Stella. She waved him off and started into the forest herself. Izzy would always be Izzy, and Stella would never try to change that.

It only took about four steps into the vegetation before the midmorning light was snuffed out, plunging them into twilight. The dense leaves blocked out most of the sunlight, enshrouding the four of them in dark, damp silence. They walked single file—Griffin leading, followed by Izzy, then Stella, with the prince bringing up the rear. Stella had to watch her feet so she didn't trip over unearthed roots or uneven ground.

It was quiet. Nobody spoke much, and there weren't many signs of life in the forest besides the annoying swarms of gnats, and the occasional flap of a distant wing or tinkling laugh of a hidden sprite. All the creatures were probably hiding, Izzy said, because they were used to humans killing them.

The silence set Stella on edge and gave her too much space to think. She hadn't really considered facing Zaria again yet. She hadn't decided if she was angry or hurt or excited when it came to her missing godmother. After all, maybe Zaria had a good reason for leaving Stella behind after the worst loss she could imagine. Maybe Zaria had been hunted by Natalia, like Stella suspected. Maybe Zaria had pressing personal issues she had to take care of, no matter how much it hurt to leave Stella behind.

Maybe she'd always planned on coming back, but had been held up somehow.

Or maybe, Stella feared, Zaria had simply left.

Stella refused to believe Zaria was dead. Zaria was the most *alive* person Stella had ever met. Always animated, vivacious, passionate, thrumming with confidence and strength, Zaria was a force to be reckoned with. She would pull Stella onto her lap and tell her stories of far-off places, forbidden romances, and political intrigue, spelling the shadows on the wall to play out the purr in her voice.

No, Zaria was alive. She was alive, and Stella would not stop until she found her.

Stella stewed in her thoughts until they broke for lunch. Once the decision was made, the boys instantly collapsed and began chowing down, unaccustomed to walking so far or going so long without eating. Stella stretched out her legs before settling down, and Izzy perched herself on a rock next to her.

"Is there any way to tell how close we are?" Stella asked. She gazed up at the trees all around her, but the forest looked the same as when they entered.

Griffin had already begun wolfing down his sandwich. Mouth full, he just shook his head.

Stella sighed and leaned back against a tree trunk. Izzy had taken out her package of biscuits and a book. She was already lost in it, chewing softly as her eyes blazed through the words, and she absently offered a biscuit to Stella without breaking her concentration. Stella took one and nibbled on the edge.

"She brought a book into the forest?" Prince Roman asked, incredulous, like Izzy wasn't there. Izzy was too absorbed to even notice.

Stella shrugged, but it was Griffin who said, "What else is there to do?"

Prince Roman shook his head and kept eating. It may have been a trick of the dim light, but Stella swore she saw the corner of Izzy's mouth twitch upward.

They took another fifteen minutes or so to break, then packed up and started again. Though it got progressively darker as the day wore on, the forest looked exactly the same no matter how far they went. The endless green drove Stella crazy, and thoughts of Zaria and her father set her on edge, so by the time they decided they should camp for the night, Stella was sore, had a headache, and was fuming.

Scowling at the dirt, she threw her pack on the ground where they'd decided to stop. Griffin took off his pack too, gently stowing the piece of the wand in one of the pockets, before he and the prince set to taking the tents out of the bags. Izzy tried to help, but Griffin insisted he could do it, so she started reading again instead. Everyone's shoulders sagged slightly with the same exhaustion and frustration that Stella felt in her bones.

"Get some firewood," Griffin called to them. "I'll create a protective barrier around us so nothing else will catch the flame."

Izzy gave a vague nod, acknowledging someone spoke but making no movement to stop reading. Grumbling, Stella stood on her knees and reached out to grab a log just a foot away. She turned around in a circle, collecting branches she thought would work and tossing them in a pile behind her. Reaching for the last one, she paused when she felt warmth on her hand. Confused, she glanced up from the dirt to find a pair of golden eyes staring back at her.

* * * * * * *

Despite what Griffin had said about fairies being extinct, Izzy's fascination with them had continued to grow. She'd read the same chapter on fairies again and again, finding little useful information, considering some of the pages had been ripped out. King Rowan had been adamant about hunting the fairies— since they looked human, they could've fit into society well, even with their enhanced magical capabilities. If one of them got away, it would be easy, relatively speaking, for them to just melt into the community and disappear.

What was the prince's view on fairy hunting? She'd have to ask.

"Izzy," Stella breathed, almost too quiet for Izzy to hear. "Izzy."

Izzy kind of nodded. "Hm?"

Stella snapped, her voice edged with fear. "*Izzy.*"

"What?" Izzy finally tore her gaze from her book to see Stella frozen on her hands and knees, one arm outstretched, reaching for a broken branch. Her eyes were wide and her forehead glinted with sweat. Izzy put down her book. "Stella? What's wrong?"

Stella hissed through her teeth, still looking forward into the darkness. Confused, Izzy stood to get a better view, but her eyes couldn't make anything out. There were two lights—sprites maybe? Why would Stella be afraid of…

Suddenly Izzy's eyes adjusted to the shadows—it wasn't a shadow, really, but a hulking dark form, growling quietly over Stella.

Izzy's limbs turned to lead and she felt the color drain out of her face. "Griffin," she said as loudly as she dared. "Griffin, we've…we've got a problem."

She heard something drop to the ground. "What's going…" Griffin trailed off, probably looking over at them now. Izzy couldn't move her gaze from the animal to check.

Stella's arms started wobbling; she couldn't hold herself up for much longer.

"Stella," Prince Roman said softly from behind them. "Back away. As slowly as you can."

Cautiously, Stella pulled herself back, one arm, then another, until she was kneeling down. She went to stand up but lost her balance. Her foot came back behind her hard, snapping a twig, and the shadow snarled.

"Get back!" Griffin shouted just as the shadow lunged forward. Izzy thought Stella would be scarfed down in one bite, but Griffin ducked in front of her and held his hands up, using magic to throw the monster several feet back.

The one snarling sound grew into an earthquake all around them, completely surrounding their little camp. The wolves were the biggest animals Izzy had ever seen, towering a head over Griffin, and once the first wolf recovered, the rest of the pack attacked.

Izzy's first instinct was to run. She tried, but only got about twelve steps before a giant animal cut her off, roaring. It swiped a paw at her, and when she scrambled away to dodge, she tripped over a branch and fell, scraping her palms. She crawled in the dirt until she got to a thick tree and pulled herself up.

Chaos ensued around her. Vicious snarls and bites and growls overpowered their bubble of silence; Izzy heard swords being unsheathed and Griffin shouting things at them, but Izzy couldn't understand him. Some snarls turned to yelps. Izzy caught a last glimpse of Griffin frantically waving his hands like a madman, using magic to pick off the beasts one by one, before a force slammed into her back, knocking her to the ground.

Izzy tried to scream, but the wolf pushed its paws down on her, taking her breath. Saliva dripped from its jaws as it raked its claws across Izzy's arm.

As quickly as it came, the creature was gone. Griffin had broken from his fight to spell it off her. Ears ringing, she reached into her pant compartment and pulled out her dagger. Her hands shook as she gripped the weapon in her fist.

Another wolf came after her, but this time she was more prepared for the blow. It knocked her to the ground again, teeth lunging for her neck, but Izzy slashed her dagger at its face in a frenzy and it batted her away. Pain pierced her back as she slammed into a tree and rolled into a little ditch.

Head spinning, she adjusted her grip on her dagger and looked up to see an animal in the ditch with her. She shrieked and held up her hands, bracing herself. No attack came. Confused, she lowered her arms to see it wasn't a wolf after all: it was a dog.

It was hurt, panting heavily, red coloring the dirty brown fur by its shoulder. Izzy moved to back away from it—she'd never been comfortable with animals—when an ear-splitting roar shook the earth beneath her. Another wolf appeared at the edge of the bank across from her, blood dripping from its jaws. The injured dog whimpered just as the wolf lunged for it.

Izzy didn't think. She reached forward, snatched the dog in one arm, and waved her dagger wildly with the other. The dog yelped at the jerky movement, but Izzy didn't stop slashing with her dagger until the wolf finally backed away. Sweaty and panting, she hoisted herself out of the ditch, while still holding the dog, to see if everyone else was okay.

Three dead wolves were on the ground, and another injured one was hobbling away. Stella and the prince were each tackling a wolf with their swords, while a bloodstained Griffin tried to take on three with his magic. He had held up well, but he was trembling, and Izzy knew he couldn't keep going like that much longer.

Izzy settled the injured dog on the ground and Stella shouted something. Izzy glanced up in time to see one of the three wolves break through Griffin's ranks and attack him from behind. Unsuspecting, Griffin went straight down and the wolf pounced, tearing into him. Izzy couldn't hear his anguished yells over the sound of her own scream.

She ran for him, slamming into the wolf on top of him and driving her dagger into its hide. The wolf howled and reeled back, collapsing and leaving a torn up Griffin bleeding out on the ground. Izzy quickly pressed on the worst wound across his chest, and Stella started shouting at the prince as she finished off another animal. There were still three left.

"Spell them out of here!" she screamed. "Griffin's down— use your magic!"

Keeping her hands on Griffin, who was now unconscious, Izzy looked up to see Stella getting pinned to the ground by one monster, and a pale Prince Roman still taking on two with his sword.

His sword? Why his sword?

"Roman!" Stella shrieked, narrowly missing getting her head bit clean off. "Roman! Magic, now!"

Roman managed to stick his sword in one wolf, sending it down. While the other geared up, he looked around helplessly, blood trickling down his face. What was he doing?

"Roman! Make a barrier or something! We're all going to die!"

The prince scraped his hand through his hair, his horrified eyes on Griffin's limp body.

Stella pushed up against the wolf pinning her down, but it just snarled and battered her sword away. She was defenseless. "Roman!"

"I can't!" Roman shouted back, his voice breaking with desperation. "I can't!"

Izzy kept one hand on Griffin and reached the other for the wolf body next to her, pulling out her dagger. "Stella!" she yelled before throwing it to her.

Stella grabbed the dagger and shoved it into the wolf on top of her. It howled and screamed before falling back, and Stella dashed to grab her sword a few feet away. Together, she and Roman finished off the last creature. Its body fell to the ground with a deafening thud, and the silence settled around them.

Prince Roman rushed to Griffin's side, a mangled gasp escaping his lips when he saw how truly injured his advisor was, and he collapsed to his knees. To Izzy's surprise, he snatched her free hand in both of his, gripping it tight.

"Is he going to die?" the prince asked her, his caramel eyes broken and imploring. "Is he? Can you help him? Please?"

Izzy glanced down at Griffin's body, riddled with deep gashes and torn flesh, blood seeping into the dirt. She didn't have a lot of medical practice—she'd read a few books and taken care of Papa when one of his delusions caused him some kind of injury. She hoped Griffin looked worse than he actually was.

Setting her jaw, Izzy held the prince's tormented gaze, trying to be as resolute as Stella. "I'll do what I can, Your Highness."

✳ ✳ ✳ ✳ ✳ ✳ ✳

Stella stood watch while Izzy patched up Griffin using the first aid package he had brought. Roman sat by his side, curled up in a ball and gazing at nothing, all his princely confidence in broken shards around him. Stella poked at the dirt with her bloodstained sword, a mouthful of questions just burning to come out.

Something moved on the ground within her line of sight. Raising her sword, Stella stepped cautiously toward the twitching lump, her heart picking up speed at the thought of a surviving wolf. When she got closer though, she realized it was just a regular dog.

"Don't hurt him!" Izzy gasped. Stella jumped and turned to see Roman staring at Izzy too. Izzy shrunk back in on herself, her red hands in the middle of wrapping a bandage on Griffin. "Please."

"It's a dog." She looked back at the injured animal, a poor little border collie with a small gash in its shoulder. "You hate animals."

"Not that one. He's mine."

Stella whipped back around, but Izzy had shifted her attention back to Griffin. "Since when?"

She didn't look up. "Since now. Bring him over, will you? He needs some help too. Be careful."

Shaking her head, Stella sheathed her sword and leaned down, scooping up the dog as gently as she could. Panting, it watched her with mournful, black eyes. She walked lightly back over to Izzy and set the animal down next to her.

"Thank you," Izzy mumbled, pressing another piece of gauze to Griffin's chest. With most of the blood washed off and bandages covering the worst parts, he looked much better

116

than he had earlier. He was still unconscious and his breathing shallow, but he was breathing.

With a sigh, Stella turned and sat on the ground next to Roman. She managed five peaceful seconds before she just couldn't take it anymore.

"What happened?"

Izzy clicked her tongue in disapproval without stopping her work while Roman's shoulders sagged and he dragged his hands over his face. He didn't say anything.

Stella gritted her teeth. After that disaster, she didn't have the patience for hidden truths anymore. "Roman, what happened? Why wouldn't you use your magic like Griffin?"

Roman ducked his head further, like her questions were too heavy for him to carry. Izzy flicked her eyes at Stella, a warning glance, but Stella just glared at Roman, willing him to answer.

"I can't," he whispered, his voice rough.

"What do you mean you can't?"

"Stella," Izzy said under her breath without breaking her work.

"What?" Stella demanded. "We're stranded in the middle of the Forgotten Forest, Izzy. We trusted in his abilities, and we could've died. We deserve to know."

Roman snapped his head up, his eyes full of such anguish that Stella felt her stomach clench painfully. "I'm a rake, Stella."

Stella's mouth gaped open and Izzy raised her eyebrows at him. "What?"

"I'm a *rake*," Roman spat, his voice breaking on the word. "I can't do magic. I've never been able to."

"But you're...you're the prince," Stella spluttered. "You...everyone knows you can do magic. Everyone...how does nobody know?"

Roman dragged his hand through his messed up hair, shifting his gaze to his unconscious friend. "Griffin is arguably the strongest magician in the kingdom besides my father," he said bitterly. "He rarely leaves my side. We make a show of it if we need to."

"Who knows?"

"Griffin. My parents. Our immediate council. The Coronas." He shook his head. "No one else."

Izzy blinked a few times, taking that in, before turning to patch up her new dog. Stella brought her legs to her chest and rested her chin on her knees, watching the prince struggle with words.

"They didn't...we didn't really discover it until I was about nine. They...everyone thought I was just slow or shy even. But eventually it became clear. My father..." Roman choked on his words, but he didn't seem able to stop himself. "My father was furious. He swore I was illegitimate and threatened to execute my mother for disloyalty to the crown. She denied it, of course, because it wasn't true, but my father couldn't accept it. She became so depressed that she couldn't be left alone. He wouldn't publicly say it, but he wasn't going to name me heir—they tried for years to have another child, but it never happened. My mother insisted I was his, that I was the rightful heir to the crown. The older I got, the more impossible it became to doubt—I look too much like him. But he's still not entirely convinced, even now, because...because..."

Because how could King Asher produce a *rake?*

"Your father is short-sighted, Roman," Izzy said softly, petting her dog with all the tenderness of a mother while it closed its eyes in contentment. "There's much more to being king than powerful magic." She glanced up at him. "I'm so sorry he can't see that."

"Elaria needs a strong king," Roman said, and Stella wondered how many times he'd been told that. "It needs a strong king, and I have to be that. If anyone...if the people knew...if other kingdoms knew...we wouldn't last a second. The kingdom would tear itself apart again before anyone else had the chance."

Stella bit her lip. She didn't know much about the politics of Elaria, but she knew the people would crucify anyone too different than what they'd come to expect. Some of the peasants might accept him, the ones that were rakes or unskilled themselves, but anyone else would see him as a liability at best. Easy conquest at worst.

Griffin took a breath and muttered something, turning his head slightly, and the simple motion stole everyone's attention from the somber silence.

Roman straightened up and leaned toward him, eyes wide and hands shaky, while Izzy gently smoothed over some of his bandages. Griffin moaned and mumbled something under his breath. Everyone tensed and waited, but nothing else happened.

"How did you two meet?" Stella asked, wanting to diffuse some of the heavy emotion in the air.

The corners of Roman's mouth pulled up, but it wasn't a happy smile. "Griffin was born a twin."

Stella blinked and Izzy gasped quietly. Elaria had some old superstitions, one of them regarding twins: people believed they were bad luck. A sign of evil. While there was no official proclamation, infanticide of one of the babies had become an issue among both the common and noble. Parents either were too disgusted with their own misfortunes or they didn't want their children to be raised under the harsh discrimination of the people around them.

"They kept him as a servant at first," Roman went on, "but as he got older, the similarities between the two boys were hard to argue. That, and the fact that Griffin's magical abilities exceeded all of theirs. One day he decided to ask them about it. His mother became hysterical and tried to kill him." He nodded at his friend. "That's where the scars came from. He must've been eleven or so because it was just after my eleventh birthday."

Again, Stella felt the weight of others' sorrows in the air, pushing on her bones and making it difficult to breathe. She wanted to ask him to stop—she didn't want to know anymore, didn't want to carry anything else—but Izzy spoke before she could.

"That's awful," Izzy murmured.

He nodded, eyes glazed over like he was somewhere else. "It was. His father is on the council. He brought Griffin to my father—he didn't know what else to do. While they talked it over, Griffin snuck out of the chamber and ran into me." Roman laughed once without humor. "He was the unwanted, disfigured son unlucky enough to come second, and I was the possibly illegitimate crown prince born a rake. We connected instantly. When they came back for him, I officially named him my advisor on the spot. It's the only order my father has ever allowed me to give and actually stood by, if only to appease everyone."

"No choice," Griffin muttered painfully, jolting them all. "You're...you're stuck with me...now."

A real smile broke across the prince's face, bright with relief. "Stuck to the end."

Izzy's hands flitted over Griffin's bandages as his eyelids fluttered, and he groaned again. "How are you?" she asked.

It took him a few tries to open his eyes. "In pain. Alive." He focused his gaze on her. "Thanks to you, I'm assuming."

She dropped her hands in her lap, cheeks turning a little pink in the darkness. "I wish I could've helped more."

Griffin sighed, then winced. "I've survived before; I'll do it again."

Roman laughed and sat back, some of the tension melting away from his shoulders. Izzy smiled and gently pulled Winston onto her lap. He didn't open his eyes, but he licked her hand gratefully, and she continued to rub softly behind his ears. Roman settled back against a tree, gazing up into the leaves. They rustled with a slight breeze blowing through the musty forest—a welcome relief. Stella reached for her pack and pulled a blanket out, wrapping it around her shoulders, and Izzy took one out of her pack and spread it over Griffin's trembling form. He tested his head, rolling it from side to side, and his eyes rested on the dog sleeping next to Izzy.

"The mutt?" he asked, bloody eyebrows furrowing.

"He's my dog." Izzy patted the dog's head like she'd done it for years. "His name is Winston."

Griffin gave a marred laugh edged with pain—Stella didn't know he was capable of laughing at all. "I still...I still don't understand you." Then he tipped his head back, another moan escaping him, and closed his eyes.

"Can I get you anything?" Izzy asked him.

He muttered something they couldn't understand, then cleared his throat and tried again. "We asked...we asked about you. Both of you. The shoes we returned...that noblewoman told us about you." He paused to take another painful breath. "Your father. How vile everyone...everyone was to you. Your friends. I don't..." His forehead creased. "I don't understand. How have you...managed to stay so...soft?"

Stella raised her eyebrows, watching Izzy's reaction. Izzy blinked in surprise. After a moment of thoughtful consideration, she took her locket in the hand that wasn't stroking her new pet.

"Some people believe being soft is weak," she started slowly. "Some have even told me that. But I think they're wrong. It might seem silly or naive, but I think we all have magic—I think kindness is magic. Every damaged person will tell you so, in their own way."

"How's that?" Roman asked, looking at her now.

She blinked at him, like it was obvious. "Well, damaged people generally are either softer or harsher because of what happened to them. They either selflessly give out the kindness they wish they'd had, or they become cold and bitter and withhold from others what they never received, ensuring nobody else can have it." She shrugged. "Either way, they illustrate the power of kindness. Compassion. Their importance."

"It's brave," Griffin murmured.

Izzy twisted her locket around her finger. "It's right. The world is too cold as it is, I think."

Stella pursed her lips and pulled the blanket tighter around her, taking inventory of their world. A world where mothers abandoned families, confidants betrayed friends, wives murdered husbands, and parents abhorred their own children.

Roman closed his eyes, leaning his head back against a trunk. With a sigh, he echoed her thoughts.

"Too cold indeed."

* * * * * * *

Once Griffin had slept for a while and eaten some food, he was able to regain enough strength to spell his wounds partway closed. By the next afternoon he was walking, albeit slowly, and they started their journey again, everyone shifting and jumping at every sound. Stella was afraid the boys would insist on going home after the wolf attack, but they pressed on with just as much determination as Stella felt burning in her own heart.

The air was frosty between the four of them. Not necessarily unfriendly, just...uncertain. Too many buried things had come to the surface during the night, and while the revelations had seemed safer in the dark, they had clung to the air and frozen over, making every breath incredibly fragile. Griffin didn't so much as look at Izzy the whole day except when he helped heal her dog, and Roman remained by his side at all times. Stella took it upon herself to lead the charge, mostly because she wasn't comfortable with everything left unsaid. She held the magic wand in her hand and walked. Izzy walked quietly after her with Winston trotting at her side. The boys stayed behind them, giving each other meaningful glances when they thought nobody was paying attention to them.

Find Zaria. Stella made that the focus of her thoughts. She didn't want to think about the prince's questionable future or Griffin's horrible past or anything else so sad and so uncontrollable. It made her uncomfortable. Those things didn't concern her anyway—she only had to concern herself with finding her godmother. Solving her father's murder. That's what mattered.

They walked on for hours, not breaking until Roman secretly told them Griffin needed to rest but wouldn't say so. It was the only time the prince spoke to Stella. She was still chewing over that when Izzy announced suddenly that her dog needed a break. Stella caught Roman giving her a grateful half smile, but that was the extent of positive interaction. Or any, really.

The forest buzzed around them, teeming with invisible life that could only be sensed and now seemed much more threatening. Stella tapped her feet against a rock while everyone else rested and ate. Each second resting was another second wasted; Stella didn't want to waste any more time. It seemed the whole day had passed before they packed up and kept going.

They'd been walking for fifteen minutes, Stella guessed, when she noticed a change in the wand. It started glowing brighter and became warmer with each step.

"I think we're getting close," Stella said, holding up the wand piece.

Izzy pointed in the distance. "I think we're here."

Stella whipped her head around to see a break in the foliage. Settled in the scene was a small cabin, crumbling and overgrown with greenery.

Purpose flowed through Stella, and she surged forward, her pulse thudding in her ears.

"Stella!" Roman called after her. "Wait! It might not be safe."

She ignored him. Stuffing the heated wand piece back in her pocket, she pulled out her sword, marched right up to the door of the cabin, and pounded her fist on it.

"Open up!" she shouted. "I know someone's in there!"

The door swung open, and Stella took a step back in spite of herself. The woman that answered barely came to Stella's shoulders and was buried in a mop of scraggly, blonde hair and filmy, wrinkled skin. Her face had been screwed up in fury, but she went rigid when she saw Stella.

"What…" the old woman mouthed. "How?"

Stella's hands trembled with her voice. "I'm looking for Zaria Rinsky. Where is she?"

Winston reached them first, panting by Stella's ankles, and Izzy, Roman, and Griffin soon caught up. Stella paid them no mind.

"Zaria Rinsky," she said again with more force, waving her sword at the lady. "Where. Is. She."

The woman glanced at all of them, her eyes lingering on Izzy, before she gazed at Stella again. It still took a few seconds for her to collect herself; she closed her gaping mouth, her beady eyes narrowing with resolve.

"I'm sorry." Her thin lips parted to reveal yellowed teeth. "Zaria Rinsky is dead."

CHAPTER 6

THE BEAST IN THEM ALL

*Z*aria Rinsky is dead.

Though the statement came quietly out of the mouth of a feeble, old woman hidden in the Forgotten Forest, the meaning hurled at them with devastating force, leaving nothing but rubble in its path.

Izzy stumbled backwards, her hand covering her mouth in disbelief. Roman muttered something very un-princely under his breath while Griffin snarled and threw what looked like a rock against a tree, and Winston plopped on the ground and whined.

Stella's shoulders shuddered, but she stared the woman down with resolution. "No. You're lying."

The old woman stared back, her small eyes gleaming with immense vitality for such an ancient lady. Her papery skin folded in on itself when she spoke again. "I'm not. She's been gone a long time now."

Griffin threw something else, snapping a tree branch and making Izzy jump. His reddening face looked like a raging animal between his pulsing scars and almost bared teeth. Roman stood rooted to the ground next to him, face pale like the moon, every muscle locked up so tense and tight Izzy thought he would shatter into pieces. She wasn't sure which of the two boys scared her more.

"No." Stella's knees started to wobble, and she held the door frame for balance. The old lady glared at her hand and took a step away, farther into her crumbling cabin. "No...she can't be. She can't. She's..." She slowly sank to the ground, the emotions playing out on her face—the conflict between hanging onto her resolve and facing reality.

Izzy shook her head in denial. Winston looked up and whined at her again, as though asking what everyone was upset about. She couldn't find the words to tell him.

Zaria's dead.

Sure, Izzy had considered that possibility. But she'd never really thought it would be true. Of all the people Izzy had ever met, Zaria was the only one who didn't seem capable of dying, who had laughed at the thought and evaded the fate, forever.

"She's gone," the old lady said flatly, the slightest shake to her voice but not a speck of pity in her wrinkled expression. "Now get out and don't come back."

She slammed the door shut on them; Stella barely had time to move her fingers before they got smashed. The forest settled into an eerie silence, like it was reeling from the loss too.

Stella was the first to break the spell. Suddenly she jumped to her feet and slammed her hand on the door. "What happened? Why did my father have your wand?"

The front door flew open again, the little old woman taut with fury. "Your father!" she bellowed with all the force of a wind storm, like she could blow Stella away. As quickly as the rage came, though, it simmered out of her when she saw the single tear falling down Stella's face. For a second, Izzy thought the old woman would break open too. Instead, she pursed her thin, white lips. "Leave, Stella. Take Izzy, go home, and forget your father and Zaria. Some things are better left buried."

Izzy gasped. Stella's eyebrows shot up, and she lunged forward only to run into the slammed door. She tried to open it, but it wouldn't budge.

"How do you know my name?" Stella shouted, banging again and again on the door. "How do you know us? Tell me!"

"Leave me in peace!" the old woman shouted back from inside.

"No!" Chest heaving, Stella folded her arms and stuck her chin out, even though the woman couldn't see her. "I'm not leaving until I get answers."

There wasn't a reply. Stella went to bang on the door again, when Izzy felt a change in the air. It pulsed somehow, almost with electricity, and a metallic taste formed in her mouth. Winston stood up and started walking in circles around Izzy's feet, whining.

Stella's fist hit the door once, then Izzy felt her body smash together into something painfully small. The world went dark, the electricity buzzed, then all at once everything came right back to her, the invisible constraints that had squashed her body instantly falling away.

Izzy doubled over and nearly heaved into the dirt, gasping, her forehead slick with sweat. Winston was sprawled out on his stomach next to her, ears flopping as he shook his head back and forth as though trying to clear it.

"What happ—" Izzy cut herself off when she looked up, her shock taking her words. Stella, Roman, and Griffin were all sprawled out on the dirt too, coughing and wheezing. A field of crops spread out before them, leading to what looked like a village in the distance. And about fifty yards behind them, as green and lively as ever, stood the edge of the forest. They weren't where they'd entered it the day before—they were farther south than their entry point—as if they'd just been spit back out.

"Whoa," Roman muttered, eyes wide when he realized where he was. "How…?"

"She…transported us?" Stella asked, still glancing around in disbelief at the unfamiliar Elarian territory. All their progress the last few days had been for nothing in just a blink of an eye.

Izzy gasped, slapping her hands against her forehead. She knew exactly what that meant.

"She's a fairy," Izzy whispered.

Roman snapped his gaze to her. "Are you sure?"

She nodded. "To do magic like that, to *transport*, especially without her wand? She has to be."

"That explains why she was hiding out," Griffin added, apparently already over the little rage fit he'd had in the forest. He gave a meaningful look to Roman. "Probably evading royal execution."

Stella gritted her teeth. "Well she can't evade me."

"But that..." Izzy scratched Winston behind his ears to calm him and give herself something to do. "Why does a *fairy* know who we are? Knowing Damon, knowing Zaria is one thing—they traveled all the time—but knowing who *we* are, recognizing us..." She trailed off, her veins buzzing painfully, and she looked at Stella. "Do you think she knows my mother?"

The drive working through Stella stopped, and she stared at Izzy with wide, conflicted eyes. Finally, she took a breath. "I...I don't know, Iz. Maybe."

Maybe. Maybe the old lady knew why Sofia had left Izzy. Maybe the old lady could tell her what Izzy did wrong, or maybe even *fix* her...there had to be some kind of magic. Love was tricky and temperamental, but there had to be some way...

Roman stood and dusted himself off, then helped Griffin to his feet. He trapped a wince underneath his scarred bravado.

"We've got to get back to her," Griffin said. "Clearly she knows something."

"And we have to do it fast," Roman added, calm and collected once more. "Before—"

"Hey!"

They all turned at the shouting voice to see several men running at them, abandoning a horse and plow, already too close for their group to make a successful getaway. Izzy's stomach clenched, and she grabbed her locket, while Winston stood at attention at her feet, his gaze on the incoming strangers.

"Before that happens," Roman finished under his breath.

✶ ✶ ✶ ✶ ✶ ✶ ✶

The men ushered Stella and her group away from the forest without bothering to introduce themselves. Stella and Griffin tried to protest, but the men just pushed them into a half full vegetable cart and sent the horse running, like there was a towering monster behind them ready to eat them all. Once they were within village borders—Doveneer, Griffin informed them—a good distance from the edge of the forest, the men stopped the horse and allowed them to exit the cart. Apparently out of danger now, the workers relaxed a little and seemed to actually look at who they had found.

Stay calm, Stella ordered herself as the men breathed sighs of relief, like they had just prevented a natural disaster. *Stay calm, and nobody will suspect a thing.*

Who was she kidding? She'd been found standing outside the Forgotten Forest with an illegal wand, a stray dog, and a dirty prince. Who *wouldn't* be suspicious of them?

Still, she forced her expression into one of mild pleasantness, like the one she'd use when she ran into Lady Pursbrough's snobby guests during work. Griffin subconsciously moved to stand in front of the prince, who slightly lowered his head, and Stella inched her way in front of him too. The last thing they needed were rumors winding through the villages and getting back to the castle.

The three men that had rounded them up stood before them now, each glancing back at the forest like they were afraid to talk about it. Several villagers had stopped to gather around them too. Stella gritted her teeth.

"Are you okay?" the first man, wearing a dirty, striped shirt, asked.

131

The second, a man in unfortunate red plaid pants, looked over them with horrified eyes. "What happened to you kids?"

All the made up excuses got stuck in Stella's throat. She'd expected enemies, not concern. A side glance at her group made her realize what the strangers saw: dirty, bruised, unsupervised seventeen-year-olds, looking dazed and pale outside the Forgotten Forest.

How do we spin this one?

Stella cracked a smile. "Sorry we scared you. Just doing some exploring—no need for any concern."

Stripes arched a skeptical eyebrow while his plaid friend gaped at them. "In the Forgotten Forest? That's a serious death wish, girl."

The third man was shorter than the others, sunburned, with a harsher expression. He turned to the few gathered villagers and said, "There's been another attack. Alert the guards."

"No!" Stella and Griffin exclaimed at the same time, then exchanged glances.

Griffin didn't hesitate to take the lead. "That won't be necessary," he said, exuding authority. "We got lost but have since found our way."

"There wasn't an attack," Stella added. All three men looked at her pointedly, and she realized she still had dried wolf blood all over her. "My fault. I thought I had the right trail, but we ended up stuck in a...thicket. Sharp and edgy, you know." She waved her hand like it was no big deal. "Nothing to get nervous about."

Stripes appraised them again with a raised eyebrow, unconvinced. Sunburn just scoffed and turned to Plaid. "We need a search party now. We can't live like this anymore." Plaid was ashen as he nodded slowly, then turned and ran, warning every person that he passed. Each one he spoke to went rigid, some pale with fear and others red with fury. They looked to the forest, then either retreated to their homes or came over to join the crowd that was forming around the group of kids.

Stella grimaced. The last thing she needed was a horde of paranoid villagers driving out her only lead.

Stripes cleared his throat. "I'll ask again: what attacked you in there?"

Stella held his gaze evenly. "I'll tell you again: nothing. You're wasting your time."

For a moment, she thought she saw reason in his eyes, and for a moment, she thought he'd let them leave in peace.

That moment ended when Griffin hissed under his breath and ducked his head. Stella looked in the direction he was avoiding and found another crowd of villagers surrounding a group of royal guards on horseback. Their leader, it seemed, was listening to the reports with a bit of animation lighting up her stone face. Her head snapped up, and she gazed at the forest with resolution.

Stripes was talking to them again, the villagers behind him all bickering among themselves, but it all melted into rumbling background noise. Stella watched as the woman on horseback gave a tiny grin, then lifted her hand in a sweeping motion, like she could reach over the entire village.

The air around her heated up, and suddenly everything smelled like it was burnt—Stella could taste it on her tongue. The people around the guards shouted in unison, like a war cry, their faces twisting up in hatred.

Stella's mouth dropped open at the abrupt change. What had *happened*?

Sunburn stepped forward, grabbing Stella's attention back, but his eyes were on Izzy. "I know you." He pointed a finger in her face, and she flinched back. "You're Merel's daughter. From Solume."

Izzy froze at the mention of her father's name, and Stella's nerves went on edge, her gut telling her to get out now. The gathering momentum of the crowd made Griffin bristle and mutter something, but Stella couldn't catch it over the buzz of the converging people. Several men came from the village carrying knives and hammers.

This was going to get ugly fast.

Sunburn sneered at Izzy's pale face, gaining ground as he spoke louder with the mounting agitation. "They finally locked the lunatic up after his pretty thing ran off on him. He was always going on and on about monsters and beasts and things that weren't there. He was dangerous." His face hardened as he watched Izzy shrink. "They said his daughter was just like him. Looks like they should've locked you up too."

"Back off," Stella barked at Sunburn as Griffin growled under his breath. "We've done nothing wrong. Leave us alone, and we'll be on our way."

Sunburn just spat at Izzy, ignoring Stella, then turned to his fellow villagers. "There's a bloodthirsty creature in that forest terrorizing us!" he shouted. "And we've lived with it for too long. I say we kill her before she tricks any more bystanders into being deluded sympathizers."

Glancing around helplessly at the unrest, Stella caught a glimpse of the woman on horseback. Her hand was still outstretched, her eyebrows pinched in concentration, but a small smirk was playing on her lips. She lifted her hand higher and snapped her fingers.

Everything descended into chaos.

The crowd rushed at Stella, shoving and yanking and jerking her around. She put her hands over her face, fighting to keep herself from falling and getting trampled or impaled by one of the weapons people were carrying. She lost all sense of space in a sea of furious and sweaty bodies.

"Lock her up!" she heard Sunburn yelling somewhere amid the mess. She couldn't tell where anyone was anymore. "She probably deserves the nuthouse anyway."

A scream pierced through the mayhem. Stella froze as her blood went cold.

Izzy.

Another scream followed with incensed barking. Stella forced her way through the mob with a new raging fervor, shoving people aside.

"Izzy!" she yelled. "Izzy, where are you?"

She desperately followed the screaming, panic pricking her nerves when the horrific sound got sharper but quieter—further away. Stella felt her stomach clench with fury and anxiety, shouting with frustration as she fought the masses between her and her best friend.

Out of nowhere, she crashed into Griffin, and he grabbed her by the shoulders before she fell to the ground.

"She's manipulating them!" he shouted at her, jerking his thumb in the general direction of where the royal guards had been. "She's a fairy hunter!"

Fairy hunter. The title echoed uselessly in Stella's brain, overwhelmed by the sound of Izzy's terrified screaming.

The throng finally broke, leaving Stella, Griffin, and Roman out in the open. She turned to see the mob disappearing in the trees of the forest. Roman moved to follow them, his face harsh with determination, but he froze when he saw the royal guards with the peasants.

Then, in the far distance, a muffled scream sounded again. Stella jumped, her nerves fraying, while Griffin let out a big breath like he'd been punched in the gut. Surging forward, she chased the horrible sound.

"Izzy!" Stella shouted, searching the village and glaring at every person that watched her warily from their shuttered windows. "Izzy, where are you?"

There was only another smothered shriek in response. Stella couldn't stand it. Her bones threatened to shatter with every scream, a sound she had never heard Izzy make, ever.

Griffin was the one who found her. His scars seemed to pulse as he yanked out the plank that was sealing two cellar doors. They opened to reveal a crumpled girl clutching her dog, her eyes wide and empty except for the ghosts that haunted her.

Stella clenched her jaw, hands balling into fists and begging to punch Sunburn over and over. Griffin's expression matched her own, but he stepped down and picked Izzy and Winston up off the floor with more gentleness than she thought he was capable of. Going slowly, he climbed back out of the cellar and set Izzy down on the ground. She curled into a tiny ball, trembling violently, and buried her face in Winston's nasty fur. He licked her arm over and over in comfort.

Stella crouched down next to her friend, which was when she realized Izzy was chanting something breathlessly, again and again: *I won't let them take you. I won't let them take you. I'm not crazy. I'm not crazy. I won't let them take you. I won't let them take you.*

I'm not crazy.

I'm not crazy.

I won't let them.

A lump formed in Stella's throat. Griffin crouched down on Izzy's other side, traces of leftover fury in his expression, and he exchanged a glance with Stella. She'd never seen him so...subdued. Timid. Like a brutish creature trying not to break a glass butterfly.

"Iz?" Stella finally asked. "Are you okay?"

Izzy didn't answer; she just shuddered harder. Griffin pressed his marred lips into a hard, angry line. Stella cautiously put a hand on Izzy's shoulder, and Izzy reached out and took her hand, gripping it so tightly Stella lost feeling almost immediately. Winston went from licking Izzy's arm to her white knuckles dutifully, like the saliva would somehow clean the hurt away.

Suddenly, Izzy snapped her head up, a speck of life warming her brown eyes. She clenched her jaw, making her bones stick out more, adding resolve to her gaunt face. Her gaze was locked on the forest.

Stella nodded to herself, knowing what Izzy saw. They had to get to the fairy. But while Stella saw her as their only lead, their only piece in trying to solve this desperate puzzle, she knew Izzy saw something else entirely: she saw a hateful village coming down on a peaceful outsider.

Though she was still trembling, Izzy's voice rang out loud and clear.

"We have to stop them. We have to save her."

They ran. Izzy's side ached and her pulse raced as she kept tripping over roots and rocks, but she didn't stop. Winston ran beside her, ears flapping and mouth open, like he somehow knew the stakes of their chase. Stella sprinted just ahead of Izzy, using the wand to guide her, with the boys right on her heels.

They had to get there in time. They had to save the fairy.

"It's a charm," Griffin explained breathlessly as they ran. "Old magic. The hunter has probably been here for weeks planting charmed objects. Now she can influence the emotional atmosphere of the village."

"She's not controlling them?" Stella half shouted back, her blonde ponytail flying in the breeze.

"No, we can't control anyone. Old magic can influence people, though. It's delicate, which is why mass hysteria is easiest. It spreads so quickly on its own anyway."

"How do we stop it?" Izzy asked.

Griffin glared at the forest ahead of him. "We can't. Even if we found the charmed objects and destroyed them, it would take time for the influence to fade. We'll just have to reason with them or try to evade them all together."

Izzy didn't know how they would manage it—it wasn't like the four of them could take on an angry mob on their own. Izzy's only hope was that the angry people would get lost in the forest, following the wand would get Stella, Izzy, Griffin, and Roman there first, and they could warn the fairy of the attack. She was a fairy after all; she should be able to take it from there, right?

Maybe the warning would soften her heart. Maybe the concern for her life would convince her to tell Stella and Izzy what she knew about their past—about their parents.

The thought of her mother propelled Izzy faster. The forest pushed in on her from all sides, trapping her in dark green the farther she went, but she didn't let her fear stop her. This was bigger than fear. She had to be brave.

Stella banked left and the four of them followed, Winston's paws skidding in the dirt to make the sharp corner. Leaves and limbs batted at Izzy, as if telling her to stop. Go back. It was useless.

She ignored them. Some things were worth the risk of failure, no matter how scary or painful the fall.

A rumble sounded in the distance, and the damp air slowly warmed with torchlight, telling Izzy they were close. Close, but maybe not close enough.

"Up ahead!" Stella shouted back at them. The trees broke open into a clearing where the old fairy's cabin was nestled peacefully into the greenery. That peace had been shattered, though, by the chaos surrounding it.

The mob had broken up, some congregated at the front of the cabin, while others had spread out in the forest, shouting and jeering and aiming their weapons in a frenzy. The royal guards were set back from the crowd, watching with interest and anticipation. The leading woman observed with hard eyes; nobody paid attention to her, and she wasn't trying to stop them. She almost seemed apathetic to the villagers' violence, as if waiting for something else.

Fairy hunter.

Izzy was several steps behind the boys and Stella—though Winston stayed dutifully at her side—so she missed whatever haphazard plan they had thrown together. She saw Stella and Griffin charge forward, while Roman snagged Izzy's arm and pulled her to the side. Winston followed, and Izzy motioned for him to be quiet.

"Stella and Griffin are going to try and drive them off or distract them," Roman answered in a low voice before Izzy could ask. "We're going to find the fairy and get her out. We can't lose her." His jaw set with annoyance, but it didn't stop him from leading her around the back of the cabin.

"You'd rather be out there?" Izzy asked, wanting to understand him. Her eyes went back and forth between his face and her feet, trying carefully to tiptoe quietly so as not to raise any alarms.

"A good king wouldn't hide behind his guards, advisors, or people. I hate to do it, but Griffin's right: that royal guard would recognize us. Korah, the woman on that horse, is a fairy hunter for my father." Roman pursed his lips grimly. "She'd recognize me, and things would get worse than they already are."

Dread coiled painfully in her stomach. "What about Griffin? He's just as recognizable. He could get cau—"

Roman shook his head. "He can spell his face momentarily to appear subtly different. The effects are brief and minimal, but it'll be enough for this."

"He can do that?"

"It's really uncomfortable and difficult to do." He rolled his eyes. "Or so I've heard. But he can hold it. Nobody will suspect it's him anyway."

They stopped talking as they reached the backside of the cabin. Roman searched for some kind of opening while Winston started sniffing at the base of the wall, like he could help too. Izzy placed her palm against the rotting wood, looking for some other entrance.

Her inspection of the cabin came up as fruitless as Roman's: there weren't any other doors and the only windows were above their heads. They both glanced up at the nearest window, and Roman offered her his hand with a raised eyebrow.

Izzy wasn't completely comfortable with the idea, and she got the feeling Roman would figure something else out if she said no, but she forced herself to nod her head and take his hand. They were running out of options; she had to be brave.

Using the wall for balance, Roman helped Izzy climb up onto his shoulders so she could see into the window, while Winston sat patiently at his feet. She wrinkled her nose when she saw the glass—it was so dirty, she couldn't see through it.

"You see her?" Roman whispered as loud as he dared.

"Hang on." Izzy wiped the glass with her arm, smudging some of the dirt, dust, bugs, and grime out of the way. The cabin was dark and cast in shadows, but Izzy could make out a figure standing in the middle of the space, hunched over and facing the front door. "I see her. She's just...standing there. Not moving. I don't know if she's going to fight or..."

Roman said something else, but Izzy didn't hear him. She looked for some kind of latch in the window, some way to open it, but had no luck. Roman precariously handed her a rock, but no amount of banging could break the glass.

"She must have some kind of spell on it," Izzy guessed. "I can't break it."

Roman cursed under his breath—for a prince, he had a broad, colorful vocabulary—and Izzy resigned herself to knocking on the window. If she could just get the fairy's attention, just let her know there were people who wanted to help, who *cared*...

Izzy heard Stella's voice rising into a shout from the other side of the cabin, and her heart raced. What if they couldn't get the mob to back down?

Izzy knocked louder. The fairy didn't turn around—she didn't even move.

"She doesn't seem very concerned that they'll get to her," she told Roman. "Maybe she has safety measures in place that—"

Suddenly, a red flame leapt from over the roof and singed Izzy's hand. She yelped and drew back instantly, knocking them off balance, and she and Roman fell in a heap on the forest floor.

Winston dug his nose into Izzy's tangled hair, checking on her. She pushed him aside, both she and Roman groaning as they sat up.

"What happ—" Roman started. The question fell away when a brilliant blaze stole their attention.

The cabin. It was on fire.

And the fairy was still inside.

Shouting, Roman jumped to his feet and surged toward the burning structure, but the old wood had caught flame so quickly that he couldn't get very close. She heard both Stella and Griffin's yells intermixed with a rise of cheers from the mob. Izzy hoped for a moment that a spell would protect the cabin, but that hope quickly went up in flames too. In a matter of minutes, the house was barely a burnt skeleton, and the fairy had either transported herself out in time or succumbed to the flames as well.

The mob. The mob had killed her. Burned her alive, trapped in her own house, quietly settled on the edge of humanity.

Roman ran back and forth along the cabin in near hysteria, trying to find an outlet, but Izzy sat frozen in the dirt, knowing in her bones there was nothing either of them could do. Winston stood in her lap growling at the flames, as though a carefully aimed bark would protect her from the fire.

Horrified, she put a hand on his back to keep him from running into the awful scene she couldn't tear her eyes from. The fire crackled and consumed the little house and everything inside, a monster in its own right.

"Papa isn't crazy," she murmured to Winston as the cabin crumbled in on itself. "There really is a beast in them all."

* * * * * * * *

Eventually the flames died down, but by then it was too late. The blaze had devoured the fairy's cabin whole, and now there were only a few charred wood pieces and a pile of ash to show for her existence.

The mob had stayed to watch their horrible handiwork, but had since dispersed, leaving the forest to its eerie silence. The five royal guards on horseback led by the fierce woman had lingered behind to put the fire out before the forest caught, and to check the rubble—Stella had hidden in the trees with Izzy, Roman, and Griffin until the woman and her entourage finally left. Now the boys were standing at the edge of the ash with stormy expressions while Izzy sat a ways off with her dog, petting him and staring at nothing.

Meanwhile, Stella paced through the remnants of the cabin, kicking up ash in her frustration while she fumed. Finding the cabin had been such a huge step forward, the first promise of real answers. Now they were left with nothing but disappointment, grief, and cinders.

Zaria was dead. The grief over that fact was only compounded by the possible death of the old fairy, their only lead. And a tiny annoying voice in the back of Stella's head whispered it was her fault.

She huffed and kicked more ash. It wasn't *her* fault. She never would have guessed that the villagers would respond with such force and violence. She never would've even wound up on that side of the forest if the old lady hadn't transported them there.

There was a chance that the fairy had survived, right? Surely, a fairy who transported four people through a forest could save herself from a house fire. Unless, of course, the strain of using that kind of magic had weakened the old creature when it really mattered.

Stella sighed and dropped her head only to see her feet, legs, and arms were covered in cinders. It took her back to just after her father died, when their money officially ran out and they were evicted. Natalia had paced around their beautiful living room in monstrous sobs so loud that Isla and Noor were huddled in the corner, too afraid and confused to move. When Stella had finally gained enough courage to ask Natalia what was going on, her stepmother had screamed in her face and shoved her into the unlit fireplace, slicing her palms and coating her skin in gray cinders.

Suddenly Stella felt very small. She wrapped her arms around her core like Izzy always did, hoping to keep herself together.

A faint shuffling sound broke through the tense stillness. Stella immediately retreated to Izzy, who was shushing her alert dog, and the boys converged in front of them. Though Griffin was haggard and slick with sweat, one of his reopened wounds dotting his shirt in spots of blood, he managed to raise his hands and create a barrier around them. Stella felt a presence of something solid in front of her, though she couldn't see anything but the forest. She guessed the barrier kept them hidden—at least, she *hoped* that's what Griffin had done.

It must've been, because when the hooded figure came into the clearing, it gave no indication it could see or sense the group of them hiding. Winston growled softly at the stranger, and Izzy put her hand on his snout, willing him to be silent as they watched the newcomer.

The figure took slow, heavy steps up to what was left of the cabin, stopping at the edge of ash. It stayed there for a second, as though breathing in the destruction, and Stella could feel the physical presence of sadness in the air.

"You always were sentimental."

Stella jumped and whirled to see the royal guards from earlier enter the clearing. The woman leading them was without her horse now, treading on foot, and had cropped blonde hair that highlighted her severe cheekbones and dangerous aura. A hunter, Griffin had said. A very capable looking one.

The hooded figure had also turned at the arrival, the movement so sudden that the hood slipped a little bit, revealing a wrinkled face underneath.

The old fairy. Stella felt a surge of excitement that her lead had survived after all. The excitement faded, though, at the realization that she was cornered in the forest by a royal hunter.

The hunter wrinkled her nose. "Old age looks awful on you."

Unfazed, the old lady just stared with a harsh expression.

"Now, come on." The hunter raised her hands. "It's been so long, I think it's only fair you drop your wrinkled pretenses."

The old lady didn't flinch when the air around her crackled and her skin started melting away. The pale, papery wrinkles gave way to a dark, smooth complexion; thin, coarse hair to a black, glossy mane; and short, hunched shoulders into a tall, wiry frame.

Zaria.

Stella had to slap her hand over her mouth to keep from crying out at the sight of her godmother. The uncertainty she'd faced for days fizzled into sheer joy at the thought of having a member of her old family back. Zaria was alive. Zaria was okay. Zaria...

Everything inside of Stella came to a slamming halt when she glanced at the hunter standing across the clearing from her godmother.

Zaria was a *fairy.*

The hunter gave a tight grin once the spell had completely melted away. She tipped her head in a lethal greeting. "Zaria."

Zaria returned with a lively smirk. "Korah."

"Clever setup you had here." Korah gestured to the remains of Zaria's cabin. "Quiet, secluded, difficult to find. Not impossible, of course."

"Of course not." Zaria's voice thrummed with the power Stella remembered, a smooth purr, like a fierce lioness always on the prowl. "Not when you bring a village down on me. You're getting desperate, Korah, to use peasants that way."

Korah shrugged. "I knew you were somewhere around here. Staging several accidents in a neighboring village was an easy way to get them looking out for a monster." The corners of her mouth curved slightly, viciously. "For you."

"Manipulating the people who trust you into committing murder doesn't make you much more. Perhaps *you* are the monster they should be wary of."

"I didn't want them to kill you—just to draw you out. I'd never deprive myself of that satisfaction."

"And what would they say if they knew their royal protection was charming them into mobbing in the dangerous forest?"

"They weren't in any real danger. I saw to that."

"It was reckless."

Korah shifted her weight, unaffected by the accusations. Instead she lifted her head higher. "Zaria Rinsky, as a fairy and therefore an outlawed monster and menace to Elaria, you are hereby sentenced to imprisonment and execution for your crimes as decreed by our late great King Rowan, who unified our kingdom after the Great War, and his grandson, King Asher, who now rules in his legacy."

"What a mouthful," Zaria muttered, stepping easily to the side. Korah matched her movement. "At least you've managed to perfect *that* speech after all these years."

Korah's expression pulled down into a savage glare that would've killed a weaker being. "Your time is up, Zaria. You can't run from this any longer. You will pay for what you are." Her eyes flashed. "For everything."

"We'll see." Spreading her arms wide, Zaria clapped her hands together, and chaos rained down on the forest.

CHAPTER 7

SEEING RED

Izzy clutched Winston, horrified, as the hunter Korah advanced on Zaria.

Zaria the fairy.

Izzy couldn't believe it. And based on the way Stella was doubled over with her hand on her mouth, eyes wide enough to hold an ocean of emotion, Izzy guessed she hadn't known about her godmother's true origins either.

"Your time is up, Zaria," Korah warned, her angled features holding a harshness that could only come from years of hunting and hatred. "You can't run from this any longer."

Zaria's full lips quirked to the side, a taunting smile that made Korah's eyes dance with fury. "We'll see." With bravado, Zaria spread her arms wide and clapped them together. Korah raised her arms in the same moment, fierce concentration on her face, and the forest came to life around them.

The attacks came and went so quickly that Izzy could barely keep up with what was happening from her cover behind Griffin's shield. Using her magic, Zaria stripped the nearest trees of their bark and hurled the shards at Korah; while she deflected, shards caught one of her guards in the face, and he went down. Unfazed by her loss, Korah sent the bark back at

Zaria, following them up with a boulder she lifted into the air with a mere gesture. Zaria spread her hands across her face just as the rock reached her and it exploded into chunks, which she shot at Korah one by one. Korah jumped out of the way, but one sharp rock grazed her cheek, leaving a thick cut.

Blood dripped into the dirt, and Korah snarled. Raking her hands through the air, she drew up the breeze into a deafening whirlwind, trapping her and Zaria in a vortex of dirt, branches, and debris. Izzy squinted against the onslaught of powerful wind, her messy bun unraveling, while Winston's ears flapped wildly.

"Zaria!" Stella yelled, one hand held up to brace against the heavy wind. Through the debris, Izzy thought she saw Zaria's head cock to the side, though she remained locked in battle with Korah. Stella took a step forward, but Roman grabbed her arm and held her back, watching the duel with a grim expression.

"Korah will kill you," Roman told her, his quiet voice barely audible above the tumult of the fight. "She won't flinch at collateral damage, and it'll only get worse if Zaria reacts and reveals she cares about what happens to you. You may be Zaria's only liability, and Korah would use that to her advantage."

Only liability. Izzy saw the words reverberate in Stella's wide eyes. Maybe Zaria hadn't abandoned Stella after all—maybe she'd left to avoid Korah's wrath coming down on the girls. Izzy barely dared to hope, but Stella's resolve hardened her face, confirming what she believed about her godmother.

"We have to help her," Stella insisted. She flinched as a tree across from them snapped in half with a deafening crack, followed by Korah's shout of frustration. "What can we do?"

Roman glanced at a pale Griffin—he did that a lot, Izzy realized—and Griffin pursed his lips in determination, then gave a curt nod. With the wind, most of his hair had been yanked out of its ponytail, and half of it was whirling in the air while the rest stuck to his sweaty forehead. He didn't look like he could hold out much longer.

Izzy shook her head at the determination in his eyes. "I don't think you should—"

Griffin cut her off with a jerk of his chin. "Make sure Roman stays out of the way, and I'll make sure Zaria walks away."

"No!" Roman argued. "I won't let you—"

"Keep him safe," Griffin went on, letting Roman's objections get lost in the wind. He shifted his stare from Izzy to Stella, and back again, like their eye contact would be a solemn oath. "Don't let him be seen or do anything stupid. I can handle this on my own."

Izzy bit her lip and nodded, hoping her eyes conveyed the same sincerity. Stella thought a moment, guarded and contemplative, running scenarios in her head, before nodding too, all three of them ignoring Roman's furious protests.

Griffin moved to step toward Zaria, and Roman planted himself in front of him, pushing him back. "Stop!" he demanded. "I will *not* stay behind as you—"

"You are the prince!" Griffin exploded, and everyone stepped back from his rage. "You are *my* prince and the future king of Elaria, no matter what your self-loathing says, and I am sworn to protect you." He took a breath, deflating slightly. "We made a pact, Roman—no matter the cost."

Roman studied his friend for a moment, pursing his lips, before finally nodding in resignation. He didn't look happy about it, but he didn't fight when Stella took his arm and dragged him away from the raging storm in the clearing.

Izzy moved to follow them, Winston pawing at her feet as if to get her to go, but she glanced back at Griffin just as he flicked his wrist at an approaching guard that had moved closer to them in an effort to surround Zaria. The guard's muscles seized up and he fell to the ground with a mangled yelp. Griffin's knee buckled with the strain of his power; Izzy rushed right back to his side. Though the sight of his bloody shirt didn't bother her, she hesitated to touch him, even to help hold him up.

"You're going to get yourself killed!" Izzy shouted at him over the chaos. "Self-sacrifice isn't always as noble as backing down and admitting you need help."

Griffin's teeth were clenched in pain or concentration or frustration, or some mix of all three. Rather than exploding in anger like she half expected, he nudged her in Stella's direction with his shoulder and met her eyes evenly.

"Izzy," he said solemnly, the first time he'd ever said her name. "I've survived before; I'll do it again. But I won't be able to concentrate if I think you might get hurt too. I can handle this. Please, just go—protect yourself and our prince."

Biting her lip, Izzy glanced over him before nodding in understanding. If anyone could handle this mess, it was Griffin. She took off running after Stella without another word, Winston at her heels, fingers winding around her locket with a silent plea to the stars to keep her people safe.

* * * * * * * *

Roman's arm was stiff and defiant as Stella dragged him through the forest. Though she was sure it wasn't completely appropriate for her to handle royalty this way, she knew that if she let go Roman would lose all reason and barrel straight back to Griffin, logic aside. If she was going to rescue Zaria, help Griffin, and keep the prince and her best friend safe, she needed Roman to do what she said and trust that it would be okay.

Also, Stella *herself* needed to believe it would be okay, but she could only deal with one thing at a time.

The forest trees calmed and stilled the farther they got from Korah and Zaria. With every step a panicked thought of her godmother pounded in Stella's head, but she forced herself onward, forced her feet to keep going. She didn't come this far just to lose now.

So why am I running away?

Once the clamor from the fight was barely a whisper in the leaves, Stella stopped, and Roman skidded to a stop next to her.

She glanced around, noticing Izzy a ways behind them, and tried to mark the place somehow with her eyes. It didn't matter though—everything looked exactly the same.

Stupid nature. Stella was never setting foot in a forest again.

"Stay here," she said to Roman. "I'll be right back."

His eyebrows shot up as his mouth yanked down into a scowl, guessing what she was planning. "No. No, you're either staying with us, or I'm coming with you."

"I'm going to help him." Stella jerked out her chin. "And you're going to stay here, *Your Highness*, where it's safe. Okay?"

"I'm a rake, Stella," Roman bit back. "Not a useless vegetable. I have just as much magic capability as you, but infinitely more training experience. Stop looking at me like I'm a wounded animal about to collapse."

"I'm *not*," she argued, but her voice fell flat on the last word. Truthfully, she hadn't known how to look at Roman since she had found out what had happened to him. "But this isn't about you, anyway. It's *my* godmother out there, and it's *my* fight. I'm just doing what Griffin asked. You are a prince, and it's our responsibility to keep you safe."

Roman scoffed. "You've *never* cared about royalty, and I know you feel no responsibility toward us now." He stabbed his finger in the air toward Griffin. "But *I* have a responsibility to my friend, and I will *not* let him die while I hide behind the trees."

"He's not going to die. I know, he's your best friend, and I—"

"He's not just my best friend, Stella! He's my brother—more than a brother. He's *all* I have left in this world, the only one I have. You don't understand…"

He trailed off when Izzy finally caught up to them, Winston running circles around their group with his tongue hanging out. Izzy stopped, breathless, and twisted her locket tighter around her finger when she saw Roman staring at her. She dropped her eyes, and that snapped Roman out of his daze.

Stella nodded at him. "I understand just fine, Roman. But the fact is, you're the prince, and you're the most valuable one here. I won't let you lose Griffin." She gave a joking smirk, hoping to diffuse some of the tension. "Or me, for that matter, since you're so concerned."

He didn't smile, but she did win an eye roll. "Well, then, I guess I can sleep soundly tonight."

"You watch mine, I'll get yours," Stella said, gesturing to Izzy. "And we can both sleep knowing the future leader of Elaria is safe. Deal?"

Izzy's eyebrows pulled down. "Hey! I don't need a babysitter either."

"Join the club," Roman muttered under his breath before nodding at Stella. "Fine. Deal."

Satisfied, Stella turned and headed back toward the mayhem.

"Be careful, Stella!" Izzy called after her, Winston barking along in agreement.

Agreement? Stella shook her head. Izzy treated that mutt like a human, and it was rubbing off on her.

Tossing the thought aside, Stella pressed on through the rustling trees, drawing her sword from its sheath. The silver blade was caked with dried wolf blood and forest dirt, but the edge was still sharp enough to give Stella a little comfort. It wasn't much, considering she was about to try and challenge talented royal hunters with a sword, but she would take any bit of comfort she could get.

After all, Zaria's life was on the line, and there was no way Stella was letting her slip away a second time.

Stella expected to hear the whirlwind before anything else, so she was surprised when Korah's exasperated shout tore through the trees, only a little farther off. Quietly, Stella held her sword at the ready and crept toward the clearing, every muscle locked with tense anticipation. When she peeked her head around the last tree trunk, she found two guards limp on the ground. Griffin was pale but fierce as he battled another guard, making sure to keep his back to Korah and his recognizable scarred face from her gaze.

Korah, however, couldn't care less about Griffin. Blood trickled from her mouth and down her face, and her eyes burned with hatred as she and the last remaining guard took on Zaria from opposite sides. Zaria's perfect hair was wild and frizzy, her eyes wide and muscles strained despite the cool confidence in her expression.

Stella paused for only a moment to take in the scene, to analyze it, wishing she was skilled enough to just go barreling in and take them all on. Then, with Roman's doubtful words echoing in her mind, she tested the now familiar weight of the sword in her hands and disappeared in the trees again.

Someday she'd be the best swordsman in Elaria. She'd make sure of it. For now, though, she would have to cheat.

Holding her breath, Stella tiptoed through the growth until she was standing just a few feet from Griffin and his opponent. She didn't give time for Griffin to react—she stalked right up behind the royal guard, slashed her sword across his knees, then slammed the hilt into his skull when he buckled. He fell to the ground unconscious like a sack of rocks. Stella kicked his head for good measure.

"I had him," Griffin muttered, sweat beading down his temple as he spit blood from his split lip.

Stella rolled her eyes. "Sure you did."

Suddenly, a scream pierced the air, making Stella jump. She turned to see the last guard lifeless underneath a fallen tree, and Korah in a bruised heap on the ground. Zaria glared vehemently over Korah with manic eyes, as if daring her to keep going, and for the first time Stella felt a twinge of fear— she'd never been afraid of Zaria, despite her intimidating nature, but she hadn't known about Zaria's powers or seen her kill someone, even if in self-defense.

Did she know her godmother at all?

Korah scowled in loathing, leaping to her feet and backing away from Zaria. "You can't hide," she spat, livid. "I'll find you, Zaria. I'll find you, and I will kill you." Then she turned and ran, using magic to bring down two trees to block anyone from following.

Rather than chase Korah, Zaria's shoulders slumped as she surveyed the carnage around her, breathing hard with exertion. She froze over when she saw Stella and Griffin standing at the edge of the clearing. Her posture straightened again, automatically regaining offensive position, but her face became completely expressionless. No, not completely. Stella could detect a hint of wariness in her narrowed eyes.

Griffin sagged against a tree, panting, but kept his suspicious gaze on the fairy. Stella felt rooted to the ground with the same murky hesitation she saw in her godmother.

She didn't know how long they stood there, staring at each other. It felt like eternities, like the endless green of the leaves had morphed and bent time around them, trapping them in a bubble of paralyzed indecision.

"So, what then?" Griffin finally grumbled, shattering the scene. "Is this it?"

Zaria jerked her chin out at his voice and took a graceful step forward. "Stella." Her tone was neither friendly nor unfriendly, but Stella noticed a slight wavering when Zaria said her name, like it had collected dust in her mouth from lack of use. "Why are you here?"

Stella blinked. "Why am I here?" she repeated, the question knocking her drive from wherever it had gotten stuck. "Why am I *here*? Why are *you* here?" Her voice grew louder and she took a step forward. "Where have you been? Why did...what...what happened?"

Zaria narrowed her eyes, irises so dark violet they were almost black, calculating with the same smooth expression. "It's dangerous to be out here."

"You don't think I know that?" Stella exploded. She raked her hands through her messed-up hair and gestured wildly toward the forest behind her. "I dragged Izzy out here with practical strangers, only to be attacked by wolves before finding you, and now...and now you're alive, and I left the prince back there—"

"The *prince*?" Zaria asked, arching a perfect black eyebrow. "The prince of Elaria is with you?"

Stella blew a piece of hair out of her face, some of her anger simmering at the thought of being reprimanded by her godmother. "Yes. He and his advisor volunteered to come help me find you. I'm trying...I heard Natalia talking. About my father. That he...that he was murdered. And I thought maybe you would...help me figure out what happened. To him."

"We aren't here with Korah," Griffin added, motioning to the fallen guards. "If this is any indication."

Zaria gave an amused half smile. "Really? Two young royals looking for a fairy, and it's completely innocent. Haven't heard that one before."

"We didn't know you were a fairy." For the first time, Stella dropped her eyes. "I didn't know."

There were a few beats of heavy silence. Stella pressed the tip of her sword in the dirt, unsure what to do.

"You, uh…you look good, Stella. Grown up."

Stella's eyes snapped to Zaria's face. The half smile was still there, her mask of cool confidence in place, but Stella could sense a slight shift in emotion—a familiar shift, one that held memories of exciting visits from her godmother, crushing hugs in her strong arms, fascinating stories of things unreal, and chocolates brought from across the kingdom.

Zaria, I've missed you so much. So much it hurts.

A sudden noise stole Stella's attention. She and Griffin turned to see Winston galloping up to them as fast as his little legs could carry him, barking incessantly, as though panicked.

"Winston?" Stella asked, crouching down. "What is it?"

The dog just barked in her face louder, like that cleared it all up, then started running the direction he'd come. The direction Stella had left Izzy and Roman.

Griffin sucked in a sharp breath and lurched forward, breaking into a run, but in his weakened state it only took a moment for Stella to pass him. She chased after Izzy's dog, the worst thoughts pulsing in her head.

The forest stretched on forever. Just when she thought she'd for sure gone the wrong way—they couldn't have gone this far—she caught a glimpse of Winston running circles around a lump on the forest floor, sticking his nose in it and whimpering. Once Stella got closer, she realized it was a person.

With a mangled gasp, Stella skidded to her knees over Izzy's unconscious body, glancing around wildly for some kind of answer. She saw nothing but Griffin searching fruitlessly in the trees while spewing panicked profanities.

Prince Roman was gone.

* * * * * * *

Everything was dark. Dark and achy and buzzy...something was buzzing. Buzzing in her ear, louder and louder, and it hurt, even in the darkness.

"Izzy?" A voice broke through the buzzing. "Izzy, can you hear me?"

Something wet washed over her face, and Izzy groaned, fluttering her eyelids in an effort to open them.

"Stop, Winston," the voice said. "Give her some space."

Finally, Izzy managed to open her eyes. She found herself on the floor of the forest, Stella and Griffin each leaning over her with pale and concerned faces, and she winced, head aching. Winston finally broke out of Stella's grasp and lurched forward, licking Izzy's cheek and plopping himself in her lap.

"Ouch," she muttered, rubbing the sore spot on the back of her head and slowly sitting up. "Where...?"

"What happened to him?" Griffin demanded. He was sweaty and spent, but that didn't stop his raging desperation, even after Stella's disapproving look. "Where's Roman?"

Izzy's eyebrows furrowed as she struggled to remember through her blinding headache. "Roman? Roman..." She got bits of memory, of her conversation with the annoyed prince of

Elaria that he couldn't do what he wanted, that he had to rely on others so heavily, and that it made him feel so weak. She remembered thinking to herself, yet again, he would make a good king, if he could ever get there, and then there was a rustle in the leaves, and he leapt to her defense, and then...

"Red." Izzy nodded slowly. "Red, everywhere."

"That would be the Red Riding Clan," a new voice chimed in.

All three of them—four including Winston—jumped and turned to see Zaria coming through the trees toward them, walking like she was enjoying an afternoon stroll rather than returning from a vicious fight with her hunter. When Izzy was younger, she used to marvel at the life Zaria emanated, how she seemed to be bigger and brighter than anyone else. Now Izzy understood where that vivacious confidence came from: magic. Izzy had known a fairy her whole life and hadn't even realized it.

But as she watched Zaria step gracefully through the shrubs, her movements nearly feline and borderline predatory, Izzy wondered if the loving woman she used to know was the same dangerous fairy she saw in front of her.

"Red Riding Clan?" Griffin repeated, not hiding his skeptical disdain, as he and Stella got to their feet. "Is that some kind of joke?"

Stella's eyes glazed over at the sight of her godmother, as if in a dazed trance she couldn't break through. Izzy knew they were thinking the same thing: could they trust Zaria?

Zaria smirked. "Now be careful. If some of them heard you say that, they'd take your hand off."

Griffin scoffed at the threat. "My hand?"

"The hand is often more effective than the head. If you take their head, they can't tell anyone else about it."

That sobered Griffin right up. Izzy paled and swallowed hard, her grip on Winston tightening. Those kind of people had Roman?

"Who are they?" Stella asked carefully, guarded. "Do you know them?"

Zaria nodded. "Red Riding clan. Extremist group. Live in hiding, work with rebels, try to bring down the infrastructures that don't do them justice. They aren't people you forget."

Izzy and Stella exchanged glances. How did Zaria get mixed up with people like that?

"The things you do to survive," Zaria said flippantly with a wave of her hand, like she heard their thoughts. "Everyone would be surprised how far their limits go when they're pushed."

"So do you know where they took him?" Griffin asked. "What they want with him?"

Zaria's eyes flashed with disdain, and she laughed once in disbelief. "What they *want* with him? He's the crown prince of Elaria. I imagine half the kingdom *wants* something with him, especially a pack of angry, suppressed royal-haters. That's probably why you don't see much royalty wandering around the forest alone, even with powerful magic."

Griffin flinched at the implications, the knowledge that he'd let his prince down. Izzy patted her dog before carefully standing up, then put a hand on the crook of Griffin's elbow. She was a little surprised when he didn't move away.

"We can get him back," she told him, then glanced at Stella. "Right?"

"Well of course we can," Stella answered, like it was obvious, and Izzy noticed Griffin relax slightly. "I can't miss the opportunity to throw my successful rescue in his face." She looked to her godmother. "Can you tell us how to find them?"

Zaria narrowed her eyes, calculating, and Izzy was shocked at how much the expression looked like Stella, despite the fact they were nearly opposite in appearance. "They are dangerous people, Stella. Are you sure you really want to find them?"

Stella jerked out her chin at the patronizing tone. "I have to. For Roman."

Zaria scoffed, but it almost sounded like a snarl. "For a selfish, arrogant prince that would give no second thought to the likes of you?"

Izzy cringed at the words, but if Stella was hurt, she only pushed back harder. "No, for a boy who only knew me for fifteen minutes before he came kicking down my door because he knew I was living in a *prison*."

Zaria stepped forward. "You don't know his—"

"I know that I'm going after him because I've done that much for you." Stella huffed, blowing a piece of hair from her face. "And he's done more than that for me." She took a breath, smoothing the edge of the crackling atmosphere. "I'm going. Not just because it's important for the kingdom, but because it's important to me. And if you can't get yourself to help us for him, then you should at least do it for me."

Zaria raised an eyebrow, the most open expression Izzy had seen on her face since finding her, then narrowed her eyes slightly at Stella. The two of them engaged in their own standoff, timeless fairy against brave girl, both a near mirror of each other, exerting their auras as if through sheer determination each could get the other to bend to her will.

The scene took Izzy back in time, to the rare occasions when Stella and Zaria would disagree while the godmother was visiting. Izzy's family was over at Stella's all the time, especially when both Damon and Zaria were there, since they traveled so much. It was like a celebration. Izzy remembered the feeling of family, of squealing next to Stella and her stepsisters as Damon unveiled the foreign gifts he'd brought for all four of them from his last trading route. She remembered making herself sick on Natalia's fresh sweet rolls, and then settling down on the floor to hear a story from Zaria. Both Izzy and Stella had watched the godmother with stars in their eyes, dreaming of being even half the person she was. Even as a child, though, Stella challenged Zaria with her perpetual stubbornness. Damon used to joke that if he didn't know better, he'd think

Stella was Zaria's. Izzy had never really thought about that until now.

The standoff lasted just moments, though it felt like much longer. Zaria broke first. The harsh concentration fell from her expression, aloof confidence filling its place, dissipating the tension in the air.

"I *have* missed your last few birthdays," she mused.

"A few," Stella cut in dryly.

"Though this brings 'asking for a prince' to a whole new level."

"You owe me."

"I'll go grab him for you. Bring him back here."

"Not a chance," Griffin bit back.

"We'll follow you," Stella added. "We're coming."

Zaria clicked her tongue with a small smile. "Always so stubborn."

Izzy saw something in Stella's blue eyes crack open, but her voice stayed smooth. "Wonder who taught me that."

A few more beats of silence sounded—Izzy thought Griffin was going to explode with impatience—but once again Zaria broke first.

"Okay, fine. You win." She shook her head, like she couldn't believe her words. "Let's go find ourselves a prince."

* * * * * * * *

Zaria led the way through the Forgotten Forest, steps smooth and purposeful like she had the rough terrain memorized. Stella trailed slightly behind her, close enough to touch her arm if she reached out, but far enough she could watch her godmother. The conflict was like a dagger in her gut, twisting to the side with every whiplash of thought: trust Zaria, or don't trust Zaria. Zaria, the loving godmother she'd been separated from. Zaria, the dangerous fairy that mysteriously disappeared after Damon died, which, Stella noted, Zaria hadn't said a thing about.

She didn't know what to think. And she hated not knowing.

Izzy and Griffin walked silently behind her, Winston trotting at Izzy's heels. Despite his haughty protests, Griffin had finally allowed Zaria to heal some of his wounds with her magic, and now he had color back in his face and could walk fine on his own. Zaria hadn't wanted to use too much magic—even fairies had limits, and she'd had a long day—and Griffin was eager to get away from her, so he wasn't completely healed, but enough, he said. Stella knew he couldn't care less about himself. He would drag his own corpse across the ground if it meant finding Roman faster.

Nobody spoke for most of the travel time, and the slight sounds of the forest set Stella on edge. She found her mind going back and forth between obsessing over Zaria's possible motives and worrying about what could be happening to Roman. The first made her feel detached from the world, a cold sadness shocking her system at the conflict she felt for her godmother; the second made her confused and aggravated. Since when did she care so much about what happened to Roman?

He helped me, she reminded herself. *He helped me when nobody else did.*

Then she glanced at Zaria, black ponytail swinging with each step, and the war in her mind started all over again.

They only stopped once—Zaria needed to get her bearings directionally, and Winston had to use the bathroom. Griffin muttered angrily to himself, while Izzy slid up next to Stella's side.

"Are you doing okay?" Izzy asked quietly, biting her lip.

Kicking methodically at the dirt, Stella kept her eyes trained on her godmother, who was several yards away. "I'm confused. To put it nicely."

Izzy followed her gaze. "She keeps looking at you. When she knows you're not looking. She does it to me too, but not as much as you."

"If you aren't looking, then how do you know?" Stella asked, annoyed, though she wasn't sure why.

Izzy shrugged. "I'm quiet. People forget how much I see."

Stella took that in stride, fighting off the irritation she wanted to aim at Izzy when she knew it was for someone else. "Fine, then. What do you see?"

"She's far away," Izzy said thoughtfully. "She's far away, and she knows it, and she can't decide how to come back."

Stella lowered her voice further. "Do you think we can trust her?"

"I think we have to."

"That's not the same thing."

"It might be, in the end."

"Found it," Zaria called, interrupting their conversation. "Get over here and stay close to me."

Griffin sauntered forward with Stella; Izzy called for Winston, who came running after them. Zaria had kneeled next to a giant boulder overgrown with vines and moss, and pressed her palm against it. Power thrummed from her body through her arm and into the rock, making it glow slightly for a split second. Then she stood and took a step back, standing at the ready in front of Stella.

Annoyed, Stella peeked her head around Zaria's tall frame to see the ground next to the boulder shuddering, like an extremely concentrated earthquake. It trembled for a moment before falling away into a cavern that opened up in the earth, revealing a path of stairs and two figures in long, blood red hoods.

Izzy gasped softly, and Winston growled underneath his breath just as Griffin did, both moving to stand in between the new figures and Izzy. The cloaks completely covered the two strangers, leaving Stella unable to see anything about them. It was unsettling. After a moment, they lifted their heads.

The one on the left, a pale man with white blond hair, gave a sharp grin, almost snake-like. "Zaria? Now this is a surprise." The girl next to him lit up at the mention of Zaria's name, and she practically glowed as she stared at the fairy from under her red hood. Stella wondered if she would start drooling.

Zaria gave one of her signature smirks. "Clegg. Raina. It's been a few years."

"It has. To what do we owe this pleasure?"

"Just looking for something." Zaria shrugged casually. "Hoping to call in a few favors."

Clegg appraised her a moment before nodding. "We do owe you a few, I suppose." He craned his head to look at the group of kids behind her, and Stella felt Izzy flinch at his gaze. "Did you bring us new recruits?"

At that, the girl—Raina, Stella guessed—broke her admiring gaze to assess them. She was at least a head shorter than Clegg, and had a soft, round face that highlighted the biggest green eyes Stella had ever seen. They were beautiful, but they seemed to see too much, and that made Stella uncomfortable.

Zaria laughed once, but the sound was more offensive than it should've been. "Hardly. I left for a reason, Clegg, and I'm not about to come back, officially anyway. This is a social visit. Sorry to disappoint."

Stella's eyes flashed to Zaria, but she ignored her questioning gaze.

Zaria was a part of this?

Stella was about to open her mouth, Griffin doing the same, when Raina's stare halted her, boring into her body. Stella felt the need to crouch down and hide.

Raina's mouth fell open, the recognition in her wide eyes probing at Stella. She elbowed Clegg. "That's Damon's daughter."

Stella's throat dried up. Zaria's smirk didn't change, but her shoulders tensed, her body going rigid.

"So it is," Zaria said, voice tight. "Now, are you going to let us in, or leave us out in the leaves? I'm getting rather sick of all this green."

Clegg's gaze went back and forth between Zaria and Stella with a raised eyebrow, curiosity blooming in his expression.

"Right, then. You know the way." With a last glance to Stella, the red figures turned and disappeared down the steps.

"Zaria," Stella forced through clenched teeth. "What—"

"Later," Zaria hissed back, enough venom in her voice to keep Stella at bay. "Don't say a word." Then the fairy started down the stairs without looking back, Griffin stalking after her. Stella exchanged a wary glance with Izzy before they followed.

The stairs took them deep into the earth, ending with a series of tunnels that made Stella's head spin just at the thought of them. Zaria didn't hesitate. She walked through the candle-lit halls like she owned them, not even pausing to think where to go.

Stella was itching to demand answers, but held her tongue, following her godmother blindly. Surely Zaria wouldn't lead them into a trap, right? Obviously they hadn't worked out the lines of their relationship yet—if they even still had one—but Zaria wasn't *that* apathetic toward Stella. Was she?

Suddenly, Zaria stopped at a wide, wooden double door to her right, where Clegg and Raina were about to enter.

Clegg grinned like a viper again when he saw them. "Oh Zaria. Always so eager to jump right into the middle of the fray."

Zaria smirked. "Life is boring on the edges."

Raina's big eyes were locked on Stella again. Stella didn't get the chance to ask any of her one thousand questions before Clegg surged through the door.

Chaos streamed through the doorway, light and pandemonium leaking into the tunnel. Clegg didn't hesitate to enter; neither did Zaria. Raina gave Stella another long look before going inside too.

Griffin only hesitated a fraction of a second. He and Stella entered together, with Izzy and Winston hanging back behind them.

The door opened to a cave carved from the earth, the space set up like some kind of council chamber. Several dozen red-clad figures lined the wooden table that circled the room, each of them talking over the other. Some looked angry, while others were calmer, sticking to logical conversation over emotional outbursts, but all of them had some kind of stake in the discussion.

Overwhelmed by the sea of red, it took Stella a second to notice the bruised figure in the center, black hair sticking out among the conformity.

Her nerves grated at the sight of the now-familiar face tied to a chair in the middle of the semi-organized madness, his expression taut with feigned arrogance that she knew hid raging fear. Griffin muttered something under his breath, confirming her suspicions.

"That's the prince of Elaria," Raina told her, like she didn't know. "A few members of the clan found him in the forest without a guard detail, and brought him here." She clicked her tongue. "Silly boy."

Stella couldn't rip her gaze from the prince. "What do they want with him?"

Raina blinked at her, surprised. "Penance. For his crimes."

"Crimes?"

"Of course." Raina turned to look at the restrained prince too, her voice grave but words too rehearsed. "The royals suppress us. He's a part of that. He's got to pay for it."

A chill ran down Stella's spine. She clenched her hands into fists, threatening to be suffocated by red, when Roman's eyes suddenly flashed to hers, as if finally sensing her presence. A small crack of relief went through his blank expression, letting her get a glimpse of his panic.

Squaring her jaw, she nodded at him, hoping he could see the resolve in her eyes.

Hang on, Roman. I'm going to get you out of here.

CHAPTER 8

THICKER THAN BLOOD

Roman looked terrified.

Izzy knew him well enough now to note the subtleties in his stance: the tension in his haughty shoulders, the ghost of a tremble in his stiff upper lip, the haunted self-loathing that permeated the entitlement in his eyes. He was so afraid, and he was desperately trying not to be. He was trying so hard to hide behind a wall of arrogant pride, a wall Izzy now knew he only built to keep in his fear, to keep out of the hateful gaze of his father. Roman had been raised in a castle where any weakness on his part could lose him his crown, in the best case scenario. Exile or death in the worst case.

Here, though, in a crowded cavern full of odd, red-cloaked people who had surrounded the helpless prince, Izzy thought he might see a different side of things—one she'd been wanting the courage to tell him since he left his castle behind for their misfortuned adventure.

"We deserve to be represented," a man with fat lips and no eyebrows was arguing. "The crown claims we have 'rights' as any other citizen, but those rights are rarely ever implemented fairly or correctly."

Many red heads bobbed up and down in agreement. Izzy twisted her finger around her locket, the heat and pressure in the room pushing in on her. Though they'd found the Red Riding Clan with the hope to rescue the kidnapped prince, Zaria had walked into the council and sat down on the back row, like she was a member too—apparently she had been at one point in time. Izzy, Stella, and Griffin saw no option but to follow her example. Winston sat at her feet, muscles taut with nerves as he surveyed the scene of strangers, but despite the clan's reputation for violence, nobody had threatened the newcomers so far.

Granted, nobody knew they were there to rescue the prince, but still, Izzy was surprised at their civility, all things considered. She thought new faces would provoke the clan, but nobody bothered them, and she wondered how much of that came from Zaria's established reputation here. One person—Raina, Izzy remembered—had even recognized Stella as Damon's daughter. Another impossible question to add to the list of things Zaria really needed to explain.

"He can't know what it's like," an older woman spat at Roman. "Living in this society, without magic. They preach rakes have a place here, but that place is down in the dirt!"

"He has all the power in the world," another echoed, jabbing a crooked finger at the prince. He actually flinched, like she'd hit him. "He doesn't understand—he can't. He'll never truly care for the likes of us."

Roman blinked in surprise, eyebrows furrowing as he mulled that over. Izzy's heart leapt at the thoughtful expression breaking through his discomfort and fear. That's what she wanted to tell him about his lack of magic, but hadn't yet found the right words or bravery: knowing weakness gives you a kind of strength—a new sight—something that powerful people, like King Asher, would never truly be able to have or understand. It was a cursed gift, Izzy knew, but she could see Roman finding the merits of it as he absorbed the accusations. He'd said he wanted to understand the affairs of his kingdom to better run it; he got more than he bargained for, but it was an invaluable experience that could shape the way the future king saw his people. Izzy had never been one for politics, and now she realized Elaria had more fractures than she'd once thought. The right king could change that.

In fact, this capture by the extremist clan had the potential to be extremely beneficial to the prince's reign if he truly wanted to bring everyone together.

Of course, he had to survive it to make it worthwhile.

Beside her, Griffin twitched with impatient anxiety, harsh jaw locked and eyes darting everywhere, like he could somehow keep tabs on the prince and every other person at the same time. Zaria was relaxed, as if watching a play, while Stella was rigid and pale, assessing the challenge in front of them.

Does Zaria have a plan? Izzy couldn't help wondering. *Does she have any idea how we're going to pull this off?*

Izzy felt like she'd just met the fairy—the *real* Zaria, anyway—but she'd known Zaria's personality for years. She was smart and quick on her feet, but tended to fire first and ask questions later. The thought made Izzy's stomach flip.

Taking a shaky breath, she glanced around the cavern again, the shouted accusations like cotton in her ears. Every gaze was focused on the prince except one: Raina. The young woman was sitting on the row in front of them, her back to Griffin, but she'd angled herself to stare at Stella. She'd been watching Stella since the first moment they'd met.

Raina sensed Izzy looking at her, and both girls jumped when they locked eyes. Izzy's automatic response was to drop her gaze, but she forced herself to be brave, to search Raina's face with the hope of finding answers. Raina just blinked at her, a new emotion Izzy couldn't place pooling in her eyes.

Izzy leaned forward to speak quietly and privately to her over the roar of the crowd, putting a comforting hand on Winston's head so he stayed still. "Is everyone here a rake?"

Raina blinked again, surprised, before shaking herself off. "A lot are, but we have others too. Quite a few members have incredible magical gifts, but they're either upset with the way the kingdom is run or are being persecuted by the crown for one reason or another." She shrugged. "We need to survive somehow."

Izzy swallowed that information. It didn't quite match with the explosive definition of extremist she had in her head. Raina herself seemed way too soft for any kind of violence, even against the prince.

"Not all of us are that way," Raina added, sensing her thoughts. "The crown likes to call us terrorists to name us enemies, but only a few hot headed members give us that reputation. Most of us just want peace. Justice."

Izzy nodded once. That made sense.

"I know Zaria said you weren't," Raina started uncertainly, "but I...are you here to join?"

Izzy wasn't sure how to answer, so she ignored the question and got straight to the point. "You know Stella."

Raina's eyes widened, if that were possible, and she shook her head. "I don't know her, no. But I'd recognize Damon's daughter anywhere." For the first time, she dropped her gaze and scratched the back of her neck sheepishly. "That's why I assumed...it's silly of me to think he would even remember me, but I thought…"

"You knew Damon well enough to recognize his daughter?"

Raina glanced back up at her. "I recognize you too. I didn't at first, but now that I see you up close...you look just like her."

A silent gasp went through Izzy, like she'd gotten the wind knocked out of her, and Winston's ears perked up, on edge for the threat. The knot in her stomach twisted painfully as she realized the implications of what Raina meant.

"She...she…" Izzy breathed, words ragged. "She was *here*?"

"Sofia? Yes, she came a couple times with Damon. It's probably been about four or five years now, though, since I've seen her."

Four years. Sofia had left Izzy almost six years ago.

Raina's eyebrows furrowed, confused Izzy didn't know the whereabouts of her own mother. "I figured you were both here to join. Damon and Sofia never did, officially, but everyone here treated them as family."

Family? Izzy couldn't decide if she wanted to cry or scream, if she should eagerly devour any bits of information she could find on her mother, or shriek that Sofia had already had a family, one that she'd carelessly left behind.

Raina put a hand on Izzy's, and Izzy had to force herself to not cringe away. "You are our family too."

"Why?" Izzy whispered, the emotion inside her threatening to tear her apart.

Why did she leave me? Why was she here?

Raina misunderstood the question. Her shoulders trembled slightly as a flash of memory danced across her green eyes. "Because...Damon saved my life. Sofia, Zaria, they helped, and..." She shuddered. "I wouldn't be alive without them."

"Damon's dead." The words were like gravel in her mouth, so she spat them out. "Sofia left us a long time ago."

Raina's eyes filled with tears of horrible sadness, and Izzy wasn't sure if the response made her touched or furious. Sofia was *her* mother. Not Raina's. Even if Sofia had...even if...

Raina's hand tightened on Izzy's. "Then my life debt will be to both of you."

Izzy nodded, clearing her throat and pulling herself together. She would get her answers; she had to believe that. Stella would probably disagree, but her gut told her she could trust Raina to say what she meant. "We need your help."

"Anything." Her expression brightened with eager devotion. "Name everything you need, anything, and I'll get it all."

The crowd pressed in on her, walls of red pulsing and suffocating. Taking a breath, Izzy willed herself to keep it together, just for a bit longer. She jerked her chin out, trying to display the same strong confidence Stella would.

"I need you to tell me everything you know about Damon and Sofia. We'll need fresh travel supplies, and an easy exit where nobody here will notice or ask questions, and I need you to keep this all to yourself." Izzy took a breath. "But first, I need something else."

Raina nodded. "Name it."

Izzy didn't respond. Her gaze traveled to the prince, still silently fighting a beratement of misplaced accusations that were meant for the rulers that came before him.

"Oh." Raina's shoulders slumped slightly and her face paled when she saw what Izzy was looking at. "Now that...that's going to be difficult."

* * * * * * *

The 'trial' lasted forever and, in Stella's opinion, was unproductive and a complete waste of time. The participating members didn't even come to any kind of resolution—they just insulted and complained and bickered among themselves about what kind of person the prince was, what they could get out of him, and what they should do with him. It might have been an interesting discussion if it weren't so futile. She had been about ready to break something when an older man said the *exact* same thing another person had said just minutes before, and the circle went on and on. For all their claims that change was necessary, they had a horrible system in place.

When they finally called the 'council' to an end, the members filed out of the cavern, talking amongst themselves, while two red cloaks hauled Roman through a separate back tunnel. He gave her and Griffin a last unreadable glance before disappearing.

Stella cursed under her breath, a word she'd learned from the crown prince himself. The prince who was gone. Again.

"Debriefing," Zaria told her just as she opened her mouth to ask. "They'll talk to him one on one now, see if they can get anything useful."

Stella had a million follow-up questions for that, with Griffin practically breathing angrily down her neck, but Zaria turned her back on them. Her long black ponytail hit Stella in the face as if shooing away a fly.

176

"I'm calling in one of those favors now," she told the pale man sitting next to her, Clegg, who had let them inside in the first place.

Clegg grinned, teeth too sharp for Stella's liking. "I'm surprised you were able to wait this long. What can we do for you, Zaria?"

The fairy jerked her chin at Roman's now empty chair. "I need some time alone with our prince." If Stella didn't know better, she would've shivered at the threat in her godmother's words. With a start, she wondered if she actually *did* know better.

What are you doing, Zaria?

Clegg nodded, not surprised. "I imagine you'd like some retribution for your persecution?"

"He'll live, if that's what you mean. I won't take that away from you." Zaria smirked. "These days, I don't get close to royals—I'd like to pay my respects to our future leader."

"I'll see what I can arrange. Until then, feel free to give your guests a tour. It'd be an honor to have Damon's daughter among our clan."

Stella froze, but Clegg just dipped his hooded head at them and stepped lightly out of the cavern, leaving them alone.

"Where is he?" Griffin demanded the same time Stella asked, "Are they going to hurt him?"

Zaria turned and rolled her eyes at them. "Your little prince will be just fine. Kercher and his band would be the only ones senseless and angry enough to actually harm a royal, and nobody will let them get near him. He'll live." She gave a wry grin. "It might be rather educational for him, actually."

Izzy nodded thoughtfully, like she *agreed*, and Stella scoffed in frustration. Even after all this insanity, she still hadn't gotten any answers about her father. Only more questions.

"It'll be a while before we get to see him," Zaria continued. "Make yourselves comfortable."

Griffin muttered something under his breath, uneasy eyes jumping back and forth across the empty space to the cave walls. He didn't look capable of being comfortable in this place. Stella hated it too. It was like being buried alive. She wanted to get Roman, get out, and finally get the answers she'd come so far to reach.

"Winston needs some air," Izzy announced, patting her dog.

No one cares about your stupid mutt, Stella wanted to scream at her. Didn't she realize what was important here?

Izzy glanced at Griffin, who looked like he was going to implode any second. "Will you come with us? We'll be back in time for Roman, but I'd rather not be alone in the forest, even if we're close."

"Take both dogs out," Zaria mumbled, so low only Stella heard.

Griffin barely even paused to think about it. With a grunt and nod, he sauntered out the door quickly, and Izzy and Winston stumbled to keep up.

"So," Zaria started before Stella could. She gestured with bravado around the cave with a smirk. "Tour, then?"

Stella clenched her teeth; Zaria knew exactly what she wanted. "I'm not interested in wasting—"

"You will be interested in this." And with that, Zaria glided out of the cave. Stella didn't see much of a choice, so she followed with a huff. If Zaria didn't give answers soon, Stella was going to take out her sword and start waving it around. She wouldn't wait anymore. Her father's ghost seemed to be calling her, pulling her toward him, begging her to bring the truth to light. He'd waited for so long. The thought caused an icy ache in her heart.

No more distractions. With or without Zaria, Stella was going to solve this, once and for all.

She followed Zaria through the dim tunnels, the taste of dirt in her mouth. Her hands formed fists when they passed by groups of red members: they'd smile and wave at Zaria or even stop to share a joke or tell a story, while they stared at Stella in awe once they recognized her. Dread and jealousy clawed at her throat with each encounter—dread for how her father met his end, what horrible lengths Natalia might have gone to; jealousy for her godmother, who fit in so comfortably here. Stella had been holed up in Natalia's attic all these years, while Zaria had a place she belonged. A family. One she'd never thought to share until she was forced.

They wandered deeper into the web of tunnels forever, grating on Stella's nerves. She was hopelessly lost and had only a small reserve of patience left. It seemed like it had been ages when Zaria finally stopped at a door. The wood was simple, but unlike the others they'd passed, it'd been carved with rudimentary yet beautiful scenes of flowers, animals, and ocean waves. The cold grief of her father settled heavier in Stella's chest.

For once, Zaria faltered just a second before entering, as though she had to prepare herself. She pushed the door open with gentle fingers, only touching as much of the door as she had to, then stepped gingerly inside. Nerves buzzing, Stella followed.

She couldn't stop the gasp that came. The room was small, cramped with a desk and two makeshift cots that were layered with dust. A few candles burned, giving the space light— probably spelled to be a forever flame, since it looked like nobody had been in here in a long time. But the walls stole Stella's attention. The little cave had been plastered with maps, some big, some small; some recent and others ancient-looking; some simple lines and others full of so many intricate illustrations you could hardly tell it was a map.

The throbbing in her heart confirmed what Stella felt: this had been his.

"I have one question for you, Stella," Zaria said as she shut the door, her voice quiet, like she could sense the eerie haunting the room held.

Stella turned in circles around the room, her mouth agape. "And I have about a million for you."

"I can imagine." The fairy stepped around Stella, moving to a smaller, oceanic map hanging above the desk, almost covered up by the others. Zaria pointed to a tiny dot on the eastern coast of Elaria. "Do you know that place?"

Forehead creased, Stella stepped forward to get a closer look. The spot on land Zaria was pointing to had the faintest black line drawn around it, hinting significance, but it was farther south than the spot Damon had always taken Stella when she was younger. It wasn't *their* spot.

Heart sinking in disappointment, Stella shook her head. "No."

"You've never been there?"

"No."

"He never mentioned that area to you?"

"Should he have?"

"He has a place there. You've really never seen it?"

Stella's jaw clamped, and she forced the words through her teeth. "No. I haven't."

Zaria appraised her with intense concentration, like she could see through Stella's skin. Stella stared right back. The maps on the wall called to her, pulled in her gut. She had to know. She had to.

"Did she do it?" Stella asked Zaria, anticipation threatening to crush her. "Did Natalia kill my father?"

Zaria's eyes glinted sharply, her mouth twisting with a kind of cruelty Stella didn't know existed in her. "Is that what you want me to tell you, Stella? Would that be easier? Would you be able to accept that your stepmother killed your father?"

"You're protecting her," Stella realized aloud, panic nearly taking her voice. Her heart hammered into overdrive when Zaria didn't argue.

She's on Natalia's side. Even more horrible, the thought drilled into Stella's brain with painful force. *What if they killed him together?*

Stella shook her head at herself. No. No, of course not. Zaria would never...*could* never...

Zaria's harsh face softened at the tears pooling in Stella's eyes. "He really didn't tell you anything, did he?"

Stella shook her head again, breaths shuddering. "Please. I need to know."

Zaria hesitated, glancing over the maps with a mournful yet imploring expression, as though they would tell her what she should do. "Damon," she started, voice wavering on the name, "was like my brother. I knew him longer than anyone else did next to your mother, but even I couldn't imagine what was coming for him." She met her gaze evenly. "I did not kill him."

"But you know who did." Stella said the statement as fact. "It was her, wasn't it?"

She shook her head once. "I don't know everything."

"But you know enough!" Stella slammed her hand on the wall. "I'm sick of these games. Tell me what you know. Help me put these pieces together, or I'll do it on my own."

"Stella." Zaria pursed her lips, unfazed by Stella's outburst. "I'm not sure it'll paint a picture you want to see. It was...messy."

"This might be news to you," Stella said coldly, "but I'm not a kid anymore. I know you missed the part where I grew up because you were hiding away like a coward—"

"A coward?" Zaria exploded, pushing forward into Stella's space. The dusty air pulsed with her fury, as though the tunnels would come down through her might alone. "Do not speak of things you don't understand."

Stella just shouted back. "How am I supposed to understand if you won't tell me anything?"

"I'm trying to protect you from the truth!"

"By shutting me out?" Stella demanded, clenching her fists in frustration. "You think you're protecting me from something so awful? Guess what, Zaria? My father is *dead!*" She spat the words at her with venom. "Nothing is more awful than that. Nothing you tell me—no matter how bloody or messy the details—will be more awful than that. And when that awfulness came, when I needed you, you were gone. You've never protected me. You've only hid from me, too ashamed to face me because even with your magic you *couldn't save him!*"

Zaria's eyes narrowed dangerously, her lips twisting with rage and giving Stella a glimpse of the monster King Rowan and Korah and all the other fairy hunters had fought to eradicate. "You know nothing! You're ignorant—"

"You left me!" Stella screamed back, her voice breaking. "I had no one, and you left me! You left me in the hands of that monster!" Tears sprung in her eyes as she remembered how Natalia had turned on her. "She treated me like a dog! She never really looked at me, never talked to me, never offered me anything except complaints that she was stuck with me. It was like she *blamed* me, like she was taking her guilt out on me."

Zaria tried to cut her off, but Stella raged on, tears streaming down her face.

"After the funeral, she locked me away for weeks. Weeks! I was twelve and scared and alone and heartbroken, and she locked me in that attic like an animal. She barely even remembered to leave food for me every few days." Stella stomped forward and glared into Zaria's dark violet eyes, throwing each word like a knife. "Where. Were. You."

Zaria opened her mouth, but nothing came out. Stella never got her answer. Suddenly the door flew open and four people stumbled in, shattering the thick tension into a million tiny shards.

She couldn't stop the relief that flooded through her when she saw the battered black-haired boy in the group. Roman was safe.

* * * * * * *

Zaria had said it might be hours before they saw Roman again, so Izzy was surprised when she, Winston, and Griffin finally descended back into the claustrophobic tunnels and ran right into Raina.

"Twenty minutes," Raina said breathlessly, lumps protruding from underneath her red cloak. "I've bought you twenty minutes. Don't waste it. Any magic will trigger alarms, but I know another way out."

Izzy beamed, her veins thrumming with adrenaline. "Thank you. Thank you so much."

They fought the urge to run, following Raina at a brisk but, hopefully, still casual pace. The young woman led them down the hall, winding them deeper into the web. Out of the corner of her eye, Izzy noticed Griffin tighten his grip on his sheathed sword, knuckles white. He saw the tunnels as cages and traps, and his anxiety showed.

Izzy hated it too, but she kept going. She had a plan. If everything went accordingly, they'd only have to deal with the tunnels for a little longer.

Raina took a last right turn, then stopped at a door. Out of habit, Izzy tensed at a red-hooded figure walking toward them, and she nearly yelped in surprise when Raina jerked her hand out and snatched the figure by the arm, then shoved them all inside. Though small, Raina pushed with enough force that Izzy stumbled over Winston and the hood fell off the newcomer, revealing Roman's face.

The door slammed behind them. Izzy patted Winston and straightened up to see the small room Raina had brought them to. Maps plastered every inch of the walls, and though Izzy wasn't a traveler, she sensed something familiar about the place. She quickly forgot the sensation, though, when she saw Zaria and Stella standing by the desk toe to toe. Zaria's expression had been swept into a cool mask, but Stella's emotion bled all over her face. Her shoulders relaxed with relief when she saw Roman.

"Thought they'd be in here," Raina mumbled to herself, staring at the walls with a sad kind of reverence. With a start, Izzy realized this cave must've been Damon's.

All the more reason to get out of here.

Griffin checked over the prince like a harried father, while Stella watched them and breathed a sigh.

"Did they hurt you?" Griffin demanded, ready to bury the tunnels at the slightest bruise.

"No, they just asked me questions." Roman shook his head, and Izzy couldn't deny she was really glad to see him when he gave a faint smile. "I guess I should be grateful my father has shut me out of all the important things. I didn't have anything to give them."

"He said he wanted to help us," Raina cut in, wide eyes on the prince in wonder. "And you meant that. I can tell."

Roman straightened his shoulders, looking a little more like a prince despite his unkempt hair and red cloak. "I did mean it." He regarded Raina kindly. "I won't forget about you, or what you've done for me. Thank you."

Raina smiled and dropped her eyes sheepishly, then started unloading lumps from underneath her cloak. They were small black backpacks, hopefully full of the supplies Izzy had requested. They likely had a long journey ahead of them.

"What's going on?" Stella asked, suspicious eyes darting from the backpacks to Zaria. The fairy just shook her head and took a step back, away from her goddaughter, illustrating she had nothing to do with it.

Izzy felt a twinge of pride. She'd done this on her own. "I made arrangements."

Stella's eyebrows shot up in disbelief as she stared at Izzy, dumbfounded. "*You* did?"

"Yes," Izzy replied, her small flicker of pride snuffed out by Stella's sour response. "We're going to find my mother."

She'd asked Griffin while they were outside getting some much needed air. The prince's advisor became more relaxed when they were free from the confines of the tunnels and crowds—like she knew he would—and he was open to discussing options with Izzy. He regarded her as an equal and took her seriously, and Izzy thought she would explode with gratitude. That had given her the guts to be completely honest about her mother and Izzy's new quest to find her.

They were going to spell her locket, Griffin had decided, like they'd done with Zaria's wand, to locate the true owner. It would take a lot of his magic, but since he'd done it before, he knew how to do it again, and he was more than willing to help her.

They were going to find Sofia.

Izzy had already constructed the reunion scene in her head. She wouldn't cry, wouldn't beg, wouldn't embrace. She would look her mother right in the eye and ask why she left. The answer she gave would dictate what Izzy would do next. If she could just get that answer, if she could just *know*, then she could fix things. Fix herself. She'd spent so much time studying the mechanics of love so she'd be ready when she became an agent of it.

She could be loved again. She had to be.

"What?" Stella's sharp voice sliced Izzy's fantasy in half. Her narrowed eyes darted back and forth between Izzy and Griffin, her expression torn between angry hurt and frustrated impatience. "Come on, Izzy, does that really matter right now?"

Izzy's skin stung like Stella had slapped her. Instantly, the hesitant atmosphere turned frosty with tension. It made her want to run and hide, to fold underneath the pressure.

"Stella—"

"We are *so* close to the truth," Stella raged on. "To him. We can't give up now."

"Look around, Stella." Izzy gestured in exasperation. "Look where he brought us. This is so...different than either of us ever imagined. Dangerous. It can't end well. We should get out while we still can."

"Don't you dare blame everything on him. Sofia was here too."

Izzy's fist clenched around her locket, and she forced herself to not buckle from Stella's force or the growing pain in her heart. "Do the math, Stella. She left us almost six years ago, just months before the trip Damon never came home from, and they've been here since then." She hesitated. "Whatever he was in—"

"He wasn't *in* anything," Stella shot back, fury writhing like an icy flame in her eyes. "He was innocent, and Natalia had him murdered. You know that."

For once, Izzy shook her head, fingers tingling with anxiety. "I don't."

Stella took a step forward, and everyone else took a step back. Her voice wavered with a dangerous mix of rage and desperation. "You *know* that."

Izzy's body trembled, but she managed to keep her voice smooth, though it was painfully quiet in the heavy air. "You are in so much denial, Stella. You hate her so much that you won't see anything else. Even the truth."

Stella blinked and recoiled like Izzy had hit her, and while her mouth stayed open as if she were still spewing arguments, nothing came from her throat. It hurt Izzy to hurt Stella that way, but, for once, compliance wasn't going to help.

"I'm sorry," Izzy said, voice soft, like a spoken bandage. "I love you, but—"

"Love?" Stella scoffed darkly. "You don't even know what love is. You spend all your time trying to figure it out, but it's just to hide the fact that you have no one but me. It's pathetic."

Izzy wrapped her arms around her waist and somehow kept herself from staggering backward. A tide of emotion—betrayal, hurt, rage, heartache—welled up under her skin, pushing against her and threatening to explode. Her whole body vibrated with the force of it.

Jaw clenched, Izzy glared into the eyes of her best friend. "Clearly I know more than you." Then she turned her gaze on Zaria, who was standing awfully quietly in the corner. "You have one chance to tell me what you know about my mother."

Zaria's face didn't change, but her violet eyes welled up with emotion—for a second Izzy thought there might be tears—and she started to say something, but stopped. Conflicted. The pity in her gaze nearly tipped Izzy right over the edge.

She didn't wait for whatever contrived answer the fairy might give. Beckoning Winston, she scooped a backpack from the floor and sauntered out, slamming the door behind her.

* * * * * * *

Izzy left.

Stella couldn't believe it. Izzy had *left*.

Her throat felt raw as she swallowed that truth, glancing around the fragile room. Griffin and Roman tucked themselves into the farthest corner of the tiny space and started muttering to each other inaudibly. Zaria stood just a few feet away, expressionless, but Stella had never felt farther away from her. In contrast, Raina was watching Stella again with those horrible, wide, green eyes. Stella thought she would drown in them.

Movements jerky, she snatched a backpack from off the ground and rifled through it. Food, water, first aid, compass, dagger, extra clothes, two cloaks, one red and one black—Raina had thought of it all. Slinging it across her back, she touched her hand to her sword still safely in place before turning and pulling back some of the maps on the wall.

"Where are you going?" Zaria asked just as Stella freed the small oceanic map from its spot.

"To his place," Stella responded gruffly, not bothering to look at her. Instead she studied the map for a moment. The thick paper felt worn between her fingertips, and she gripped the lifeline as tight as she dared.

"I'll meet up with you after, then."

Stella gave no indication she'd even heard her godmother. She was about to move for the door when Griffin broke his conversation with Roman. He gave the prince a meaningful look before nodding in gratitude to Raina and picking up a backpack. Then he shot Stella a heated glare and stepped out himself. She wanted to punch him.

Raina glanced timidly at Roman. "I don't want to tell you what to do, Your Highness, but you have about ten minutes

187

before the guards realize you're gone. You should take the back exit I showed you. Now."

Roman nodded at her. "Thanks Raina." Then, to Stella's surprise, he looked to her, gesturing to the map she clutched in her hand. "You're going to keep tracking him." He said the statement as a fact, unsurprised.

Stella's throat felt thick with things she didn't want to deal with, so she just nodded.

"Then I'm coming."

She blinked, her voice cracking. "You will?"

"Yeah. I told you I would help you, and I will keep that promise. We decided Griffin will go with Izzy, and I'll go with you." He didn't continue the sentence, but the words hung in the air, unsaid: they would meet back up eventually. While Stella only felt hurt and anger toward Izzy, something buried deep underneath told her that's what she really wanted.

"Besides," Roman added with a faint smirk, "who will protect you from the sea monsters?"

Stella rolled her eyes, finally composing herself. "I don't know—my fencing teacher was a complete moron."

Roman actually laughed, and the sound warmed up Stella's icy core a few degrees. She took the red cloak out of her backpack and put it on, just as Roman pulled his hood over his head again.

Before they could exit, Raina took Stella's hands in her own, green eyes full of imploring compassion. "Your father saved my life. I hope you find peace for him and yourself."

Stella took a breath. "Thank you. Now where do we go?"

"I'll just take them out the front," Zaria said, surging forward. "Nobody will suspect me if we're stopped, and I don't want to be around to see Clegg's face when he puts the pieces together."

Somewhere, a twinge of guilt vibrated through Stella, but she ignored it. Zaria didn't have to come with them to get Roman; she had chosen this herself.

"Understood," Raina said with a nod. Though several years older than Stella, Raina's big eyes and eager devotion made her look much younger, and Stella couldn't help but wonder how someone with her innocence got mixed up in a place like this. "Good luck, Zaria."

The fairy gave her a fond smile. "Take care of yourself, Raina."

Raina nodded rapidly. "I will. I will."

Zaria didn't look back as she surged out of the room. Stella pulled her red hood over her head. She couldn't make out much of Roman's face, but he gestured to the door with bravado.

"Ladies first."

Taking a moment to steel herself, Stella followed after Zaria.

"Goodbye," she heard Raina whisper on their way out.

* * * * * * * *

The dim tunnels threatened to crumble underneath Stella's feet. Keeping her head down, she counted every step, flinching at every sound, waiting for someone to shout after them. Many members of the clan had instantly taken to Stella because of her father, but she doubted they'd be nearly as hospitable if they knew she was smuggling out the prince.

No, they would make it. They'd get out, and nobody would know until they were far away.

True to what Zaria said, nobody they passed gave them a second glance unless they were greeting the fairy. Every slight sound, every silent breath, echoed off the walls, and Stella felt too cramped in the small space. The feeling of Roman walking next to her was the only comfort she had, but she could sense his nerves too. Zaria walked in front of them, confident as always, and Stella tried not to follow too close behind. These clan members were strange, but there was still a level of casual Stella had to maintain to keep from drawing attention.

189

We'll make it. We'll make it. We'll make it. We'll make it. How long were these tunnels anyway? They hadn't walked this far on the way in, had they?

"Zaria!" a voice called from behind them. "Zaria, wait up!"

Stella's blood went cold, and she heard Roman take a sharp breath. Zaria stopped and turned gracefully, not even a flicker of panic in her eyes.

"Stay calm," she muttered through unmoving lips. "If it comes down to it, I'll get you as close as I can."

Stella was struck with indecision—should she and Roman keep walking or stick with Zaria?—but the choice was made for her.

"I didn't know you were back," the same man said. "Who are you travelling with now?"

Stella nonchalantly sidestepped in front of Roman and lifted her head up to see a handsome man with olive skin and playful eyes, and Clegg trailing behind him.

We'll make it we'll make it we'll make it we'll make it.

"Roscoe," Zaria greeted with a genuine smile, real excitement in her eyes. "It's been ages, my friend."

Roscoe stepped forward and gave Zaria a hug—Stella had to fight to restrain her shock—momentarily enveloping her in red.

"Seems like you're fitting in just fine," Clegg commented, eyes on Stella wrapped in a cloak. He inclined his chin toward Roman. "Which of your friends decided to stay with you?"

"They were both trying to decide," Stella said casually. "The tunnels are a little difficult to stomach."

"Don't we know it," Roscoe chimed in. "I'm afraid one of these days I'm going to be as pale as Clegg." He elbowed his friend playfully, but Clegg's suspicious gaze was on the hooded figure behind Stella.

Just leave us alone.

"I'll have to catch up with you later, Roscoe," Zaria said, and she sounded truly sad about it. "I'm just finishing a tour for these new—"

A commotion sounded from far down the tunnel, but it seemed to vibrate in the earth around them.

"Seal the exits!" someone was shouting. "The prince is gone!"

Three things happened in the next sixty seconds: Clegg narrowed his eyes on Roman, then turned the glare on Zaria, a mix of shock and betrayal in his expression. Roscoe saw Clegg's face and glanced at Roman in disbelief before gaping at Zaria. The fairy stepped to the side, seizing Stella's wrist in one hand and Roman's in the other. Face reddening, Clegg was opening his mouth to shout when the air around Stella crushed her into nothing, and the tunnels disappeared.

A rocky landscape unfolded around her, and she fell to her knees in a heap, panting. Goosebumps rose on her neck as a brisk wind kissed her skin; she glanced up to see a vast expanse of stony terrain ahead and what looked like a mine entrance in the distance. Behind her, the earth rose into snow-capped peaks that touched the sky, higher than Stella could see.

"The Isslotts," Zaria said, her voice low and nearly overtaken by the wind.

She offered Stella a hand. Stella ignored it and stood, dusting herself off. To her left, Roman did the same, eyeing the fairy warily.

Zaria regarded Stella for a moment, then pointed ahead. "Head east. Keep the mountains on your right. Don't bother the miners and they won't bother you." Her words faltered for a moment. She opened her mouth, then closed it, then opened it again. "After...find me. If you need to. We can...we can talk about it."

Stella just gave her an empty glare and turned her back, her boots crunching on the gravel as she started walking away.

The air crackled. Stella turned to find Roman alone, Zaria gone.

Zaria, who had betrayed her friends to save a prince she hated.

Zaria, who had lied and ran while Stella had to face unbearable suffering alone.

Zaria, her godmother, the last family she had left.

Clenching her jaw, Stella pushed all thoughts of Zaria to the side. Her godmother had just done what she owed Stella— nothing more than that—and she couldn't think about the rest now. That was for later.

Now it was time to find answers.

Stella took a breath and reached underneath her cloak, pulling out her father's map.

"So," Roman started, glancing at the paper in her hands and giving her a half smile. "To the ocean, then?"

The sorrow in Stella's chest deepened at the thought, every nerve buzzing in fearful anticipation and the thirst for truth.

"To the ocean."

CHAPTER 9

ROSES AND CINDERS

Izzy's fingers trembled as they clutched her locket. While the metal around her neck had given her a sense of pained peace for years, the magic it now contained pulled her forward down the winding dirt path. The half locket had once belonged to Sofia, and now, along with Winston and Griffin, it was going to bring a mother and daughter together again.

Stella should be here. The thought echoed for the thousandth time since she'd left her best friend in the tunnels of the Red Riding Clan. *Stella should be here too.*

A sharp stone settled in her gut at the thought of their fight. Stella and Izzy had been best friends forever, and while they definitely had their arguments—Stella's personality often gravitated toward conflict despite Izzy's allergy to it—never had they fought like that. Never had things gotten so personal, right where it hurt the worst.

It seemed her heart was split in half: one part yearned for the companionship of her best friend, knowing they'd make up eventually. The other half, though, couldn't shake Stella's hurtful words. Stella knew better than anyone what Sofia's abandonment had done to Izzy. She knew how much it meant to her. She *knew.*

Shouldn't their years together count for something? Shouldn't their love for each other protect them from such harsh and bitter battles?

Of course, years of knowing and loving hadn't stopped Izzy's sweetheart Gannon from leaving her too. Sofia, Gannon, Papa, Stella...could Izzy keep anybody that mattered to her?

Automatically, she glanced at Griffin walking next to her, a bit slower than usual, as it had taken a lot of his energy to spell the locket. Izzy had nearly overflowed with gratitude when he'd caught up to her and said he was going with her. It wasn't until then she realized the strange attachment she'd acquired for him. And while it warmed her core to have him faithfully at her side when she needed someone most, the cold thought repeated in her mind that it wouldn't last forever. Like everyone else, Griffin would leave too, eventually. She had to be prepared for that.

Find Sofia. If she could talk to her mother, she'd be one step closer to discovering what truly happened, what drove her to leave. If Izzy could fix herself in time, then maybe she had a chance with Griffin. Maybe she could have at least one person.

Winston gave a quiet whine at her feet, as if he could hear her thoughts. She smiled down at the dirty dog. She couldn't forget Winston—if anything, Izzy knew he would be with her until the end. She'd never thought to study love between humans and pets, but now she was starting to think it might be the purest kind.

"Have you talked to her?" Griffin asked suddenly, breaking their easy silence and pulling Izzy out of her head. "Since she left, I mean."

"No." Izzy's eyes scanned the trees of the forest as they continued on. "She kissed me goodnight and when I woke up the next morning, Papa said she'd left us."

Griffin grunted in response. The air around them buzzed with life, but it didn't have the same vitality as earlier—they were on the edge of the forest rather than in the middle of it.

"Have..." Her gaze turned to him timidly. "Have you talked to your mother? Since...then, I mean."

His jaw clenched, highlighting the scars that his mother had given him. "No. I have nothing to say."

"Do you...do you have to see them often? Since they're nobles and you're at the castle?"

"It happens. Roman works to make sure there's limited contact, but I can't avoid it every time."

She nodded, then bit her lip. "Do they…do they still hurt? The scars?"

He gave a half shrug as he pondered that. "The memory hurts worse than the injury, I think," he decided. "If I could just take the physical pain, I would."

Izzy shuddered at the thought, at the memories that must've haunted Griffin since he was eleven. "You must hate her," she whispered.

Griffin pursed his lips, confirming her statement, then looked at her. "Do you hate *your* mother?"

Izzy couldn't even begin to sort through the swell of complicated emotions that came when she thought of her mother; she hadn't understood them for years. So she settled with an uneasy, "I don't know."

She took a breath, changing direction slightly when the locket influenced her. The Forgotten Forest still all looked the same. If spelling the wand to find Zaria hadn't worked, Izzy would have little faith that the magic knew where it was going through all these trees.

"Roman loves you a lot, you know," Izzy said, hoping to diffuse some of Griffin's pain. "The bond you two have is very special. I don't know if I've ever seen anything quite like it."

Griffin gave another impartial grunt. "He took me in when nobody else would."

Again, Izzy felt a pang of hurt. *So did Stella.*

They walked for a while, sometimes talking, sometimes not. Izzy was so grateful for their easy companionship. There was no pressure or any kind of expectation that Izzy couldn't hope to measure up to. They talked about life at the castle compared to life in the villages she'd lived in, views on the issues in the kingdom, and the best books they'd read. When they stopped to eat and Winston sat dutifully at Izzy's feet, Griffin told her all about his horse Ewan and his favorite place to ride on the castle grounds. When they started walking again, the locket guiding their way, Izzy decided to ask him one of her favorite questions.

"What do you think love is?"

Griffin nearly stumbled in surprise, glancing at her with furrowed eyebrows. "What?"

"Love," Izzy repeated, twirling her locket absently. "How would you define it?"

"I...uh..." Griffin took a breath and shook his head, jostling more of his hair loose from its ponytail. "I don't...I..."

Izzy tried to curb her grin so he didn't think she was making fun of him. "There's not really a right or wrong answer. I know what I think, and I'm always curious to know what other people would say. It's such an important question." When it looked like he was going to protest, she added, "Differing opinions help the research."

Griffin watched his feet. He took a few steps before he cleared his throat and answered quietly, "I'm not sure I know what love is."

Now it was Izzy's turn to almost trip. "Well of course you do. You love Roman, don't you?"

"I suppose." It sounded more like a question than an answer.

"He's like your brother, isn't he?"

"Well, I..." Griffin laughed once, a dark sound. "I grew up believing I was an orphan until I discovered I had a brother, and now he wouldn't hesitate to kill me. So that phrase doesn't mean as much to me as it does to Roman."

"Oh." Izzy took that in thoughtfully, filing it away in her brain. She'd never considered that. "That makes sense."

"In the traditional sense of the word, though, yes," Griffin amended. "Roman is like my brother. I don't know...I don't know if that counts."

"Well," Izzy started, reasoning through what evidence she had, "I've seen you risk your life for him multiple times, and not just because it's your civic duty. And you would do it again. Right?"

Griffin pursed his lips and nodded without hesitation.

"You care about his wellbeing and happiness. You would do anything to make him better and happier and live the life he deserves, right?"

"No matter the cost," Griffin agreed with a flicked glance at her.

"And being around him makes you happier, right? You feel a little more at home when he's around, and you know you can trust him."

Again, Griffin nodded.

Izzy beamed. "Well, then, I'd say you have a great grasp on love."

The corner of Griffin's mouth pulled into a small smile at her enthusiasm. "And you're an expert?"

"No, not an expert." Izzy shrugged. "More like a working apprentice. Someday I will be, though. I've been researching a long time."

Griffin's smile grew. "I see."

They continued to debate the mechanics of love as they walked and what constituted genuine love for another person. The traveling wasn't nearly as bad with such enjoyable conversation, and it was easier to press on through their exhaustion. After the horrid encounters with the wolves and villagers, Izzy wasn't inclined to stop for very long, even to sleep, and Griffin didn't complain. As one day melted into two, she'd stopped paying attention to where they were going until they were nearly there.

It was well after dark on their second day. They'd made their way out of the Forgotten Forest and had traveled along the edge of Doveneer, skirting the village's work lands and being careful not to run into any people.

Eventually the glimpses of civilization had faded away, and they found themselves wandering in the middle of nowhere. She caught sight of glorious Mount Brenne in the distance, giving her a soft mark of where in Elaria they were, and that led to a debate over the different legends surrounding Mount Brenne. Izzy forgot all about her quest and aching feet until the locket started to vibrate ever so softly. She skidded to a halt and looked up, tearing herself away from the engaging conversation.

A giant stone building loomed in front of them, crumbling and worn. The iron gate had broken off its hinges and hung at an odd angle, allowing for people to pass in, and part of the right tower had collapsed on itself.

"I know this place," Griffin said quietly, like he could sense the ghosts haunting the building too. "It's an old prison. The crown discontinued its use after a deadly riot took the east tower down a few years ago. They haven't had the resources to fix it since, so they moved the prisoners somewhere else."

He stopped talking abruptly and looked at Izzy with a creased forehead, as if realizing what he'd just said. Izzy felt the color drain out of her face at his words.

"It's been several years since then, though," he went on quickly. "Since the crown abandoned it, a lot of drifters use it for shelter. Maybe that's why she's here."

Izzy barely heard him. Suddenly, she didn't care why Sofia was here, why she'd chosen a broken down prison for a place among the homeless when she already had a home, or why she hadn't come back in so long. Because now that Izzy was here, now that Sofia was in reach for the first time in years...Izzy knew what she wanted.

She wanted her mother back.

And she was going to get her.

* * * * * * *

Stella smelled it before she heard it: saltwater, growth, and life. The second the familiar scent touched her nose, she broke into a run, leaving the prince behind mid-sentence.

Sweat beaded down her back, and her muscles ached from all the walking she'd done the past few days, but she didn't feel anything besides the wind on her face, the air holding a taste of seawater. Within a few minutes, she burst through a thicket of brush to find the sun sparkling over a massive blue that stretched on forever: the ocean.

She couldn't stop herself. Stuffing the map in her backpack, Stella threw it on the ground, then kicked off her shoes and stowed her socks in them. Then she ran forward, yanking her pant legs up on the way. The sand was warm and scratchy, but she didn't care. The second the water hit her toes, she gasped, both from the shocking cold and the familiar sensation of the sea rolling over her feet in slow waves.

Her soul sighed in relief. She was home.

Kicking her legs, she splashed herself with sprays of water, then scooped some up in her palms and let it run down the back of her sweaty neck. The tip of her blonde ponytail was soaked within seconds, and it smelled like brine every time she turned her head. It was amazing.

Spinning around, Stella looked out over the water, trying to pinpoint where the sky touched the sea. Ever since she was a little girl, she'd felt such a deep connection to the ocean. She remembered telling her father she wanted to be just like it, and he had laughed and ruffled her hair and said, "That's my girl."

But Stella had meant it. She still had that connection to the water, the longing to be like it. It was beautiful and constant and mysterious yet honest. It got angry. It swelled up. It caused damage. But at the end of the day, it would retreat back to its place and begin the constant roll of the waves again.

Stella loved that. The constancy. The power. The fact that the ocean had such a solidified place in this world that nothing had real, absolute control over it. It didn't answer to anything. It just was.

She'd been splashing around like a little kid for a few minutes before Roman finally caught up. He came through the trees with searching eyes, then broke into a smile when he saw her. She beckoned him to come closer. He did so carefully, still keeping a safe distance from the waves, reminding Stella that most people in Elaria were terrified of the ocean. She had never understood that.

Roman had her backpack slung over his shoulder next to his, and held up her boots with his other hand. "Do you have an issue with shoes or something?"

Stella didn't answer; she just splashed him. He skittered away like a startled puppy, and she burst into laughter.

"What?" she said, giving a teasing half curtsy. "Are you afraid to get wet, Your Highness?"

"I'm not a fan, no," he answered, eyeing the water as though he could see every possible danger in it. "But you have fun. Let me know when something tries to bite your leg off, and I'll come right to your aid."

Stella rolled her eyes and muttered, "Coward," just loud enough for him to hear. In response, he threw one of her boots at her.

"Hey!" she complained as she ducked and the shoe sailed past her head. "I need that!"

Roman just smirked at her. She made sure to kick up a lot of water while she retrieved her sopping boot.

They continued that way down the shoreline for a while, Stella trucking through the water up to her knees while Roman walked next to her safely on the dry sand. The sun was beginning its dive into the ocean when they came upon the house.

Stella had been so lost in her overwhelming giddiness that she had nearly forgotten why they'd come in the first place. Seeing the property, the reminder, sobered her right up and wiped the grin from her mouth.

The house was *huge*. Okay, no, it wasn't huge, but it was at least twice the size of Natalia's shack in the village. The walls were made from a gorgeous, smooth, dark wood that seemed to grow right out of the ground, and had such a majestic and earthy feel.

Stella had a bad taste in her mouth as she stared at the home that was never hers, but so clearly *his*. Why had her father never shared this with her?

Even more confusing: where had he gotten the money for something this nice?

Roman glanced from the house to her, gauging her reaction. Biting her lip, she felt the request build up in her throat and get stuck there. She knew what she wanted—to tackle this alone—but she couldn't get herself to ask that of Roman without sounding rude, especially after all he'd done for her.

He nodded at her, knowing what she meant, and gestured to the house. "Take your time. I'll be on guard out here."

She gave him a grateful smile. He turned and settled himself onto the sand a ways away, careful to give her space and keep himself a healthy distance from the crashing waves. Stella watched him for a moment before turning back toward the house. Her toes squished in the prickly sand as she dragged herself around the far side and found the front door.

There wasn't a lock on it. Once she got closer, she sensed some kind of barrier—had Zaria put up magical security measures for Damon? How was Stella supposed to get in?

Hesitating, she gently pushed her hand against the door. The air around it rippled and crackled, then the force was gone. Stella pushed the door open without any resistance, and a spark of hope flickered in her heart.

Maybe he meant for me to come here after all.

The musty air was stifling compared to the fresh air of the sea, and Stella had to choke back a cough at the dust. Her wet feet threatened to slip on the stone floor. She stepped softly, so as not to fall or awaken the ghosts she felt lurking in the corners.

A chill ran down her spine that had nothing to do with her wet legs. Something told her this place was her father's, but she would not find the father she knew here.

Pull it together, she reprimanded herself. She didn't come this far to quit now. She owed this to her father, and to herself.

It only took her a few minutes to explore the first floor. The compact but beautiful kitchen held nothing but a few dishes and a couple bowls of moldy fruit, and there was so much dust in the living room that she knew nobody had sat on the chairs in ages. Her fingers tingled when she entered the bedroom, but there was nothing discernable or personal or out of the ordinary. Nothing that spoke of her father.

Again, she felt a pang of betrayal in her chest. This place was a stunning home and he had hid it from her. Why?

Her frustration required an outlet, and during her fourth inspection of the house she found something she hadn't noticed before. In the kitchen, between the stove and a tall cupboard, there was a slight dent in the ceiling. Not bothering to be careful anymore, Stella climbed on top of the stove and pushed against the discrepancy. It took some work, but it finally came open, revealing a set of retractable stairs that led to the attic. The attic must've been spelled or something, as she'd only seen one story from the outside. Curiosity piqued, she pulled the stairs down and climbed up without another thought.

The sight of the attic took her breath away—this was *definitely* her father's.

A giant window took up the far wall, showcasing a beautiful scene of the ocean, and she caught sight of Roman sitting dutifully on the beach, scrawling something on a notepad, his sword at his side. What wasn't glass was covered in paper: maps, illustrations, photographs, and so many notes. A huge desk took up most of the space, and it was littered with notebooks and loose papers, all covered in the small, methodical handwriting she recognized instantly.

Tears welled in her eyes at the sight of something that was his, that he had touched. After he died, Natalia had thrown away everything that had anything to do with him, like she was trying to erase him from their lives. Another point of evidence for her guilt.

Suddenly, Izzy's voice echoed in Stella's head: *you hate her so much that you won't see anything else. Even the truth.*

Stella shook her head with vehemence, as though Izzy were still here and they were still arguing. Izzy was wrong. Stella would prove it now.

Lurching forward, she started rifling through the pages on the desk, her eyes scanning over the familiar writing. She blazed through the first few pages without blinking. By the fourth she had slowed down. The fifth had her confused. By the eighth, the chill down her spine was back and an uneasiness had settled in her stomach. By the twelfth, she was shaking at the common words that ran through all the pages.

Spies. Attacks. Rebels. Blood.

Spies, attacks, rebels, blood, spies, attacks, rebels, blood, spies, attacks, rebels, blood.

War.

Tyranny.

Dethrone.

Stella sucked in a sharp breath at the last page she looked at. Big words had been written across it with thick black ink, and a symbol had been drawn on either side of the message. Hands trembling, Stella patted her pant pockets. In the left one, next to the sheathed sword at her hip, was the other broken piece of Zaria's wand, safely tucked away. Instead, she tore open the pocket on her right leg and pulled out the blue crest she'd found in her father's box. Both she and Izzy had noticed its similarities to the royal insignia, but the color was wrong and the shape was different. Sharper. Defiant.

She held up the metal crest to the paper. They matched. Written in between each symbol were four words.

LONG LIVE THE QUEEN

Stella's gut told her it wasn't referring to Roman's mother, Queen Sarafina. Somehow she knew it meant something much worse.

A ringing sounded in Stella's ears, and she suddenly felt dizzy. The paper fell from her grasp and she doubled over, trying to breathe, trying to keep herself stable.

This didn't make sense. None of this made sense. There must've been a mistake—this couldn't be her father's place. He was a simple merchant, a loving father and doting husband, tragically murdered for his money by his greedy new wife.

What money? The thought was all she heard over the ringing in her ears, getting louder every second. *He didn't have any money to steal. He married Natalia for* her *money.*

Stella's blood went cold. She'd never thought that statement before, never believed it. Damon loved Natalia. Everyone knew that. Everyone...but how could he afford to build a house like this?

It's not his. It's not. It can't be.

What was that awful ringing noise?

Growling in frustration, Stella spun around to the window, where the sound seemed to be coming from. What was Roman doing?

She looked out to see the prince had abandoned their backpacks—and her boots—on the shore and was walking toward the sea. She was almost excited at the thought of him giving it a try, but then she noticed his shoulders. He was too straight, too formal, steps too purposeful and heavy. His jaw was slack as he lurched forward, his eyes focused on a spot in the ocean. And bopping in the water with long black hair and pale skin, mouth open in song...

Siren.

Choking on terror, Stella slammed the crest back in its pocket without bothering to close the flap, and ran for the stairs.

"Roman!" she shrieked the second her feet hit the sand. "Roman!"

He was already ankle-deep in water and continuing on. The siren just smiled a devastatingly beautiful smile and crooned more of that awful ringing, but Stella knew she wasn't hearing what the prince was.

"Roman!" she screamed as she sprinted across the beach. "Roman, stop!"

Roman's head cocked to the side, but he kept walking, knee-deep now. The siren noticed Stella advancing and scowled at her, not breaking the song, before turning back at the prince. Then, faster than Stella could blink, the creature launched itself at him, dunking them both into the water. It turned red almost instantly.

"Roman!"

Stella didn't hesitate. She ran straight for the water and dove in. Everything blurred as her hands felt hair and scales and fabric, and her eyes burned from saltwater. She tried to yank the monster off of Roman; the siren just snarled and lunged at Stella instead. Stella didn't know where her strength came from, but they fought mercilessly underwater. She managed to come up for a split second, desperately needing air, but the siren just dragged her back under. She felt her skin tear but she didn't stop flailing, hoping the red water around her wasn't from Roman, begging the stars that he was able to get himself free.

With a shriek of hate, the siren gripped Stella in her claws and slammed her body against the ocean floor. Water rushed into Stella's lungs, and everything went black.

* * * * * * *

"...st...el..a..."
"...stel...la..."
"...Stella…"
"Co...ome on...Stella...plee...ease."

The voice she heard was distant, murky, like it was under water. She was too far away, but she wished she were closer. The voice sounded scared.

"Stella! Come on, Stella, wake up. Please."

A painful bubble rose in her chest, and she coughed. Water spurted out of her mouth and trickled out of her ears, bringing the voice into focus. It was right next to her. The crashing of the ocean waves sounded in the background, farther away than she'd thought they'd be.

"Stella? Stella, can you hear me?"

Her throat blazed like it was on fire, and her body twitched, longing for the water again. Anything to put out the grainy heat.

Something pushed against her chest once, then twice, three times, rhythmically. The last push seemed to squish the rest of the water from her lungs. She convulsed again and coughed half the ocean up, the saltwater burning her raw throat.

A soft hand smoothed her plastered hair back from her forehead. "There you go. Breathe. Breathe."

The harsh coughs nearly ripped her fragile throat in half, but they allowed her to get air into her starved lungs. She took a couple ragged breaths before cracking her eyes open. The first thing she saw was Roman—actually, he was the *only* thing she saw. He was sopping wet too, leaning over her with his face screwed up in panic. His shirt had ripped to reveal a deep bloody gash in his shoulder that stretched dangerously close to his neck. Red slashes dotted his skin and face, but he was alive.

He relaxed when she met his gaze, nearly losing his balance with the force of the relief that crashed into his expression.

"You're okay." He mumbled the words under his breath, as if reminding himself. "You're okay. You're alive."

"Wow, Your Highness," Stella said, some of her sarcasm lost in a coughing fit. "I didn't think you cared so much."

"I...I don't." Roman shook his head, as if trying to clear it, to convince himself of what he was saying. But then his eyes found hers again, and she saw a different story in them. "I don't at all."

"Clearly." She only got halfway through the word before her body convulsed painfully again, and she spat out more water. How could there *still* be water in her? The sharp sand pressed into her back and her left arm stung. She glanced down to see her forearm red from the siren's sharp claws. "What happened?"

"You dove into the water without a weapon, like a halfwit," Roman growled, but it was more out of desperate respite than anger. "When I came to my senses, the monster was trying to slash you to bits."

"How did you stop it?"

"I didn't," Roman admitted. He still hadn't moved from his hovering over Stella, each hand braced on either side of her. He nodded his head to the right; she glanced over to see her father's blue crest in the sand. It must've fallen out of her pocket. "It stopped when it saw that. It was the strangest thing: the siren just swam away. I dragged you to shore and behind some brush, waiting, but it hasn't come back."

"Huh." A shudder went through Stella, rocking her, and she coughed again. "Thank you."

Roman's gaze snapped back to hers. "No. Thank *you.*"

Stella opened her mouth to say something snarky back, but the look in his eyes rendered her speechless. She saw herself in them, but her best self: strong, smart, enduring, resourceful, brave. Her throat became thick at the thought that maybe he saw all that in her.

Though she wasn't prepared for it, she saw the second his eyes shifted, the moment he lost rational thought and made the decision. All at once, he leaned down and pressed his mouth against hers.

She was sure he had meant to be carefully soft, but too much desperation leaked out of him, spilling into her. She felt the 'almost' of the siren encounter, how differently it could have ended, and how devastated she would have been. Not just for losing a prince, or a human life, but for losing *him.*

Suddenly, he went rigid, like he just realized what he was doing. His mouth broke from hers, and he glanced over her sheepishly, breathless. "That...that couldn't have been the appropriate thing to do."

Still gasping saltwater, Stella met his eyes evenly. "I've never really cared about the appropriate thing to do." Then she took a fistful of his torn wet shirt and pulled him down to her, and her lips found his in an instant. She forgot all about her father and Izzy and the siren and everything except for the prince's tantalizing mouth.

She didn't know how long they were tangled up in each other—it was probably only minutes, but it felt like seconds and hours at the same time—when Roman finally pulled away from her. This time, he helped her sit up, eliminating the temptation.

"Sorry," he said once she was stable, running a hand through his hair nervously. "I guess I had to do that at least once."

Stella smirked at him. "Twice."

Roman's lips quirked into a half smile, and he leaned forward to kiss her gently. "Three times," he amended. Then he narrowed his eyes slightly at her violently shivering body and chattering teeth. She hadn't noticed it until now.

Stella started to reach for a backpack, but Roman waved her off. Instead, he pulled out three of their cloaks from the Red Riding Clan and wrapped two of them around Stella's shoulders. He wrapped the third around himself before gathering dry brush and making a small fire for them. When he finished that, he took two apples and a package of dried meat from their supply and told Stella to eat, but she refused until he let her bandage his shoulder.

She couldn't suppress the happiness that came when everything was finished and he sat behind her and pulled her into his arms, draping his cloak around both of them. It felt so good.

She'd been taking care of herself for so long, she'd forgotten what it felt like to be looked after. Shivering still, she pulled the cloak tighter around herself and settled further into Roman's arms. He just held her closer, resting his chin on her head.

"Did you find what you were looking for?" he asked softly, as if afraid his voice would shatter the fragile scene.

Stella sighed at the thought of the house and the crest now back in her pocket. She still hadn't really digested what she'd found, and she wasn't ready to talk about it. "For now."

He didn't press the point. She could feel his uneasiness too, the nagging fear that a new catastrophe was just at their door, ready to knock it down and ruin their brief moment of delicate peace. Neither of them mentioned that fear, though, as they watched the sun disappear under the horizon.

* * * * * * *

The old prison was cold. It reminded Izzy of the mental ward Papa was in, and she instantly hated it.

Griffin insisted on walking just ahead of her, wary of any potential threat, and Winston's fur stood on end as he followed the advisor, second in command in her protection. If she weren't so emotionally occupied, she would smile at how sweet they were to her.

They passed three people on their way in: one dirty man scowled at them without getting up from his corner, another barely interrupted his scavenging to give them a glance, and the third was a woman too drunk to notice they were even there. Izzy held on to Griffin's elbow, gently guiding him as the locket guided her. She stepped lightly over rubble, careful not to kick up dust, afraid to make any sound. The anticipation built in her chest, so heavy it threatened to suffocate her.

The locket took them down a dank staircase and through a dim hallway. Izzy shivered, whether from the cold seeping from the stone or her nerves, she wasn't sure. The necklace in her hand continued to get warmer and vibrate harder until it brought her to a door: a thick, stone door of the third cell on the right with a broken lock. Her mother should be on the other side.

Griffin glanced at her in question. Nodding, she stepped in front of him to face the door herself. Her heart pounded wildly in her chest and her fist shook as she raised it to the door. It took several moments before she could make herself knock.

Nothing happened.

She tried again, harder. No response.

Buzzing with suspense, Izzy took the wide doorknob in her clammy hand and pushed the door open.

The cell was tiny, even smaller than the attic at Natalia's house. The rank smell attacked her nose with a vengeance; she had to breathe through her mouth. A barred, square window near the ceiling let in a bit of moonlight, allowing Izzy to see the dirt that lined the edges of the stone walls, the matted straw on the ground next to a small mattress, and the broken shackles.

Empty. The cell was empty.

Izzy surged forward, prepared to search every nook and cranny for some clue as to where her mother went. Maybe the locket had gotten it wrong, maybe this was where she lived but she had made a trip for the night, maybe there was a hidden door somewhere that led to a place better than this horrible cell.

Griffin dug a match and candle out of the backpack from Raina. The small flame was enough to light the entire space. He checked underneath the mattress while Winston sniffed the floor and Izzy felt her hand along the walls.

She'd made three passes around the cell before she found something: a loose stone in the wall, one that had been extracted and pushed back. Heart leaping, she used her fingernails to pry the stone from its place, coughing at the dust that went flying into the air. She discarded the rock and Winston instantly started licking it. Griffin brought the candle over, kneeling next to her, just as she stuck her hand in the secret hole.

A silent gasp escaped her when her fingers brushed against thick parchment. She pulled out a small package tied together with a piece of straw.

Izzy knew it—Sofia had left a note detailing where to find her. She'd wanted Izzy to come back after all.

Her heart was still in overdrive when she pulled the straw free, and a piece of paper fell from the bundle. She moved to grab it, but a familiar shape in the package snatched her attention, so Griffin picked it up instead to study it.

Even in the odd shadows of the candlelight, he went pale. "Izzy," he said, soft voice filled with understanding and regret. "Izzy."

She barely heard him. Her fingers fumbled with the folded paper until it came free, a flash of gold tumbling into her palm: the other half of her locket.

"Izzy." Griffin finally pushed the paper in front of her face. She recognized the shape drawn on it: the crest Stella had found, the metal one she carried in her pocket. Griffin's mournful voice matched his face. "This is a rebel crest, Izzy. She...she must've been arrested."

Izzy's pulse thudded in her ears; she couldn't get enough air. Her hand swatted the paper out of her face with desperate denial. "That wasn't hers. That was Damon's."

Griffin said something else, but Izzy wasn't listening. Instead she stared at the locket for another moment, feeling sick, before she turned to the last thing in the package: a letter, several pages long, full of her mother's swirly cursive handwriting. Her eyes devoured the words despite a nagging in her stomach that told her to turn away.

It was a letter for her. For Izzy. From Sofia. Written in this cell, eight months after her arrest. Izzy felt lightheaded as she read the letter, the most painful lines jumping out and scorching what was left of her heart.

Damon was a liar. A hideous liar.

I thought magic could help your Papa. He was getting worse, and I knew he wouldn't want me to go, so I didn't tell anyone.

I left with Damon and Zaria to find people that could help him.

Damon manipulated me—everyone. All of us, for years.

When the guards caught up to us, he ran and let them arrest me instead of him.

They think I'm a traitor. A spy for a rebel alliance. They don't believe me.

I just wanted to save your Papa.

I never meant to leave you, not forever. But these prison conditions are harsh, and I know I won't live much longer—I have only days left on this earth, and I wish more than anything I was home instead of trapped in this hellish place.

Izzy read the last line again. Then again. By the third time, her hands were shaking so hard and her eyes were blurry—she couldn't read anymore. But by then, she had memorized it already.

Please understand, my darling Isabelle, that I love you, and everything I ever did, I did for you.

Shuddering, Izzy doubled over, clutching the letter to her chest next to her locket, and sobbed.

* * * * * * *

She should've told Stella everything.

Zaria knew that now. She should've told her goddaughter the whole truth from the beginning the second she showed up at her cabin door.

But how could she have done that to her? The girl loved her father so much, telling her would've been like murdering Damon all over again. Truthfully, the deep wound of betrayal still bled in Zaria all these years later, one she knew would never really heal.

Damon had nearly been her brother. And nearly everything she knew about him had been a lie.

She should've never been suspicious of Stella, but how could she not? Even Natalia had been, for a while. The girl was so close to her father, it was impossible to know whether he had planted ideas in her head, even if she didn't realize it. It was a miracle the crown hadn't executed her with Damon, just for being his daughter, like they'd nearly done to Natalia. Just in case.

Just like Sofia.

Sofia.

Zaria's heart ached at the thought of her dear friend, one she hadn't been able to save. And when it had come down to it, she couldn't make herself tell Izzy the awful truth about her mother's death—a slow, painful death inside a dreary cell that was meant for someone else.

Zaria had figured it out too late. She tracked down Sofia's cell only to find she had died a week earlier.

Self-loathing rose in her throat like bile. All the magic in the world, and Zaria hadn't been able to see Damon for what he was, protect Sofia from a fate that wasn't hers, or properly shelter either of their daughters. She was a fairy, immortal in a sense. She'd seen generations come and go, and she should've had plenty of more time to find Stella and Izzy, to explain, to take care of them the way they deserved.

She should've told them everything. And now it was too late.

Clenching her jaw, Zaria yanked against her restraints again, but nothing gave. The metal shackling her was special, despicable, designed to painfully dull her magic. Already, she felt lightheaded and sick. Weak. Unable to fight, her magic just beyond reach.

After leaving Stella, Zaria had been so distracted. She should've been quieter. She should've been more careful. She should've known the hunters would be right on her trail after finally smoking her out of her cabin, chasing a bloody vendetta, a century-old hatred, bent on giving her the fate they believed she deserved just for what she was.

In the ancient stories—the ones nobody spoke of anymore—fairies were revered and treasured. Now people taught their children that fairies were demons, that they should be blacklisted and hunted, marked as murderers.

Even after all these years, all she'd seen, all she'd lost, she wasn't sure if they were right.

Now, with everyone she'd ever loved gone, a deep hole of loss and regret in her heart for each one, she wondered if she truly was the monster of the story.

The towering royal guard with uneven eyebrows and a brown moustache stood over her, reading the charges she knew by heart in a booming voice that carried over the torchlight flickering in the night. As always, Zaria kept her chin high, even as he read her death sentence. They could chase her, beat her, make her bleed, but she'd never let them see they got to her. She could take that victory to her grave.

Once the guard had ordered her execution to be carried out in the morning, he retired to his tent, leaving Zaria painfully bound in between two trees with a handful of guards watching over her. One of them kneeled in front of her, hateful eyes boring into hers.

Korah punched her once. Twice. Five times. Five punches for the five years she'd made every breath about finding the fairy that knelt before her. Five strikes for the five years lost.

Then one savage punch to her ribs—one for the year they knew each other before the hunt began, before they became cat and mouse, when they were just two young women aspiring to be something more, desperate for the taste of glory. Before everything shattered into pieces.

Blood dripped from Zaria's mouth as she doubled over, panting. Korah reached down and roughly took her smarting face in one hand, crushing her jaw as the shadows from the flames danced along her face, illuminating her triumphant loathing.

"Say your last prayers to the blasphemous gods that created something like you," she seethed, her nails drawing blood from Zaria's chin. "Because when the sun rises, your life will end, and like a witch, you will burn."

CHAPTER 10

THE LAST PETAL FALLS

Mornings were always different.

Stella had never realized that until she left Natalia's house. Ever since she'd started trekking through the Forgotten Forest, she noticed that while situations rarely changed overnight, they always felt vastly different when she woke up the next day.

Nights were dark, either making you desperate and hopeless, or comfortable and honest. Secrets thrived in the dark, and people often spilled their deepest truths when tucked underneath the safety of the night sky. A bleeding wound, for better or worse, that wouldn't stop gushing.

Mornings were different. They were crisp and sharp and bright. Too bright, sometimes. It made it harder to hide, which was good if you were seeking clarity, but bad if you wanted denial. A congealed wound, precariously closed with dry blood and fragile skin, that gave you a fresh start but threatened to split back open with the slightest wrong move.

If Stella had been shaken and wounded from the siren attack last night, she only felt annoyed and sore this morning.

If Stella had been overwhelmed and confused about what she found in her father's study last night, she only felt raw and empty about it this morning.

And if Stella and Roman had felt comfortable sleeping all tangled up in each other on a deserted beach last night, the feeling had completely evaporated when she opened her eyes this morning.

Roman woke her up early. She had groaned when she saw the sun barely peeking over the horizon, but the prince paid no mind to her complaints. Instead, he urged her up and started packing their supplies into their backpacks methodically, while obviously trying not to look at her. She'd been perfectly warm in his presence—and arms—last night, but now Stella felt a chill in her bones that had nothing to do with the cool ocean breeze.

He regretted kissing her. She could see it written all over him.

And how could he not? Roman was responsible and determined and faithfully dedicated to his crown despite everything that came against him. Playing around with a peasant rake wasn't exactly royally sensible. It could only end in heartache, for both of them, and she could sense him hesitantly snipping the attachments they'd made to each other for both their sakes.

She'd been so *stupid.*

Neither of them spoke much as they got their stuff together. Roman offered her fruit for breakfast, but Stella felt sick and declined. He didn't eat either. She couldn't decide if he was eager to get going or dragging his feet—somehow a mix of both—but they'd started their journey again before the sun had cleared the horizon.

Stella didn't want to leave the ocean, but she didn't want to stay near her father's house either. She turned her back on it and felt it looming over her shoulders, willing herself to forget about the documents she'd found inside.

A mistake, she'd convinced herself last night. *It's all a mistake.*

That had been easier to believe in the dark. This morning, though, thoughts of her father only filled her with dread that she'd gotten everything all wrong.

She needed to talk to Zaria. She needed to talk to Izzy.

Izzy. Stella's already queasy stomach dropped at the thought of her best friend. She'd said awful things to Izzy, just for wanting to find her mother—just like Stella had wanted to find her father. She hoped Izzy had found better success.

Roman led the way, keeping a good distance from a mine entrance. Stella was lost in her own thoughts for a while before she broke their sturdy silence.

"Where are we going?"

He flinched at her voice, and Stella's stomach clenched painfully. "Meeting up with Griffin and Izzy," he said gruffly, as if addressing a stranger.

Her shoulders slumped, both from the thought of facing Izzy and Roman's low, strained tone. "How do you know where to go?"

"We talked about it."

"How?"

He sighed. "Enchanted paper. He gave it to me a long time ago. We can write back and forth no matter how far apart we are."

"Huh." Stella bit her lip, debating whether to ask if Griffin happened to mention how he and Izzy felt about her. The glare he'd given her after she'd yelled at Izzy could've scorched anyone to ash.

He cares about her. He cares about her a lot.

Stella scowled at the trees. Surely the prince's advisor didn't have the same relationship restrictions Roman did, or at least not nearly as strict. He probably could be with Izzy if he chose to. And based on the way he looked at her, he would choose her.

Would Roman choose Stella?

Stop it. This line of thinking would get her nowhere. *Stay focused.*

Stella glanced around the endless trees and huffed to herself. It was going to be a long day.

They walked for miles in the direction they'd come, eventually coming upon the rocky terrain again, and Stella got increasingly perplexed by and frustrated with the prince. One second she'd accept his quick pace and cold shoulder as evidence they needed to cut ties, and the next he would be dragging his feet and stealing glances that held so much veiled emotion, and the flame in Stella's heart would splutter to life again.

Stupid prince. Stella gritted her teeth, hating that a cute boy had such power over her and her emotions. She and Prince Roman were friends. Good friends that had seen a lot together in their brief time knowing each other. Good friends that were so different, yet balanced each other out perfectly, and kissed on occasion…

Stop it.

She couldn't deny the attachment she felt toward him, though. There were so few people in the world she had a real, positive connection to, and she couldn't ignore that. It was so easy to lose people, to lose *important* people, and Stella had to grip them as tightly as she could while she had them. She'd start again with Zaria. She'd try to fix things with Izzy. And there was no way she was letting Roman go, prince or not.

As if sensing her resolve, Roman slowed his pace again, so he was walking next to her. Stella stole a quick glance to see his harsh yet blank expression. She knew that practiced mask was only there to hide a tidal wave of emotions.

I know how you feel, she wanted to tell him. *I know you're conflicted, but I'm going to fight for this.*

"I lied to you," he started quietly, keeping his eyes straight ahead.

Stella blinked in surprise. "What?"

"When we first came and broke you out of your stepmother's house, I told you that I couldn't get any information on your father's murder. That wasn't completely true." He hesitated for a half second. "There wasn't a murder case, but there was an execution order. That's all it said. I didn't know what the order was for." He gestured to her pant pocket, where her father's blue insignia was safely stored. "Once that crest fell onto the sand, I knew exactly what happened to him."

Stella's limbs felt like lead. Here she had been hanging on to some desperate hope that the papers in the attic had been a mistake, some kind of elaborate joke, even. But hearing him say it out loud made her want to sink into the ground and never come out.

He was executed. My father was executed.

"Even that first day with you," Roman continued, "I knew things...I knew things wouldn't end well for you. They couldn't. And I made peace with that. I never considered...never imagined..." His eyes flicked to hers for a moment, the gaze edged with pained conflict.

"I know," Stella said solemnly. "I thought that if I found the truth, proved Natalia guilty, that...that somehow it would fix everything. Deep down I knew it couldn't, not really. My father is still dead no matter what I find."

Roman didn't reply. Stella waited a moment as they walked, letting the courage build up inside her.

"About last night," she began, "I—"

"Last night was a mistake." The bite in his tone was empty, making it harder to believe, though Stella still cringed. "I never should've done that."

She wasn't going to let him get away with that. "I don't believe you."

"You don't have to."

"Is it because I'm a rake?" Stella snapped back. "Because that would be awfully hypocritical."

"No, of course not. It's...there's a lot...I can't—"

"Be with a peasant? Honestly, Your Highness, I thought you preached equality."

Roman laughed once without humor, matching her bitter tone. "Yeah? You want to be queen?"

The arguments prepped in Stella's mouth dried up into dust. She stared at him a moment with her jaw hanging open, unable to answer.

He scoffed at her thick silence. "Yeah, that's what I thought."

"That's not fair," she argued, but her voice lacked its usual strength.

"What, that my hateful father will leave me a broken kingdom to put together on my own without so much as his blessing? No, that's not fair at all." Bitterness hardened into firm resolve. "But that's *my* future. And I'm going to take it."

She took four steps before he spoke again, his voice so quiet she almost didn't hear. "Besides, they wouldn't see you like I do. My court, my people, my father...nobody would."

A sharp lump formed in Stella's throat, and she felt like she was bleeding out all over. "Roman, what if...what if we—"

"No," he cut her off, closing his eyes like he was trying to tune out the rest of the world—trying to convince himself he was right. "We can't. I can't. I'm going to be king of Elaria. I'm going to be a strong king—stronger than my father—and I'm going to fix this kingdom. We made a pact: no matter the cost." He took a deep breath through his teeth and opened his eyes. "This is my cost."

Tears sprang in her eyes and she fought to keep herself together. "So, what? After all this, you're just going to let me go?"

Roman fixed his face so it was expressionless again. "No. I can't do that either. That's the problem. You..." He choked on the words for a moment. "You know too much."

Out of everything he'd said, that one hit her hardest. Despite everything they'd done together, everything they'd been through, he still didn't trust her to keep the biggest secret of his life: the secret that could destroy Elaria and get Roman killed before his disastrous reign even started.

Roman pointed ahead of them, to a path that led up a rocky ridge. "They're waiting for us up there," he said, tone clipped. He hesitated a moment before rushing ahead.

Dumbfounded, Stella darted in front of him, blocking his path, and met his gaze evenly. "Roman, I would never *ever* tell anyone, I swear."

Stella's skin tingled as he stared at her, and again she could see herself reflected in his caramel eyes. But, unlike the beach where he seemed to see the best in her, now she feared he only saw the worst: stubborn, quick-tempered, reckless, angry, vindictive. He didn't touch her, but he might as well have slapped her.

He doesn't believe me. He thinks I'll tell.

Eternities raged on in just a few moments. Roman stared at her a second longer before taking her hand and leading her up the rocky path. Every part of Stella seemed to be throbbing.

"A king has to make so many hard decisions," he said after a minute, though it sounded like he was talking to himself. "I didn't want it to end this way. I really didn't. But, honestly, I only found you after the ball because of her. I didn't expect I would...think of you this way."

Because of her? The question echoed uselessly in the back of Stella's chaotic mind.

"Stopping here wasn't part of the plan." His tone darkened with buried emotion, dripping with hateful regret. "But they threatened my life and offered me a deal—a deal that would solve a lot of my problems. I...I had to take it."

"Threatened you?" Stella breathed. "Where are we going?"

Roman hesitated before answering. "It's an old headquarters for a rebel group. They cause a lot of headaches for my father—their work makes the Red Riding Clan look like fumbling toddlers."

"They made you a deal?"

He nodded, the motion jerky and painful. "One of their spies found me when I was held in the tunnels, before I knew you...before you got there. They'll limit their attacks and pull back some of their inside forces once I'm crowned. It'll put me several huge steps forward. I...I had to take it."

Even amid her wrecked heart, she couldn't help but feel a swell of pride for him. He was so dedicated, solving problems before they were really his.

A group of men met them at the top of the ridge. There were six total, each big and strong enough to snap a person in half. Their designated leader was at least a head taller than everyone else—probably two heads taller than Stella—and had a gnarled stumped wrist instead of a right hand.

Stella swallowed hard, heartbreak forgotten and nerves taking its place.

Roman stopped a few feet away from the group and nodded at the leader. "Carn."

Carn spat on the ground, not quite at Roman but almost. "Prince." Then his piercing blue eyes turned on Stella with bright interest, and her blood went cold. "She looks like him enough."

Roman nodded again, the muscles in his neck straining, tightening his grip on her hand. "She's his."

"Well, then, you have yourself a deal." He gave a sinister smile. "We'll behave ourselves."

Roman nudged her forward, and she stumbled toward the men. "Then she's yours."

"What?" Stella gasped. Strong hands seized her, and she started kicking her legs and screaming. "No! Let me go! Roman!" She was able to knee one man in the stomach and kick out another's leg, but there were too many of them, and with every one that went down, another grabbed her twice as hard.

"No! Let me go! No!" Craning her neck, she turned to catch a glimpse of the prince watching her with a blank face and hollow eyes. "Roman! *Roman!*" Then they picked her up and threw her in a giant bag like a vegetable, and she lost sight of him.

She punched and flailed and shrieked as they carried her off. The thick burlap scratched against her skin and somehow the harsh particles were in her throat, rubbing it raw with each scream. Eventually she had to stop thrashing to catch her breath, which was when she noticed the tiniest hole in the fabric.

Forcing herself to calm for a moment, she closed one eye and put the other against the peephole. One of the men was carrying her over his shoulder, like a sack of potatoes, and with each step she swung slightly to the right. It took a few steps for her to make out the structure they seemed to be going to, a fortified building that had been built into the side of the mountain. It blended in so well in the middle of nowhere, Stella almost missed it.

Who were these people? What could they possibly want with her?

All too soon, they were inside the building. The man carrying her opened the sack and dumped her out onto the floor, and Stella's chin grated against rock.

"Stella? Stella!"

Stella whipped her head up to see a cavernous area filled with all kinds of equipment, from weapons to maps to supplies. Hanging on the far wall was a giant blue replica of the crest in Stella's pocket, and halfway across the space, fighting ruthlessly against her own captors, was Izzy.

"Stella!" she shrieked, face red with exertion. "Stella, run!"

But already Stella had nowhere to go. Sack Man dragged her across the room to a large table, then threw her to her knees. Her head smacked against the edge of the table and she saw stars for a moment. Then a thick hand gripped her jaw, forcing her to look up.

"Well, Miss Madeus," the one-handed man—Carn—sneered, his breath rotten. "I've been waiting a long time to meet you."

"Get off me!" Stella tried to wrench herself free, but he just tightened his hold, and she choked.

"I know you don't know me," he went on, oblivious to her squirming, "so let me introduce myself. I'm Carn." He extended his stumped arm, then gave a malicious grin. "Oh, right. That. You might have noticed I'm missing a hand."

Stella finally got her feet underneath her, but then Carn slammed her head against the table again, and the room started spinning.

"Truth is, sweetheart, I know your old man. Or knew him, I guess. He was part of our rebel alliance since we were kids. Didn't ever tell you that, though, did he? He didn't bring his family here like the rest of us did." He smirked. "Did you know Daddy was actually a rebel spy?"

Stella didn't answer. She just glared.

"Thick as thieves we were, Damon and I. Blood brothers. Until the day he decided to betray us and save his own skin. Lost my hand that day; barely made it out with our lives. I was disappointed to hear the crown finally chopped his head off, only because I wanted to return the favor while he was still breathing. Alas, he was buried with two hands. You'll just have to take the favor for him."

"Stop it!" Izzy shrieked, her terrified voice echoing in the vast space. "Let her go!"

Carn obeyed. Stella slumped to the floor, gasping, but before she could get her bearings, two of Carn's men yanked her up and shoved her against the table, the edge digging painfully into her stomach. Sack Man grabbed her left arm and stretched it across the surface, holding it down. She thrashed around, trying to get away, but they held her firm. Terror crashed into her, threatening to overwhelm her whole being.

Carn's eyes glinted with dark hatred as he grabbed a wicked dagger from his belt. "I used to be the best in the business until that day—now the stump makes it hard to blend in. I've adjusted though. You will too."

The dagger gleamed as Carn raised it above the table, and Stella squeezed her eyes shut just as Izzy screamed.

* * * * * * * *

Izzy couldn't stop shaking.

She'd tried deep breathing. She'd tried counting. She'd tried telling herself to stay calm.

The shaking wouldn't stop.

Despite her trembling hands, she kept wiping the blood away, though the rag was so saturated already it was mostly just smearing red around. She didn't care. She kept doing it. She didn't want to think. She *couldn't* think, not rationally at least, not without hearing Griffin's cracked voice when she ran and Stella's awful scream when they—

Stop, she commanded herself, trying to block out the memory of Stella's screams woven together with hers. She just shook harder.

After they had...done what they did to Stella, one of the men used magic to seal her wound up, essentially forcing her muscles and skin to grow over her wrist to make a stump so she couldn't reattach her hand. Stella lost consciousness halfway through, and the men had dragged both of them down a hallway to a makeshift cell made of mismatched metal pieces that had been welded together. With a warning to stay quiet, they'd left them alone.

Now, Izzy had Stella's head in her lap, wiping their red-stained clothes with a soaked cloth Carn had put on Stella's bleeding arm once the horrible deed was done. Distant voices vibrated from afar, and some kind of scratching sounded a few feet from their cell, but besides that it was quiet. A few kids had already walked by—she'd pleaded with a thirteen-year-old boy to let them out, but he'd just spat at them and kept walking.

How are we going to get out of here?

Suddenly, Stella stirred, turning her head. She started crying before she was fully awake, a broken sob bubbling on her lips, and she whispered Roman's name. Izzy pretended not to notice.

"Stella?" she whispered as she smoothed Stella's dirty blonde hair off her forehead. "Stella, it's me. It's just Izzy."

"Izzy?" Her ragged voice cracked and tears streamed down her face. "Oh, Izzy."

Stella cried for a minute while Izzy stroked her hair, her own eyes swimming in stinging tears.

"He left me here," she cried quietly. "He left me here. I never should've gone with him. I never should've trusted him. I don't trust anyone. Why...why?" Then she took a shuddering breath and opened her eyes to look into Izzy's. "Izzy, I'm *so sorry.*"

"I know, Stel. I know you are. I'm sorry too."

For a moment, Stella hesitated. "Did you...did you find her?"

Izzy's breath hitched and she nodded hastily. "I found...where she...she's..."

Stella's eyes widened in horrified understanding, and then she started sobbing again.

Izzy bit her lip, unsure if she should leave it at that, or tell Stella the truth about what she found. Would Stella believe such a harsh reality about her father? The memory of their fight made her think not.

"She never said his name," Stella said suddenly.

"What?"

"Natalia." She sniffed and shuddered. "After he died. She never said his name again. She was afraid to. Like someone would hear."

Izzy nodded to herself solemnly, a heavy weight in her chest next to both locket pieces around her neck. Stella knew.

Steeling herself, Stella lifted her head slightly and started to survey the room, but her eyes caught her mangled arm and she went pale and yelped. Izzy gingerly lowered her head back onto her lap.

"He left me here." Stella had stopped sobbing, though tears still fell down her red cheeks. "He kissed me, and then he left me here. I really thought that he might...that we would work. I should have never...I didn't think that he...and he thought I would tell, that I..." Her breath caught again. "How could I have been so stupid? He's a *prince*! What did I...what could possibly...what did I do?"

"You're human, Stel," Izzy told her. "It's not stupid to want a prince, or to love one. Not at all. There's nothing weak or pathetic about wanting love. You did nothing wrong."

Through her tears, Stella's blue eyes burned with icy rage. "Never again. He'll never control me like that again. Nobody will." She raged on in fractured whispers and angry half sobs about the prince who had left her so brutally broken—on the inside and out. Izzy didn't think herself capable of true hatred, but what she felt toward Roman now felt pretty close. The loathing was even sharper because of how much she'd come to love Roman in her own way.

As much as that hurt, though, it wasn't what mattered most. Not right now.

Cautiously, Izzy cut in. "Stella," she said softly. "They're going after Zaria."

Her eyebrows furrowed in confusion. "What?"

"Roman and—and Griffin." She nearly choked on the advisor's name, but forced herself through it. "They're going after Zaria."

Instantly, the sorrow cleared from Stella's expression, that icy determination taking hold of her. "Tell me everything."

So Izzy did. She told her brief details of finding her mother's cell and discovering what happened. She told her that they spent the night under a tree next to the prison, and Griffin woke her up the next morning, saying they had to go. While they walked, he told her the truth. He had been studying magical creatures for years, specifically fairies, because he'd heard an old legend about them: fairies were immortal, but they could pass their life essence on to another person, transferring their magic as well, as a way of ending their immortality should they see fit. Several books hidden deep in the royal library had confirmed the theory, and he came to Roman with a solution to their rake issue.

They needed a fairy.

Izzy told her that she'd been horrified when she realized what he meant. Griffin shamefully explained that they had set a trap for Zaria, and she'd been caught by Korah and the royal guards after they'd left the Red Riding Clan. She was scheduled to be executed tomorrow morning. Roman and Griffin were planning on saving her at the last minute, then tearfully explain that the girls had died in the rescue attempt, and use Zaria's grief as a means to pressure her into giving her life essence to Roman, therefore transferring her magic to him. Fairy magic was taboo in the kingdom—they wouldn't tell anyone the true origins—but it would make the prince more powerful than his father and give him the reputation he needed, securing his throne and Griffin's title. Griffin's established status as advisor to the king would ensure he could never be executed for his birthright, and give him the power to go after his wicked parents and guarantee the revenge he'd been craving since they'd tried to kill him.

Both boys would get what they wanted. It was a crazy plan, with many possibilities for failure, but they were desperate and had no other option.

Izzy didn't tell her how Griffin had broken down and told her he'd never cared for anyone the way he did for her. She didn't say how he had told her he could save her, that he could keep her safe if she left Stella behind. She didn't say how he'd taken her face in his hands and begged her to come with him, but instead she ran and let herself be imprisoned with Stella, and it shattered what was left of her heart.

Stella was clenching her teeth in fury by the time Izzy was done. "He said that to me. Right before he left. He said 'I only came after you for her.'"

Izzy nodded. "She's on the fairy registry. They recognized her when they first saw the photo at the ball."

"And the prince of Elaria went after the magic." She shook her head in disgust. "Of course. Would the transfer process kill Zaria?"

Izzy shrugged. "He said there have been rumored survivors, but if it's true then they're very few and they're usually younger fairies. If she did survive, though, they were planning on killing her anyway. No witnesses."

"Snake," she muttered vehemently. "So what do you know about this place? How can we get out?"

Tilting her head, Izzy mentally rifled through her observations. "I've seen twelve different men and five different women, plus a handful of kids. I think they all live here too, on the other side of this bunker. The main hall is filled with crates of weapons—I don't know exactly what's in them, but I did hear someone mention a device that explodes. They also threw your sword and our supplies in the pile, once you were unconscious."

Stella nodded to herself. "I'm going to need that sword back because I'm going to stab Roman with it."

Izzy pursed her lips, forcing herself not to look at Stella's left arm. "Fair enough."

Stella carefully sat up, her face still too pale but her eyes much more alert. She motioned to Izzy, and together they started examining their cell to find a way out. The distant voices had quieted, though the scratching still sounded near them, and Stella crawled closer to it, investigating.

"This place is impressive, but it's practically crumbling off the mountain. I guess rebel spy work isn't a goldmine."

Izzy nodded in agreement, surveying the vast space again. The structure seemed to have been carved right out of the mountain, and while it must've been a strong defense years ago, it had since fallen into disrepair.

Stella reached her arm in between the bars toward the scratching sound on the wall, then flinched when she saw her stump. She quickly switched so her right arm was sticking through instead.

"I'm right-handed," she muttered, sardonic, trying to cover up her devastation at her new disability. "How thoughtful."

Izzy knew worrying over the injury would only make Stella mad, so she let the girl work. Stella pushed against a weak place on the wall where the sound seemed to be coming from. After a minute, part of the rock wall crumbled away and a spot of sunlight streamed in—something was working on it from the other side too.

"What…?" Stella trailed off, and Izzy leaned forward to get a closer look.

Suddenly, a furry head popped through the hole, searching eyes resting on the captive girls.

"Winston!" they both gasped in delight at the same time.

Winston whined softly and panted with excitement, trying to push the rest of his body through the hole. Izzy scooted forward, and she and Stella started brushing away bits of rock, widening the opening, until Winston squeezed all the way through. His fur was matted and bloody, though Izzy couldn't find any wounds on him.

"How'd he find us?" Stella asked. "Unless someone…" She trailed off, glancing uncertainly at Izzy.

Izzy didn't have the capacity to deal with that. Maybe someone had sent Winston to them, maybe they hadn't. She didn't care. She *couldn't* care, at least not yet.

Reaching through the bars, Izzy gave Winston a hug, pressing her face into his dirty fur. "Thanks for not giving up on me," she whispered to him before straightening up. "Okay, boy, I need you to listen carefully, all right? We have to save Zaria."

* * * * * * *

Breaking out took longer than they anticipated.

Izzy still hadn't stopped shaking, but now it was more out of nerves than trauma. Based on the little spot of sun leaking through their hole, they only had a few hours left until dark. The advisor—it stung too badly to think his name—had told her Zaria wasn't going to be executed until the next morning, but she didn't know how much she could trust that timeframe. Plus, she didn't know when the boys would get to the fairy. They could almost be there.

They could be with her now.

She could already be dead.

"No, Winston!" Stella slumped in frustration, raking her hand through her lopsided ponytail. "That's not it either."

Izzy's furry friend was sitting on the floor outside their cell, tail thumping against the ground with pride. He used his muzzle to push the rock he'd found at Stella. Though they'd kept sending Winston to retrieve them a tool or weapon—anything they could use to get out of this cell—the dog wasn't getting the point. First he'd brought back a dirty sock. Then an empty canteen. Now a rock.

Forcing a breath through her teeth, Stella picked up the rock and started smacking it against the cell lock, hoping something would give. When it didn't, Izzy stuck her hand through the bars to pet Winston, then pointed in the distance.

"Go get it, Winston," she said, feigning excitement so the dog would get excited too. "Go get it."

Winston jumped to his feet and bounded away. Izzy sighed.

"What if we don't make it in time?"

Of course we'll make it. Izzy heard Stella's predictably determined response in her head, and it took her a second to realize she hadn't said it out loud.

Instead, Stella was hunched over herself, tracing a trembling finger over the new skin on her deformed wrist. Her mouth twisted with a mix of horror and disgust, and her voice shook, even in whispers.

"I don't know."

A slight screeching sounded—metal against concrete. Both girls jumped and straightened up, preparing for the next obstacle, but it was Winston that came around the corner, dragging Stella's sword and backpack in his mouth.

"Yes!" Stella pumped her fist in the air, shedding her anguish and putting her tenacity back on. "Good dog! Very good dog."

Izzy smiled. "Told you."

Stella rolled her eyes. "No you didn't."

Stella jammed the sword into the lock and wriggled it around—Izzy had to help keep her balanced—until the cell came unlocked. The two of them stepped out of their prison, and Izzy knelt down to properly hug Winston while Stella reattached her sword sheath to her hip and slung the backpack over her shoulder.

"So what now?" Izzy asked.

Stella gave a wicked grin. "Now, we make an explosive exit."

Hugging the walls, Stella, Izzy, and Winston stole down the hallway, footsteps silent except for the soft padding of Winston's paws. Izzy bent halfway to keep a hand on him so he wouldn't run away as Stella led them down the corridor.

"Was the entrance this way?" Stella whispered.

Izzy glanced around at the brown walls that all looked the same. "I'm not sure."

They kept going, avoiding voices and moving away from their cell, until they came to an open room filled with crates. Once Stella confirmed they were alone, she gave Izzy her sword and opened the crate closest to her. It was full of a bunch of metal contraptions.

"I heard a few of them talking about machinery like this," Izzy murmured. "It allows you to do things without magic. The metal parts work together with some kind of other power source to do tasks for you."

"That's amazing," Stella whispered back in awe, rifling through metal gears and stowing a few in her pocket. "Why don't people have it?"

"Other kingdoms have already developed it, but our kings have outlawed manufacturing it for years. These people are working on it in secret to bring more equality."

Abandoning the machinery, Stella took her sword back. "Yeah, well, if they hadn't cut off my hand I might be more inclined to help them. Let's go."

They searched through each crate, leaving the lids off of the ones that held weapons or something that looked like it might explode. When they had about ten open, Stella had Izzy dig into their backpack and take out a few matches.

"Hey!"

Izzy jumped, dropping the matches, and Stella cursed under her breath while Winston started barking at the intruder. The boy that had spit on them earlier was running at them, two men at his heels. They did not look happy.

"Stop!"

Stella fumbled for the matches, dropping her sword and trying to balance the small box on her stump hand. Izzy kept an arm around Winston, securing him, and then joined Stella in frantically trying to light something. The footsteps pounded closer.

"Yes!" Stella finally caught a spark and her match lit up with a flame. With a maniacal smile, she tossed the burning match in the closest open crate, then shoved it toward the approaching men, shouting in pain when her injured arm hit the box.

The men cursed and ran away from the crate. The boy stopped and gave Izzy and Stella each a murderous glower before he ducked away too. Then the crate exploded.

The ground rumbled underneath them, the walls shuddering from the explosion. Screaming and yelling sounded down the hall, though there was a blaze in between them now. Izzy, Stella, and Winston ran the opposite direction, dropping matches on crates as they went and leaving destruction in their wake.

Izzy helped Stella push another crate against the wall, then they blew it up, effectively bringing down the wall and causing the building to start collapsing. Winston barked at the flames, and Izzy had to yank him out of the base before a slab of ceiling fell on him. Fist clutching the nape of his neck, she dragged him over the rubble and outside.

They ran. Izzy's feet threatened to come out from under her as they raced down the mountain, but she managed to keep herself upright while watching Stella closely, just in case. Stella was slightly wobbly as her legs pumped her faster, but Izzy didn't know if it was from blood loss, shock, or an imbalanced body. Meanwhile, Winston barked next to them in delight, happy to be running with them and probably thinking it was a game.

Izzy shook her head. While she and Stella had never thought of this quest as a game by any means, the search for truth had led them places they'd never imagined and cost them way too much.

Stella slowed down at the base of the mountain, then stopped and turned around to watch the building crumble on itself while she caught her breath. Izzy leaned over next to her, panting, and patted Winston's head.

Straightening up, Stella spat on the ground. "Good riddance." Then she turned to Izzy. "We have until tomorrow morning, right?"

Izzy glanced up at the sky. It was late afternoon now, nearing evening. "Until Korah executes her. They plan on reaching her before then, though. They could be there now."

"No," Stella said fiercely, like her word was law. "They're not. We'll make it."

"How are we going to find her? She could be anywhere."

Grinning in triumph, Stella sheathed her sword and reached into her pant pocket, pulling out a piece of Zaria's magic wand that they'd found in Damon's box by the sea. Though that was barely two weeks ago, it felt like a lifetime.

"They never took the spell off it," Stella said. "It should still bring us to Zaria."

Izzy nodded, glancing doubtfully at the sky again. She didn't want to be pessimistic, but the boys were hours ahead of them—how were they going to beat them to Zaria?

Stella pursed her lips, reading the doubt on Izzy's face. She opened her mouth to speak, but a loud guttural noise cut her off. The three of them ducked behind a bush and peered over the leaves.

A man traveled down the dirt road toward the building they'd just destroyed, riding some kind of vehicle: it was long and skinny, not enclosed, and had one wheel in the front and one in the back. The air smelled metallic and smokey, and the piercing sound seemed to be emanating from the machine itself—the gears working to make the wheels turn.

She'd never seen anything so wonderful.

"Machines without magic?" Stella asked, wonder and excitement coloring her tone.

Izzy nodded, transfixed. "That's what they said."

Her eyes glinted, locked on the approaching vehicle. "I think I know how we're going to catch up."

* * * * * * *

Now, Stella could get used to this.

Izzy had her reservations, so Stella was the one who threw the rock at the rider, throwing him off his non-magical contraption. She was also the one who knocked him out, but Izzy had to help her drag his body off the road. It took a few minutes to set the machine back up, poke at it, and get it working again. They stuffed Winston in a basket hooked to the back of the vehicle, then Stella got on. Izzy was hesitant, but they had no time for fear. Eventually she climbed on behind Stella and held her tightly, using her left hand to control the handlebar that Stella couldn't grip anymore.

Then they flew.

The wheels stayed on the ground, but it was just like she imagined flying would be. The wind whipped against her face and through her hair, the mountainous landscape zipping by on either side of her, and both she and Izzy shouted in exhilaration. It was so much better than the carriages that ran on magic, which most people couldn't afford anyway.

Izzy gripped Zaria's wand in her free hand, gently guiding the vehicle to where they needed to go as the sun started disappearing under the horizon. Stella was a little nervous once they passed through secluded corners of Racine and Doveneer before finally reaching the edge of the forest, but despite the changes in terrain, the machine adjusted accordingly, and they zipped by too fast for anyone that might have noticed to follow.

Stella loved it. After they got to Zaria, she was going to ask her godmother where to find parts for a machine. Surely, the fairy had been exposed to it in all her travels. In fact, now that Stella knew the truth about Zaria's origins and Damon, there were so many stories Stella wanted to hear. So much mending in their relationship that needed to be done.

She stole a glance at her missing hand, nauseated every time it caught her eye. Some things couldn't be fixed, but she'd fix everything she could and live with the rest.

I'll get to you, Zaria. I promise. And after she saved her and got her revenge, she'd dedicate her life to manufacturing this technology and sharing it with everyone, no matter what traitorous, lying princes had to say.

Once the thick trees of the forest swallowed them in endless green, it was harder to tell how much sunlight they had left. Stella pressed forward, the leaves blurring around them, chanting to herself that they'd get there in time.

They drove for what seemed like forever. Stella's legs were unbearably sore from straddling the metal contraption for so long, and though the wound was closed, her hand—or lack thereof—hadn't stopped throbbing.

Suddenly, Izzy gasped. "The wand is getting warmer!" she shouted over the roar of the vehicle. "We must be close!"

Stella frowned as she glanced over the machine, realizing a new problem.

"How do we stop this thing?" Izzy yelled.

Stella looked closer at the controls on the handlebars. None of it made sense to her. She only knew how to make it *go.*

"Stella?" Izzy's voice was edged with nerves. "Please tell me you know how to stop."

She kept studying the controls. It couldn't be *that* hard, right?

"Stella?"

Stella huffed. "Well it's not like I got a training course on this thing!"

Izzy gasped again, pointing the wand. "There they—" Then she cut herself off with a scream, jerking the handlebar to the left. Stella shouted in surprise and looked up from the controls just in time to watch them barely avoid colliding with a tree.

The momentum from the sharp turn rolled their vehicle; Winston yelped and jumped from his basket, but Stella and Izzy couldn't get free in time. They tumbled to the ground with an undignified *thud* while the machine skidded across the forest floor and came to a stop.

Stella groaned, fighting back tears at the pain vibrating across her body and the dizziness in her head. She started to push herself up, but her left arm buckled the second she put pressure on her wound, and she gasped at the stab of pain. Izzy caught her before she fell back to the ground, wrapping an arm around her and leaning her up against her shoulder.

"What an entrance," Stella muttered to herself. She'd wanted to make a better impression than that.

Steeling herself, she glanced up to face the scene framed by the forest trees: her insides burned with anguish and hatred when she saw Roman gawking, gaze darting between her and their vehicle. Griffin was standing loosely next to him; his eyes glazed over when he saw Izzy, and Stella heard her take a sharp breath when she saw him. And kneeling before them, looking so pale and sick and just *broken*, was Zaria, gaping at Stella with welled up tears forgotten in astonished relief.

"Stella," she breathed, words ragged. "Stella, you're alive."

And in that moment, hearing those fragile words spoken by such a strong creature, Stella understood how Roman had thought his plan might work. The confirmation of Zaria's devoted love for Stella only fueled her resolve and gave her strength.

"No thanks to them," Stella spat as Izzy helped her to her feet. A collective gasp sounded, and she momentarily lost her confidence, her pulse thudding in her ears and her fists clenching, except now it was just one.

Swallowing her scalding humiliation, Stella raised her injured arm, refusing to let herself be bullied by it.

She scowled at the spineless traitor. "You owe me something."

Zaria was on her feet instantly, back on offense and forgetting her moment of despair. She seemed sunken and...dull, somehow, like someone had literally tried to suck the life out of her through the wounds on her arms. Stella felt sick at the thought of what Korah had done to Zaria—and what she *would* have done—but the fairy's eyes burned with her usual intensity as she backed away from the boys. Roman just gaped at Stella's disfigured arm in horror, while Griffin had moved his stare back to Izzy.

"You deplorable, wretched creatures," Zaria murmured, infuriated, understanding without an explanation. Her steps lacked their usual grace, but she kept backing up until she stood by Stella and Izzy.

Stella just glared at the prince, waiting pointedly for him to speak. Though even just the memory of his voice felt like an excruciating electric shock, she wanted to hear what excuses he would make for his betrayal.

Roman finally shifted his gaze from her missing hand to her face. "I need that magic," he said simply, like it was all the defense in the world. "I have to save Elaria. I have a kingdom to inherit."

She scoffed at him. "A pathetic one. Fitting, for such a pathetic prince."

He ignored the jab. "Stella." She was glad he choked slightly on her name. "Step aside."

Each word came forced through her teeth. "I'd. Rather. Die."

"Zaria is going to die anyway, eventually." He looked at the fairy now. "You know Korah is going to catch up with you someday. Wouldn't you rather end things on your own terms, for a great reason, rather than have someone decide to waste your magic? Why not leave a tremendous legacy in the name of the crown?"

Stella was afraid that argument would resonate with Zaria, but the fairy just sneered at the prince.

"Since it's done so much for me? You forget, boy, that I fought loyally for the crown until your great grandfather turned his back on my kind and ordered our execution. And you seem to have already forgotten what you've done to my goddaughter." She jerked her chin defiantly. "I'd rather Korah skin me alive and let me bleed out than do *anything* for the likes of you."

Roman pursed his lips and straightened, puffing himself up with arrogance and power—a glimpse of the haughty boy she'd first met at the ball. "As your future king, I order you to give me your magic, or I'll...I will..." He trailed off, eyes flicking to Stella.

"Or you'll what? Kill me?" Stella laughed darkly. "You couldn't do it yourself this morning. You won't do it now."

They glared at each other in a standoff, each running through possible scenarios. Stella wanted to take on the prince herself, and if she didn't have Griffin's magic to worry about, she would. Who would be able to face him? Izzy was out of the question, Stella didn't stand a chance, and Zaria was already weakened—how long would she hold up against Griffin? Would she be able to run fast enough if she couldn't dredge up enough power to transport?

The scene settled, everyone sizing up the challenge ahead. Out of all of them, though, it was Izzy who moved first. She stepped forward, angling herself between Stella and Zaria and the boys. Her pleading voice was soft but strong as she placed a hand on Stella while looking at Roman.

"We don't have to fight. We don't." She turned her gaze to Griffin, and both of them flinched at the eye contact. "Please. Let us walk away."

Roman stepped forward, determination hardening his expression. Stella used to think that determination was for her. "I can't."

As if on some unseen cue, Griffin raised his hands, preparing himself. His scarred face held its perpetual indifferent frown, but his eyes bled with conflict, locked on Izzy, who was standing in the line of fire.

He loved her. He really did.

"Move." Griffin's voice was so quiet, Stella almost didn't hear, but the pleading command wasn't for her anyway. "Move. Now. Please."

Stella felt Izzy tremble, but her tone held firm, and knowing what kind of torturous heartbreak was coursing through her veins, Stella had never been prouder of her. "No."

Griffin flicked his wrist and a force blew Izzy to the side; she landed roughly on the ground several yards away. Then a thrumming power surrounded them, dividing them, trapping them: a magical barrier. Roman, Griffin, Zaria, and Stella inside. Izzy and Winston outside.

"No!" Izzy yelled, pounding her fist against the invisible wall. "No, Griffin, stop! Please!"

Griffin winced, but didn't hesitate aiming for Zaria. Stella pulled out her sword and lunged at him, but Roman cut her off. Metal clanked as his sword met hers.

"I have to do this," Roman told her, and he sounded truly desolate. "I'm sorry."

"You will be," Stella snarled back. She pushed against him with all her force, knocking him back a step, and then their duel began.

Metal clashed with metal as Stella and Roman fought, and the air buzzed with electricity as Griffin and Zaria engaged in magical warfare, with Izzy's anguished shouts and berating fists in the background. Stella couldn't break her concentration to check on her godmother; she fought the prince with all the hateful intensity she had. While much more trained, he held back, whether consciously or not, and Stella had enraged grief on her side. She only got angrier when he stole glances at her mutilated hand that knocked her off balance every few steps. He had the audacity to look appalled.

For a second she was transported back in time, to when they were staying with the Coronas and the prince offered to teach Stella to defend herself. They had traded jokes and laughs and smiles, building the first new friendship Stella had accepted in a long time.

Fake. It had all been fake.

"I didn't mean for this to happen," Roman told her again, voice strained with the effort of dueling. His eyes darted to her hand again. "I just needed you busy until my secret was no longer a threat. That's it. I didn't even know if you'd *want* to leave them since they worked with your father."

Stella feigned a jab to the left, but went right at the last second, slashing her blade across his cheek. "They magically sealed the wound. I'll never get it back."

The wounds you gave me will never heal.

He barely raised his sword fast enough to block her next blow. "I didn't know they would do that to you!"

"Well, what did you *think* they were going to do?" she seethed. "Invite me in for tea?"

A deafening cracking sounded, and a force nearly knocked Stella and Roman off their feet. Both Griffin and Zaria cried out, and Stella felt the magic barrier crumble around them. Winston barked erratically and Izzy once again shouted for them to stop.

The barrier was gone. They were free.

Roman scowled and surged forward, hitting so hard and fast with his sword that she stumbled away, barely keeping up. "You have *no idea* what I've been through. You have no idea what I've endured, the pressure on my shoulders. I sacrifice because I *have* to, not because I want to." She tried to get ahead of his blows, but he didn't let her. "If I thought you would've stayed out of my way, if I thought for one second you would've stayed quiet and stepped aside, I *never* would have left you."

Left me? Furious tears burned Stella's eyes, and she found a new rush of energy, retaliating with ruthless drive.

"I trusted you!" she screamed at him, landing a solid gash across his forearm. He automatically pulled back, and she used the slight hole in his strategy as a window to mercilessly seize the advantage. "I trusted you, I fought for you, and I could've loved you, you *treacherous, backstabbing prince*!"

She faked losing her balance again, so he lunged for her weak side, but she turned and drove her sword into his shoulder, where the deepest part of his siren wound was. His knees buckled and he grunted in pain—she secured her place by successfully disarming him and kicking him to the ground in front of her.

Zaria cried out again from behind her, and Stella heard her collapse. To her right, Griffin rushed toward Stella, aiming a reckless and deadly bolt of magic at her before she slashed Roman to bits.

But she didn't care. She only wanted Roman to feel what she had.

Stella brought her sword down on Roman's neck just as Griffin shouted in raging panic and sent an attack at her, but she knew he was too late. Roman raised his arm above his face and Stella knew she'd won.

A force shoved her out of the way, and her sword slashed clean through air. Stella fell to the ground hard, the impact scratching up her face and making her dizzy. Groaning, she spat out dirt and blood as she tried to get her bearings and sit up.

"No! *No!*"

The anguished scream wasn't Roman's, like Stella had hoped.

It was Griffin's.

"NO!"

Stella pushed herself up to see Roman still bracing himself in the dirt and Griffin slumped on his knees several yards away. His agonized eyes were focused on a heap of black clothes, bronze hair, and red. So much red.

Izzy.

Stella's jaw dropped open and a mangled cry escaped her. Faster than she could register, Zaria dove forward from her place on the ground behind the girls and bellowed with exertion. The air around Stella converged on her, crushing her bones together. Then it flattened out again, and she looked up to see they were alone now, in a different part of the forest. The boys were gone.

Panting, Zaria collapsed in the dirt, her pale face slick with sweat from the weight of her capture, fighting Griffin, and transporting them all—Winston included. The dog whined and pawed at Izzy, who was laying on her back, breaths shallow and face gaunt, trembling as she bled out. A porcelain angel, dressed in red.

Stella scrambled to her best friend, tears falling down her face. She took one of Izzy's bloody hands. "Izzy...you jumped in front of me. You pushed me out of the way." She cried harder. "Why did you do that? *Why did you do that?*"

Izzy's glassy eyes shifted, finding Stella's. She managed a weak grin, but her words were laced with so much pain. "I figured it...out. I figured it out."

"Figured what out?"

"Love." She coughed, and they both flinched. "If you...if you love someone...you would do anything for them. I spent...my life looking, but...I had it...already. I had you." Her eyelids fluttered, threatening to close forever.

"No!" Stella shouted desperately, squeezing Izzy's hand like that could force life back into her. "No, Izzy, please stay with me. Please!"

Zaria finally managed to push herself up on her arms, dragging herself across the dirt with her elbows. Even on the verge of passing out, she was strikingly beautiful, and that beauty cracked with deep fault lines when she laid eyes on Izzy.

"Isabelle," she crooned softly, a mix between a song and a plea as she caressed her bloody cheek. "Isabelle, I'm so sorry."

"Zaria." Stella's cracked voice was saturated with tears. "She's going to die."

The fairy watched Izzy with tender adoration, a lifetime of love and sorrow passing in her eyes. Then she took a breath, steeled herself with resolution, and met Stella's gaze evenly. "I can save her."

Stella felt the wind had been knocked out of her. "What are you waiting for? Do it!"

"I can save her." Zaria's face hardened with resolve. "But on one condition."

"Condition? She's going to *die*!"

"She threw her life away for you!" she shouted back. "I won't save her just so you can throw it away again."

Stella's eyebrows furrowed. "What are you talking about?"

"I will save Isabelle's life if you swear to me you will leave the prince alone."

Shock shook Stella. Her jaw dropped open, feeling a slight pierce of betrayal.

Zaria continued. "You leave this place. Leave Elaria if you have to—it's immensely difficult, but not impossible. Take Izzy, forget the prince, and *get out*. Live a life you both deserve."

"But…" Stella stammered, overcome with resentment at the thought of Roman getting away unscathed. "But how can I forget? He took everything from me!"

Zaria jerked her chin at the dying Izzy. "He hasn't taken her. Not yet."

"But—"

"But what? What are you going to do? Kill the crown prince of Elaria? Even if you manage to succeed, it will tear you apart and you'll spend your life in prison or evading it. Then what? Take his kingdom? You don't want that. You're not Damon." She leaned forward, forcing Stella to meet her fathomless violet eyes. "Revenge consumed your father. It consumed me for most of my life. It's consuming Roman and Griffin. Do *not* let it consume you too."

Winston whined and plopped down in the dirt, resting his head on Izzy's shoulder. It was barely moving. She was barely breathing.

Izzy was *dying*.

But how could she let Roman get away?

"Stella," Zaria snapped. "Decide now. Promise me."

Stella clenched her teeth, battling the two sides tearing her soul in half. Her missing hand throbbed though it wasn't there, a constant reminder of the fissure in her heart that would never go away. Overpowering that, though, was the pulse in her remaining hand—Izzy's hand, slick with blood.

If you love someone, you would do anything for them.

"I promise," Stella said through her teeth. "I promise."

Zaria searched her eyes, then nodded when she decided Stella meant it. Stella opened her mouth to ask how she was going to save Izzy—and tell her to hurry—but she stopped when she saw Zaria's dark skin begin to glow.

Then she remembered. The fissure in her heart widened until it broke her clean in half.

"It's a way to live on," Zaria told her, as if sensing her thoughts. "It's a little-known legend, but fairies can pass on their immortality, should they choose to." She laughed once without humor. "Forever can get boring after a while." Then she looked over Izzy with all the love of a childless mother. "It'll be difficult for her to adjust. You'll have to help her. If Korah ever discovers what happened, you'll have to run from her too."

"Zaria…" Stella's breath hitched into a sob. "Zaria."

Zaria's body glowed, dotting in specks of gold that lifted into the air and floated toward Izzy. With every dot transferred, Izzy's skin gained color while Zaria's turned gray. Gray and withered and crumbling into dust.

Gently, the fairy took Stella's face in her hands, smearing Izzy's blood on her cheeks. Zaria's eyes welled up with tears as she looked over Stella again and again, as if committing her to memory for the brief time she had left. Stella sobbed louder and Zaria brushed her tears away with her thin fingers.

"For the record, I wanted to take you with me." Zaria's weakening voice broke and a single tear escaped her eye. "I wanted to so badly, but Natalia thought the crown would come for you. They were already suspicious of you, already considering killing you just for your father. She knew if you disappeared with me they would lose all restraint, especially if Korah found out about you, and I had to agree. She thought the only way to save you was to make you as insignificant as possible until they stopped watching you."

Stella shuddered, sobs racking her body. Zaria leaned forward and kissed her on the forehead.

"I'm so sorry," she whispered. "I'm sorry it all happened this way. I love you. I always have. I always will."

"Zaria, please." She didn't know what she was begging for, but she was desperate to keep her, to keep everyone, to just make them *stay*. "Zaria, please, please, please."

But the Zaria she was used to wasn't with her anymore, not the brilliant, lively, confident godmother she knew. This Zaria was gray and withering, literally falling to pieces right before Stella's eyes. She lowered herself to the ground next to Izzy, who was becoming more vibrant by the second, and Stella watched as bits of her skin and hair crumbled into dust, decades of age shining through after years of immortality. She turned into wrinkles and soot with protruding bones—a decaying image of the vengeful old hag she'd been masquerading as when Stella had first found her.

But she was content. She had found peace.

"They'll get their kingdom," Zaria told her in strained words, eyes shining. "You go make yours." Then her eyes closed, and she gasped her last breath. Her papery body collapsed into dust, leaving fragments of a skeleton.

"Zaria!" Stella screamed through her tears. "Zaria!"

When no answer came, Stella bent over the bloody body of her best friend and cried.

* * * * * * *

The soft breeze was laced with the scent of saltwater and damp fabric, fluttering through Stella's loose ponytail. She stopped to take a moment and breathe it in, letting it soak into her body and seep into her soul, relaxing her as it went. Though she could barely contain her excitement, the constant paranoia in her gut hadn't been silenced in weeks—the relaxation was a welcome moment.

Elaria's small northern port was quiet and subdued, nothing like the glamorous and bustling vision Stella had always carried in her head as a child. The dock was big enough to house at least fifteen ships, if not more, but only four were anchored and all of them were as shabby and worn as the dock itself. The crews were even more depressing: they were all sunburnt and hardened, speaking in low voices with each other.

Stella caught a conversation between two passing women: two more of Elaria's ships had gone down just this week and dozens of people had died. There was serious talk of the council shutting down the ports altogether, though the logistics of acquiring goods was an issue. Elaria had become as self-sufficient as possible due to its isolation, but how long could it hope to survive completely on its own?

The question faded from Stella's mind as the conversation faded from her ears. At least she knew the northern port would never close, not completely anyway, because the black market ran around it and it was the easiest way to slip through the locked kingdom borders. That was why she wasn't afraid of the three royal guards she counted—if they were here, they'd already been paid off, which was why she'd picked this port in the first place.

As she surveyed the scene, she wrapped her blue scarf tighter around her left wrist, hiding her deformity. She hadn't yet decided how she was going to create a makeshift hand, but she was confident she'd find something. But that something wasn't here.

She gazed over the ocean, to the point where the horizon met the water.

That something was out *there*.

"Are you sure this will work?"

While so much had subtly changed about Izzy since she'd nearly died, she was also exactly the same. She looked like herself, just...brighter. Vibrant. Lively. She possessed a new grace she didn't have before, and her skin almost glowed with the power now pulsing in her veins. Stella was surprised to find herself so relieved when Izzy's voice sounded the same as it always had—she hadn't known that was a worry of hers. It seemed silly now, but she couldn't help but be reassured every time she heard her best friend speak.

Stella's tone didn't waver. "Of course I'm sure."

"There are three royal guards here," she commented coolly.

"I know."

Izzy didn't say what she was thinking, because Stella already knew, and it was too risky to talk about it out loud with so many people around. Couldn't have anyone knowing there was a fairy in their midst.

Izzy leaned down to pat Winston on the head. The dog had undergone his own transformation, and they found he looked completely new when he was clean. He had three shades of fur—dark brown, light chestnut, and white—but in the forest they'd just known him to be hopelessly dirty. Now he sat shiny and dutiful at Izzy's feet, surveying the scene himself. If he sensed the new power his adopted owner possessed, he didn't treat her differently for it.

Stella planned their route in her head: which stairs they would use, the path they would take, the sailor they would talk to. While she had her sword at her hip, she didn't want to have to use it. They'd risked a lot in these last two months to barter for passage on a ship, and she wasn't going to squander that opportunity for an unnecessary fight.

"I've got it." Stella glanced at Izzy. "You ready?"

Izzy bit her lip, the only evidence of anxiety on her face. Her trembling fingers twirled the lockets around her neck. She hadn't stopped shaking since she had woken up, still hadn't adjusted to her new body. Stella had to watch for the moments she'd get dizzy and collapse, or get sick and vomit, or get so shaky and overwhelmed and scared that things would start exploding around her. That hadn't happened in five days, and neither of them were itching to break the streak. Especially on a boat.

But despite the immense struggle Stella could only guess at, Izzy kept going. Like a flower that had been stepped on, crushed, wilted, and frozen to death, only to have the quiet audacity to grow again the next spring.

That was Izzy's talent. Surviving.

"I don't think it's possible to ever be completely ready for anything," she answered softly. "But let's go."

Stella nodded. Steeling herself, she led the way through the solemn harbor. The cobblestone path was rough under her boots, and she used the sensation to keep her grounded, refusing to succumb to the fear gnawing in her stomach. While she'd always longed to be here, boarding a ship with the promise of adventure, now that she was here, actually doing it...she couldn't shake her nerves.

Dozens died. The entire ship, everyone on it, lost to the waves forever.

Stop, she ordered herself. Panicking would get her nowhere, and she knew she had to leave Elaria, at least for a few months, in case a certain royal was working to track her down. Besides, she had a theory—a theory regarding how her father was so successful and safe on the ocean—and despite everything, she wondered if his luck was hereditary, if he'd passed it on to her.

Izzy hadn't been as hopeful, but, then again, Izzy had a lot on her mind lately. Despite having enough power in her pinky finger to level the whole port, she was pale and clammed up, her locket fisted in one hand as her glassy eyes darted everywhere.

Sensing her panic, Stella slowed enough to talk quietly to her. "This is just the beginning. Think of all the places we're going to see, the people we'll meet. And, of course, the food we'll try."

"Mhmm."

"And the stories we'll hear."

At that, Izzy's eyes lit up. "The books we could find."

"Of course." Stella grinned. "Eventually you'll be able to write your own book of all our experiences. It will be unlike any book anyone has ever read."

"We could find an island," Izzy went on dreamily. "Or a cabin in the mountains."

"Not a forest, though."

Izzy made a face. "Never."

"And we'll come back someday with all of our stories, all of our adventures, and carrying all the technology we can find." Stella smiled proudly to herself. "We'll be legends."

Izzy took a shaky breath before whispering, "Legends."

Once they got to the dock, they found the captain manning the ship they were taking. He barely gave them a second glance once he realized they'd already paid their way, and he ushered them on.

They stopped at the edge of the dock to admire their vessel: the brown wood was chipped, the faded gold paint flaking, and the sails looked like a grandmother's patch quilt. Izzy gave a side glance to Stella, but Winston barked his approval, which made both of them smile. Sure, it wasn't the biggest ship in the line, but it didn't look like it would sink. Hopefully.

Stella nodded to herself. Someday, she'd have a ship all her own.

"Who knows?" she said, watching as the sun reflected off the water like thousands of tiny crystals. "Maybe we'll get hooked on the sea."

Izzy pursed her lips thoughtfully, debating against Stella despite them having made this decision together. "We could get lost. Our ship could go under. We could drown."

"We could." Stella smirked at her. "But wouldn't that be an awfully big adventure?"

The corners of Izzy's mouth pulled into a smile. "For adventure, then. And the books."

"And the books."

Beckoning Winston, Izzy linked arms with Stella, both of them taking a breath. Then, together, they took their first step onto the boat—their first step into their new beginning.

Emilee King is the author of the Arie's Story survival series and the Elarian Chronicles. She loves fairy tales, superheroes, and murder mysteries, and is constantly on the hunt for good stories. When she's not writing, you can find her reorganizing her bookshelves, eating food, beating the high score on Galaga, or spending time with her family.

@emtheauthor

www.emileeking.com